WATCH YOUR BACK

OTHER BOOKS AND AUDIOBOOKS
BY CLAIR M. POULSON:

I'll Find You
Relentless
Lost and Found
Conflict of Interest
Runaway
Cover Up
Mirror Image
Blind Side
Evidence
Don't Cry Wolf
Dead Wrong
Deadline
Vengeance
Hunted
Switchback
Accidental Private Eye
Framed
Checking Out
In Plain Sight
Falling
Murder at TopHouse
Portrait of Lies
Silent Sting
Outlawyered
Deadly Inheritance
The Search
Suspect
Short Investigations

CLAIR M. POULSON

WATCH YOUR BACK

a suspense novel

Covenant Communications, Inc.

Cover images *Castle Rock Reflections* © Eric Foltz, iStockPhotography. *Floating Feet* © Matjaz Slanic, iStockPhotography.

Cover design copyright © 2019 by Covenant Communications, Inc.

Published by Covenant Communications, Inc.
American Fork, Utah

Printed in the United States of America
First Printing: February 2019

26 25 24 23 22 21 20 19   10 9 8 7 6 5 4 3 2 1

ISBN 978-1-52440-780-3

To Marsha and Scott Peterson

PROLOGUE

"MY BOYFRIEND WAS JUST SHOT!" the frantic voice said.

"Where is the victim?" the dispatcher asked.

"He's with me," the caller answered, her voice shaking as she hurriedly gave the address. "He's dying! I don't know what to do for him. Please hurry."

"Officers and an ambulance are on the way. Is the shooter still there?" the dispatcher asked.

"No, he shot him and sped away," the woman said. "I thought he was going to shoot me too."

"What was he driving when he left?" the dispatcher asked.

"A dark-blue Cadillac Seville."

The dispatcher quickly put the information out to officers to be on the lookout for the Seville, surprised the woman's description of the car was so specific. Then she asked, "What's your name?"

The caller was breathing heavily and sobbing intermittently. "Brea Burr."

"And what is the victim's name?"

"Duane Trahan. He's bleeding badly. I need help now!"

"Help is on the way. Be calm and try to stop the bleeding."

"I'm trying, but it's gushing out."

The dispatcher spoke calmly, professionally, but Brea was getting increasingly upset. "Do you know who the shooter was?" she asked.

"It was that radio guy Bronson Melville. He's my ex. He was jealous of Duane."

That explained why Miss Burr was so sure of the vehicle.

Only when an officer arrived at the location did the dispatcher allow the call to be disconnected. She then placed a call to the police chief, who listened to what she had to say and then told her to send a detective to the scene.

***

Detective Gage Tipton arrived at the scene, and Detective Sergeant Jon Hanks responded a few minutes after him. Gage was the younger of the two, but he was assigned as lead investigator.

Gage found the victim deceased and Miss Brea Burr hysterical when he arrived.

That evening, after completing the crime-scene investigation, Gage went to the alleged killer's home. Melville's car wasn't present, and no one answered the door. No one had seen the man or his car during the first few hours following the murder, but shortly after leaving Melville's home in the Bloomington area, Gage passed a car going the other direction. It was not the blue Cadillac, but knowing what Melville looked like and thinking it could be him, Gage turned his Explorer and caught up with the vehicle.

He followed it for a moment, and then he hit him with his red light. The car, a light-green Toyota, sped up. Gage stayed right on its tail as he called for backup. To his surprise, the car screeched to a stop against the curb at Melville's home. The driver jumped from the vehicle and ran for his front door. Gage leaped from his own vehicle and ran hard after the man he was now positive was Bronson Melville. Gage was younger than Melville and in much better shape—Melville was somewhat overweight and ran slowly—and had him by the collar as the fugitive attempted to unlock his front door while at the same time attempting to pull a pistol from a shoulder holster.

Gage slammed him against the door and slapped cuffs on his thick wrists. The suspect's Glock fell to the ground, and Gage kicked the gun out of the way. Then he spun Melville around and informed him he was under arrest for the murder of Duane Trahan. But before Gage even had a chance to inform the suspect of his Miranda rights, he blurted, "Duane had it coming. He stole my girlfriend from me." No sooner had the words left his mouth than he apparently came to his senses and said, "You can't use that against me. You didn't inform me of my rights."

"You didn't give me time," Gage responded, pretty sure that what Melville had said would be admissible in court as a spontaneous utterance. He read him his rights at that point, and Melville continued to insist Gage couldn't use the earlier admission against him. By then a patrol unit had arrived at the address, and two uniformed officers joined Gage and his prisoner on the front porch. "He has blood splatter on his jacket," Gage told them. He glanced down and added, "And on his pants and his shoes. Take him to jail and hold him until I get there. I need to have his car towed, and then I'll come in to interview him."

Two neighbors approached Gage and told him if he needed them to testify, they would. Both claimed they had heard Melville say the victim "had it coming," an admission of sorts, so Gage took their names and phone numbers and asked them to make written statements and give them to him before he left Melville's home.

After he had received the statements, he spoke to several other neighbors. One of them claimed that just the previous evening Melville had threatened to "take care of Duane Trahan." A couple of others had heard the same thing. They all spoke of Melville as a loud, dishonest man most of them didn't like, despite his popularity with his radio audience. They made it clear to Gage that Melville's radio fans didn't know him like they did. They also mentioned Bronson had a brother, a shady ex-con who often came around, frequently with some rough-looking friends. They knew only two names: the brother was Alvin, and there was another guy they knew only as Dwight. They also mentioned that once in a while a guy in a loud, fancy silver pickup truck was there.

At the jail, the accused killer was placed in prisoner clothing, and his clothes and shoes were confiscated as evidence, along with the pistol that had been taken from where he'd dropped it at the arrest scene.

Before the defendant was locked up, Gage, assisted by Detective Lieutenant Bill Dollison and Detective Sergeant Jon Hanks, ushered him into an interview room for questioning. Melville declared his innocence loudly but refused to answer questions. He was allowed to call an attorney, and a few minutes later JC Hass, Attorney at Law, strode in and informed the officers that the interview was over. Gage groaned. *Anybody but Hass,* he thought.

The lawyer was allowed a few minutes alone with his client, and then Melville was taken back to a cell, continuing to loudly assert his innocence.

The officers conferred for a few minutes and then returned to the police department, where the lieutenant and the police chief joined them. The captain missed that meeting, as he was overseas on vacation.

Gage explained to the others how the arrest went down and reviewed the evidence he had collected. He mentioned the confession, the spontaneous utterance, Melville had shouted before he'd been informed of his rights. He then produced the signed statements of the man and woman who had heard him say it from the yard next door. He also showed his superiors the statements of those who had heard the accused say he was going to take care of Duane Trahan.

"I never did like the guy," Lieutenant Dollison said. "And it sounds like, from what you gathered from his neighbors, they don't like him either. Apparently he doesn't have very classy friends. It looks like we have a solid case against him. Good work, Gage."

That night, on radio and television newscasts, Attorney JC Hass stated that Melville was innocent and that the arresting officer was jumping to clearly erroneous conclusions when he'd made the arrest.

"The inexperienced young detective is trying to make a name for himself," Hass said. "He just returned yesterday from a three-day scuba-diving venture at Lake Powell. He should have kept diving for another day; maybe then an experienced officer would have handled the case, one who isn't so gullible. Detective Tipton actually believed the lies of a very shady woman by the name of Brea Burr who was angry at Melville for ending their relationship and accused him falsely in retaliation. I will prove Melville is innocent. Tipton has no credible evidence. Bronson Melville will soon be free and back on his very popular radio program."

No mention was made of the other witnesses, but JC Hass most likely didn't know about the statements Bronson's neighbors had made.

Contrary to what Hass had declared, however, Melville was soon charged with murder and held without bond in the county jail.

CHAPTER ONE

Three weeks later

IT WAS AN ORDINARY MONDAY evening in late May and an extraordinary first kiss on the doorstep. I'd been dating Denadene Stegner for several weeks, and I probably should have kissed her before tonight, but I didn't get to be twenty-eight and still single by being overaggressive. I'd dated a fair number of ladies over the years, but until I met Denadene at a regional young single adult activity in St. George, I simply had never felt the buzz.

Old habits are hard to break. I was in no hurry and had no intention of pushing the relationship. I liked her a lot, but I was not in love with her—not yet, at least—and maybe I never would be. Denadene seemed patient enough. She still dated other guys. I knew about her dates because she'd mentioned them to me. She'd even named one of them: Isaac Sparks. She'd actually mentioned him three or four times. Seemed to think he was a pretty good guy.

Like Denadene, I'd been on a date with someone else too since our first one. But for the past few weeks, I hadn't asked anyone else out. I told myself it was just because I hadn't really had the opportunity to date others, but I had to admit I enjoyed her company a lot.

I figured I had time to find out for myself if she was *the one* and to move the relationship forward if that's what I wanted to do. That first kiss had me thinking maybe I *should* move it forward. It really was nice. I supposed taking my time would also give her time to decide if I might be a mistake in her life or if Isaac Sparks or the other guy she'd dated might be a better prospect than me or if she was even interested in a serious relationship with anyone. She was twenty-four and had been through a very bad, childless marriage that had ended two years ago. She had told me a couple of times she didn't intend to ever make the same mistake again. So even though deep down I thought I wanted to, I didn't push her. That first kiss had been a big step for me. I had never been the kissing kind. That kiss had surprised me. I wondered, though, if she kissed the other guys she dated like she had kissed me. But I didn't think I really wanted to know.

We'd been to dinner and a movie and talked about taking an overnight trip to Zion National Park the following Friday and Saturday—I had those days off work—but Denadene wasn't sure if she had to work on Friday or not. She told me she wanted to go, although I wasn't sure she meant it. I hoped an overnight date (I was more than happy to pay for two rooms) wasn't pushing too much. She'd spoken to her boss, attorney JC Hass, that morning about getting the day off, but he'd told her to check with him in a day or two, as he might need her for some work on a high-profile case in which he was defending a local radio personality, Bronson Melville, charged with murder.

Melville was popular with some of the local folks, and his arrest had stirred a lot of gossip and even anger among his fans. His neighbors and a lot of other people were glad he was in jail. They were not fans. But the general public had no idea how solid the evidence we had collected against Melville was. So as not to stir things up further, we kept that information quiet, as did the prosecutor's office. Attorney Hass denied we had any credible evidence against his client and claimed I had fabricated it or, in the alternative, that I believed a witness Hass said was lying. We didn't care what Hass thought. What mattered was what we could prove in court, and we had what we needed and more to convict his client of first-degree murder.

Denadene and I had both tried not to let it happen, but the murder case was a bit of a thorn between us. She was a legal secretary and was loyal to her boss, whom I considered to be a first-class jerk. I had trodden lightly with her about my feelings for the guy. Hass and I had tangled in court before. Like the public, Denadene didn't know how much solid evidence we had against her boss's client. I discussed none of the particulars with her. All I could tell her was that I was confident we would get a conviction. On the other hand, JC Hass repeatedly told Denadene it had been a very bad arrest and kept insisting the *supposed* witness, Brea Burr, was a known liar who had it in for his client and would be destroyed in court if she was foolish enough to testify. He also told her the arresting officer was trying to make a name for himself.

Of course, I was the officer Denadene's boss repeatedly tried to tear down, and she knew it. I had arrested Bronson Melville, and I had no doubt about his guilt. Melville was a very bad man, one who had pulled the shades over the eyes of much of the public. As JC Hass spread his lies, I, with the help of some of my colleagues, continued to build on the already-solid case.

But Hass didn't know I was the man his legal secretary was dating quite regularly and for whom she wanted the day off. At least, that's what Denadene had told me, and I had no reason not to believe her. She had expressed no desire to tell her boss, which was fine with me. He was a competent attorney but was blatantly dishonest, and he had an extremely overinflated ego. If he'd known Denadene's date was to be with the arresting officer on his high-profile case, he would have, I was certain, told her she had to work on Friday.

"I'll call you," she told me shortly after that sweet kiss on her doorstep.

"When?" I asked.

"I should know by Wednesday," she said, smiling at me. "I made JC promise to let me know by then."

"That'll work," I said. Then I grinned at her. "Bat those pretty baby-blue eyes of yours, and he'll be sure to let you have the day off."

She punched me lightly on the shoulder. "You know I have no intention of encouraging him."

Hass was also a divorcé, except he'd been through three marriages. The man was more than twenty years older than Denadene, but that hadn't stopped him from asking her out several times. She told me she kept their relationship strictly professional, but I knew he'd take her out if she showed the least amount of interest.

"I know," I said. "I was just kidding. I'd better go. I have to interview a couple of people tomorrow about the Melville case. One of them is expecting me early in the morning."

She smiled. "Okay. It's been a wonderful evening, Gage. I promise I'll call," she reiterated. "I think I will be able to persuade JC to give me the day off. I really do want to go with you."

"I'll be anxiously awaiting your call," I replied. I thought about kissing her one more time, but that would be pushing it, and I was not a pusher in the romantic arena. So I simply waited until she had gone inside and shut the door to her apartment and then headed back to my blue Ford pickup.

Denadene did not call me on Wednesday, nor did she call me on Thursday. I was anxious to know if she could go with me, and I was already feeling disappointment. Maybe she didn't want to go after all. But I tried her cell phone a half dozen times anyway. It went to voicemail each time. I had optimistically booked a couple of rooms and needed to cancel them soon if we were not going. I was feeling desperate, so I called the JC Hass Law Office early on Thursday afternoon.

I didn't recognize the voice of the woman who answered. After telling her I needed to talk to Denadene, she said, "Ms. Stegner did not come to work yesterday, so Mr. Hass asked me to come in and help out."

"And you are?" I asked.

"My name is Lily Kwick," she said. "I've covered for Ms. Stegner a number of times before."

"She didn't come in? That makes no sense," I said anxiously. "She promised she would call me either yesterday or today and she hasn't."

"I'm sorry, but I didn't catch your name," the temp said.

"I'm Detective Gage Tipton," I said reluctantly. I hadn't wanted to identify myself to that particular law office.

"Oh," Lily said in a tone that indicated my name was an unsavory combination of nasty words. "Mr. Hass would not want her to speak with you, Detective Tipton. Any communications he has about the Melville matter will be with the prosecutor in the case. But I'll tell him you called."

"No, that's okay," I said. "Please don't bother. I can speak with the prosecutor as well." I added that last bit because I didn't want to let her know my interest in speaking with Denadene was personal and had nothing to do with the murder case. Mrs. Kwick could think what she wanted. "Thanks for your time, Mrs. Kwick."

"*Ms.* Kwick," she said with a bit of a growl and ended the call before I could apologize for my blunder.

I stared at my phone for a moment, my mind in a whirl. I wondered if I'd been mistaken to think Denadene enjoyed my company and wanted to continue to date me. But I also wondered if Hass had discovered *who* Denadene wanted to go with on Friday, and if he had dismissed her from his one-man law firm because of his intense dislike of me.

But that didn't make a lot of sense. I mean, if he had fired her, she would still have called me. I believed her to be a woman of her word. The worry that had been eating at me became a distinct discomfort in my stomach. I put my phone in my pocket, walked out of the police station, and drove directly to Denadene's apartment in my official, unmarked, tan Ford Explorer. Her dark-blue Volkswagen Jetta was not in her assigned parking space.

I parked my car in her designated spot and ran up the stairs to her apartment. I stood where we had shared our first kiss on Monday night and rang the doorbell. I waited, wondering if I cared for her more than I had let myself believe. Maybe she was giving up on me and didn't want to talk to me. I thrust that uncomfortable thought aside and rapped on the door with my knuckles. There was no answer.

I finally gave up and walked back down the stairs to my Explorer. I had met Denadene's parents and felt comfortable with them, even though they knew that at that point Denadene and I were just good friends who were dating and nothing more. She'd grown up in Cedar City, and her parents still lived there. I sat in the driver's seat and found their home phone number and called. Her mother answered, and I said, "Hi, Mrs. Garford. This is Gage Tipton."

"Hello, Gage. I'm glad you called," she said. "Perhaps you can tell me what's going on with our daughter. We can't get her to answer her cell. It's not like her."

That statement did not relieve my angst in the least. "I'm sorry," I said. "That was why I was calling you. I can't seem to reach her either. I haven't spoken with her since Monday. She was going to call me about a trip we had planned for the weekend, but I haven't heard from her."

"She told me about the trip," her mother said. "She was very excited. Her father and I thought maybe you two had decided to leave early. I even tried to reach her at the law office yesterday, but some other woman answered the phone. She was quite rude to me."

"I got the same treatment," I said. "She told me Denadene had failed to come to work yesterday morning and she was filling in for her."

"She told you that?" Mrs. Garford asked. "She told me Denadene had quit and she had taken her place." Mrs. Garford was starting to sound frantic. "I've been trying to reach her since I spoke with that woman yesterday afternoon. I know Denadene is uncomfortable with her boss, but she is loyal to him. She would never just quit and leave him hanging unless she felt threatened in some way, and I don't believe she has."

As she spoke, I found myself wondering why Ms. Kwick would tell me one thing but Denadene's mother another. Which of the two versions was the truth? Or were they both lies? I also wondered why Denadene had never told me about her discomfort around Hass. She had only told me he'd asked her out and she had declined. As far as I knew, that was the end of it.

"Would you mind going by her apartment to make sure she's okay? Maybe she's sick and her cell phone is dead," Mrs. Garford said.

"I'm actually here now. Her car is gone, and she didn't answer her door," I said.

There was a long silence, and Mrs. Garford was breathing heavily into the phone. "Gage, I'm really worried. I'm afraid something has happened to her. I don't know what to do." I could hear soft sobbing.

"It's been more than twenty-four hours since anyone has seen her, so I can list her as missing. We'll find her."

The first thing I did after getting back to the office was put an attempt to locate (ATL) out on Denadene and her blue Volkswagen Jetta. Just in case, I called the Dixie Regional Medical Center. I had to identify myself as an officer before anyone would tell me she was not a patient there. I officially filed a missing person report with my department. Finally, despite knowing I would not be well received, I headed for the law office of JC Hass.

A short, plump lady in her mid-fifties, whom I assumed must be Ms. Lily Kwick, said with a smile as I stepped in, "Good afternoon, sir. Are you in need of the legal services of Mr. Hass?"

"Just answers from him will do fine," I said as I pulled out my ID and showed it to her. "I'll need a few minutes of his time."

The woman let her smile slip. She straightened her short grayish-brown hair with a quick snap of her wrist. "Detective, Mr. Hass has no desire to speak with you. I thought I made that clear when you called. It would be highly improper since he is defending the man he told me you falsely arrested."

I stepped close to her desk—Denadene's desk, actually—and leaned toward her. "Ms. Kwick, you seem like a very nice woman, but you are wrong on two counts. First, Mr. Melville is guilty of murder, and we will prove it. Second, I don't want to talk to Mr. Hass about his client's case. I want to speak to him about Ms. Stegner. Now, you can either buzz his office and tell him I'm coming back to speak with him, or I will announce myself when I go back."

"Don't you dare! That is not allowed," she said testily.

"This is only your second day, Ms. Kwick, and you are temporary, so I don't think it's up to you to decide if I speak to Mr. Hass or not," I said, trying hard to restrain my growing anger. "Either buzz his office and tell him I'm here to see him, or I will go back there unannounced."

I stared at her, and she stared back, stubbornly shaking her head but not allowing her eyes to meet mine. Finally she said, "He's not in, Detective."

I didn't believe her. Surely she would have told me that right away if it were true. I straightened up, turned, and walked past her desk toward the office with the brass nameplate that read *JC Hass*.

"You can't do that," she shouted after me.

I did not reply—simply knocked on the door. "Who is it?" a male voice called from inside.

I grabbed the doorknob, turned it, and stepped inside. As I suspected, Ms. Kwick had been covering for Hass. "I'm sorry to bother you, sir," I said as Hass pushed his chair back from his desk and frowned. I wasn't sorry in the least.

"Who are you, and what do you want? You have no business barging in here like this. I told Ms. Kwick I was not to be disturbed," he said angrily as he rose to his feet and pointed a finger at me. "If you need an appointment, schedule it with her."

So he didn't even recognize me. That actually made me angrier than I already had been at the guy. "I am not here seeking legal advice, Mr. Hass. If I needed legal advice, you are the last person I would come to. No, I'm the officer you've been so busily maligning," I said. "I'm Detective Gage Tipton. But I'm not here to discuss the Melville case. I'd like to know why Denadene quit her job with you."

A puzzled look came over his face, and he plopped back into his chair. "What are you talking about? She didn't quit. She didn't show up for work yesterday morning, which is very uncharacteristic. I'm worried about her. She's not answering her phone. She would have given me appropriate notice if she were going to quit, but she likes working here. She likes *me*. What makes you think she quit?"

"That's what Ms. Kwick told Denadene's mother," I answered, jerking a thumb toward the front office. "Either way, Denadene is missing, and I am trying to locate her."

"Missing?" Hass said as he leaned forward in his chair. "I figured she was home with the flu or something."

I nodded. "A formal report has been filed." I didn't think he needed to know I had filed the report myself. "Her car is gone too. Her parents are distraught. They were particularly upset when your temp told them she had quit her job. Denadene hadn't mentioned she'd intended to quit."

"Lily said that?" Hass asked. He was staring past me, but he jerked his eyes back and said, "Denadene did not quit; that I can assure you. She's a good friend and an excellent legal secretary—the best I've ever had. I'll straighten out the misunderstanding with Lily."

"That's between you and Ms. Kwick. I'm concerned about locating Ms. Stegner. When did you last see her?"

"That would be Tuesday at about six when we closed the office for the evening. I walked with her out to her car. She seemed just fine. She gave no indication she might not be in the next day."

"I'm told she was planning to call a friend about whether you were giving her the day off on Friday," I said. "They had plans to go out of town."

"Do you know that for a fact?" Hass asked.

"Yes, I do. I'm taking her disappearance very seriously, speaking to people who might be able to help me, people she knew."

"I'm surprised she didn't call her friend." He hesitated, as if thinking about what he wanted to say next. Finally he went on. "I told her she could have Friday off, and she thanked me. When she didn't come in yesterday, I tried reaching her two or three times and finally phoned the temp agency and asked them to arrange for Ms. Kwick to cover for her."

My stomach roiled, and I felt chills on my arms. Something was very wrong.

I had never been invited to sit, so I turned toward the door. Then I stopped and turned back. "Please call me if you hear from her, Mr. Hass." I pulled a card from my pocket and dropped it onto his desk.

I was halfway out the door when Hass said, "You believed the lies of a scorned and unsavory woman and arrested an innocent man, Detective. You need to wise up and arrest the right person, if you're smart enough to figure out who that might be."

I did not turn around. "We'll see who needs to wise up," I said over my shoulder. I stopped a moment later at Denadene's desk, where Ms. Kwick was squirming uncomfortably. "In the future, don't lie to me," I growled. "And don't lie to Denadene's parents."

I left her red-faced and stammering as I went out the door and slammed it behind me.

CHAPTER TWO

I WAS DRIVING WHEN LIEUTENANT Dollison called me. "Where are you, Gage?" he asked.

"I'm on my way to Hurricane to see Ms. Stegner's ex-husband," I said. "I tried to call him but got no answer."

"Sounds like a good idea," the lieutenant said. "But I'll need to have you wait on that for a little while. I just got a call from Mark. JC Hass would like to speak with you and Sergeant Hanks about Bronson Melville, but since Jon won't be back from Salt Lake for a couple more hours, it'll have to be just you."

"Can't it wait for a couple of hours?" I asked. Mark Stansel was the deputy county prosecuting attorney, and I was irritated Hass had contacted him for a meeting and hadn't said a word about it to me.

"He said it's urgent," Lieutenant Dollison said. "Hass is already there, demanding to speak with you and Jon. Mark tried to get him to make an appointment for tomorrow, but he won't consider it. He said it has to be now."

"Okay, I'll head back, but it'll take me a few minutes," I said grudgingly. All I needed was to have to deal with the Melville case right now. I couldn't imagine what Hass could possibly want. He had been given a list of all the evidence we had on the case, and a preliminary hearing was set for the following Monday.

"Apparently Hass is pretty wound up," the lieutenant said.

"I was just there, and he didn't mention anything to me about the case," I said as I took the next exit so I could head south again. "Well, that's not exactly accurate. He did remind me Melville was innocent. He's got to know that isn't true."

"We have an airtight case, Gage. Don't worry about that. Just get in there and help Mark settle the guy down and send him on his way."

"I doubt my presence will settle him down. We're not exactly friends."

Dollison chuckled. "I understand, but the guy did ask for you, so go in and see what's up."

A few minutes later, in a rather sour mood, I entered Mark Stansel's office. "Sit down, Detective," he instructed me. There were three chairs in front of his desk. The center one was already occupied by Denadene's boss. Hass looked up at me and scowled. I sat in the chair to his right because it was a little farther from him than the chair to his left.

"Took you long enough," Hass growled.

"I was on my way to Hurricane."

"What's in Hurricane?" Hass asked, staring at me with undisguised dislike.

"Denadene's ex-husband," I said.

"What do you want to see him about?" he asked.

"I didn't come to get cross-examined," I snapped. "I thought you wanted to talk about the Melville case."

"I do," he said. "I'll be making a motion to the district court first thing in the morning to dismiss. I presented a copy of the motion to the court clerk today. I expect the judge to rule on it Monday morning before we begin the preliminary hearing."

"And we will strongly resist that motion," the prosecutor said.

"The judge will grant it when he sees what I have to say," Hass said with a cocky shake of his head. "It's like I told you, Detective. You arrested an innocent man and do not have a case."

"You know very well we do," I said. "Surely you've seen the evidence by now."

"Which is what I've been explaining to him for the last fifteen minutes," Mark said. "I've responded fully with his request for discovery. He knows everything we do."

"Read the motion," Hass said. "The judge will grant it."

"This doesn't explain why you wanted me here," I said. "If I need to do further investigation, I will. But I can assure you there is more than enough to get your client bound over for trial."

A sneer crept across the defense attorney's face. "You have a lot to learn, young man," he said. "You've been trying to make a name for yourself at my client's expense, and I've been saying all along you don't have a leg to stand on. I am a man of considerable influence in this community, and I will see to it that you lose your job before this is over."

I addressed the deputy county attorney. "Is that what I came all the way back here for? I don't have to sit here and listen to this man make personal attacks against me. I have other things I need to do, such as finding Ms. Stegner."

"If I'd known she was dating you, I'd have told her she had to work tomorrow," Hass began before Mark could answer my question. "You should have told me that when we spoke a short while ago, but I had to learn it from someone else." He didn't say who that someone else was, and frankly, I didn't care. "None of that is of any consequence now. As shocked as I am, it seems Denadene did quit. I just didn't know it when I talked to you."

"What are you talking about?" I asked as I got a sinking feeling inside.

"Ms. Kwick isn't quite as efficient as Denadene. She hadn't opened all my mail when you barged into my office this afternoon," he said. Then he smirked and let me sit and wonder what Ms. Kwick had found in the mail. I didn't ask him. I wouldn't give him the satisfaction. Finally he went on. "There was a letter of resignation from Denadene. I still find it hard to believe she didn't give me any notice, but then I suppose if she was actually going out with the likes of you, she wasn't nearly as reliable as I thought she was."

"She's a great legal secretary, and you know it," I said defensively. "Did you bring the letter with you? I'd like to see it."

"It's in her personnel file now, Tipton. It's really none of your concern," he said. "But I will tell you this much: it was postmarked yesterday in St. George. She apparently mailed it first thing yesterday morning."

My mind was reeling. "What did it say?" I demanded.

"That she quit," Hass said, emphasizing each word as if he thought I was dense. "That's all you need to know."

"Did she sign it?" I asked as doubts swirled through my mind. "She would have told me if she was going to quit. She liked her job, and she was loyal to you, although I can't imagine why."

Hass chuckled. "I guess we both misjudged her, didn't we? Of course she signed it, you fool. I know her signature. And her loyalty was a facade, wasn't it? Apparently it was you she was loyal to, the stupid girl."

I ignored that remark. "If Denadene wrote it, she would have given you reasons for her sudden resignation," I pressed. "What did she say her reasons were?"

"It's none of your business," he said again, his face turning red.

"Actually, I think it is. I am officially investigating her disappearance. I have a missing person report to follow up on. If you have evidence that can convince me to close the case, you need to present it to me," I said.

Hass turned back to Mark and said with a smirk on his face, "Well, I'll be going. Read the motion, Counselor. I'll see you in court on Monday. There will be no need to go through with the preliminary hearing." With that he stood and marched out the door, shutting it firmly behind him.

"What a jerk," I said.

"I won't argue with that," Mark said with a frown. He picked up the motion and started to read. I sat quietly, waiting and fuming. He finally set the papers back on his desk and looked across at me with a frown. "It seems your friend is not the only person missing."

"Who else is missing?" I asked.

"Our star witness, Brea Burr. At least, that's JC's claim."

"I don't believe it. I spoke to her just yesterday," I said. "She admitted she was frightened, that she feared Melville would get out and come after her, but she said as long as he was locked up, she'd be okay. He's not out, is he?"

"I'm sure he's not. He's being held without bail."

"Even without Brea we have a case," I said confidently, although I had to admit I was concerned over this revelation.

"And a good one, unless the judge chooses to believe the garbage that JC put in this motion," the prosecutor said.

"What garbage?" I asked.

"Read it," he said and shoved the motion across the desk toward me.

I felt my collar burning as I read. The motion, for the most part, was an attack on my integrity. In it Hass accused me of manufacturing evidence, of coercing a confession, and making a couple of Melville's neighbors lie about him. He also accused me of forcing the now-missing witness to lie. Hass even claimed he had received good information that the witness had fled the area to avoid being forced to perjure herself in court. I finished reading the motion while I tried to extinguish the flames of my anger. I finally said, "This will never fly with the court."

"That's right, but I would suggest you see if you can find our missing witness, Gage." Mark paused, thinking as he scratched his chin. "I wonder what's happened," he muttered. I didn't say anything. I just gave him time to put his thoughts together. Pretty soon he pulled his hand from his chin and looked at me. "Either she's been dealt with violently by someone of Melville's acquaintance, or like Hass claims, she got scared and ran. I hope it's the latter—that she's been intimidated, not killed."

I shivered. "Who are some of Melville's friends, or do you know?" I asked.

The prosecutor slowly shook his head. "I have no idea. You're the detective. Maybe you can figure it out. Let me know what you learn."

"I'll get to work on it as soon as I check with Ms. Stegner's ex-husband in Hurricane." I stood and turned to leave Mark's office.

"Don't worry about this motion to dismiss," he said to my back. "It's dead in the water." He chuckled. "You have the defense counsel running scared, Detective. You and Jon Hanks have built an outstanding case."

I turned back. "Thanks," I said.

I was worried about Brea Burr, but I was more worried about Denadene. I hit the freeway north, intent on talking to Denadene's ex-husband, Randall. Once I got to Hurricane, I quickly located his house. To my astonishment, Denadene's dark-blue Volkswagen Jetta was parked in his wide driveway, pulled up near the closed doublewide garage door.

I parked on the street and walked toward the front door, wondering if for some insane reason Denadene had decided to go back to her ex-husband. She'd told me a little about the abuse he'd heaped on her during their ill-fated marriage. I felt a surge of anxiety rush through me as I stopped my approach to the front door and instead stepped over to her car and peered in. It was empty—no suitcase or bags of any kind, no purse, no trash, nothing. It was clean—the way Denadene always kept it.

I walked to the door and rang the bell as I wondered how Randall had ended up with their house from the divorce. I'd never asked Denadene, and she had never mentioned it. In fact, I'd never given it any serious thought before. I really hadn't cared to hear a lot about her divorce.

There was no answer, so I knocked firmly on the door. Same result. I looked around and then walked to the side of the house. There was a window in the garage, so I put my head close to the glass and looked in. There were no vehicles in it—just a lot of junk. I had no idea what Randall drove, but whatever it was, it wasn't parked in his garage or by his house.

I walked back to my vehicle, thinking I might as well head back to St. George and see if I could locate my missing witness that evening. But I had no sooner buckled my seatbelt than I changed my mind. I decided to check with neighbors about Randall and Denadene before I left. I knocked on the door to the home just east of Randall's house. A woman with a child in her arms answered the door. She was probably in her thirties.

"Hello, my name is Detective Gage Tipton of the St. George Police." I showed her my ID.

"Becky Currier." She nodded in lieu of a handshake and shifted the child from one arm to the other.

"It's nice to meet you, Mrs. Currier," I said.

"Please, call me Becky. Mrs. Currier is my mother-in-law." She smiled warmly. "I don't mean that as an offense to my husband's mother; we get along marvelously. It's just that when people call me Mrs. Currier it makes me feel old."

"Becky it is, then," I said. "I have some questions about your neighbor, Randall Stegner."

The woman's face went dark. "He's a creep, if that's what you want to know. The smartest thing his ex-wife ever did was leave him," she said.

"Is that so?" I asked. "Do you know what her car is doing at his house?"

She looked over at Randall's place. "If you're talking about that blue Jetta, I didn't know that was hers. She drove an old white Nissan when they were together. She must have purchased that after the divorce," she said. "I'll tell you, that guy really took her to the cleaners when they split up. He got the house and the truck, and she got the old car."

"Surely she got something else," I said.

"Well, I suppose I was exaggerating, but she didn't get much. She told me she didn't care, that she was just desperate to get out of the marriage. She also told me there was so much owed on the house that she could never have made the payments anyway. The same was true of Randall's truck. My husband and I were already living here when the Stegners moved in. For a short time, they seemed really happy. She went to church every Sunday, but other than the first couple of weeks, he didn't attend with her. Anyway, after a while I noticed she became withdrawn, unhappy."

"How long after you noticed this change in Denadene was it until she left him?" I asked.

"Too long," Becky said with a bite in her voice. "I'm sorry. I really don't care for Randall. But it was maybe four or five months. She was pretty depressed when she finally had taken all she could from the creep. I know she talked to our bishop several times. Of course, she never told me what he counseled her."

"Let's talk about the car some more." I pointed at the Jetta. "I guess you didn't see Ms. Stegner park it in the driveway."

"No, Randall did. That was yesterday around noon. I guess I assumed he'd just bought it, although now that I look closely, I see it doesn't have a temporary sticker. Like I said, I didn't know it was hers. Are you sure it is?" she asked.

"I've seen her drive it," I said. "She referred to it as her car." But now I wasn't sure. I wasn't sure of anything at that point. I decided as soon as I finished speaking with Becky I would run the license plate number, and then I'd know for certain whether the car was Denadene's. I continued. "You mentioned a truck. What is it?"

"Randall drives a really big Dodge Ram. It's silver, jacked up really high, and is really loud. It drives my family and me crazy. When I saw him in that VW, I thought maybe he was finally going to drive something a little quieter once in a while," she said with a frown. "I guess we'll still have to listen to him rev that obnoxious thing up all hours of the day and night."

"Becky, did you or your husband see Ms. Stegner here during the past day or so?" I asked.

"No, this is the last place I'd have ever expected to see her," she replied.

"Have you seen anyone over there you wouldn't expect to see besides Denadene?" I asked.

"Now, that I can answer yes to. This morning, after getting home from the doctor with the baby, there was a black van with tinted windows parked in Randall's driveway right next to the Jetta." She pointed in that direction. "A man I'd never seen in this neighborhood before was just coming out of the house with Randall. They looked in the back of the van as Randall put his diving gear in. He's a scuba diver. Did you know that?" Becky asked.

"I didn't," I said. Diving was one of my hobbies too. I couldn't believe I had anything in common with Denadene's ex. She and I had never talked about my hobby, or she would probably have mentioned Randall was a diver. "What happened then?"

Becky shrugged. "After he had finished loading, Randall got into the passenger side and his friend took the driver's seat, and they drove off."

"You said you'd never seen the driver in *this* neighborhood. Does that mean you recognized him from elsewhere?" I asked. I said nothing about the diving equipment but found myself with a gnawing worry over it.

"Oh yes," Becky said as she once again shifted the baby from one arm to the other. "It was Alvin Melville. I had no idea he was friends with Randall."

"Melville, as in, the brother of the accused killer Bronson Melville? The guy who has been repeatedly on the news with Bronson's attorney, JC Hass?" I asked.

"Yeah, that's him. Seeing him being interviewed on TV is the only reason I recognized him," Becky said. "I've never met him or seen him in person before this morning. I know I shouldn't say this, but just from the way he acted and spoke on the news made me dislike him. He's creepy." She forced a laugh. "I guess I shouldn't be surprised he and Randall are friends. They're both creepy."

I wondered what besides his diving gear Randall had in the van. Or *who* else. Could Denadene be tied up and gagged back there—or worse? But then my mind skipped to the missing witness, Brea Burr. Maybe she was in there.

"Has the van been back that you've noticed?" I asked.

"I haven't seen the van or Randall's pickup," she said. "I don't know where his truck is, unless it's in the garage."

Becky's information didn't help my worry. My murder case and my missing person case merged. Somehow Denadene's ex and the killer's brother were tied together. That could mean Bronson Melville and Randall were also acquainted. The very thought made me sick. And angry.

After speaking with Becky for a couple more minutes and learning nothing else of substance, I checked at several other homes in the neighborhood. I only actually spoke with three more people, and two of them were oblivious to anything going on at Randall Stegner's house. They even seemed surprised when I pointed out the blue Jetta.

One neighbor across the street and a couple of houses to the east, however, had more light to shed on the situation. The wife was still at work, and the husband, who worked nights, was just getting ready to go to bed so he'd be ready to work that night. I apologized to him for keeping him up, but he assured me I wasn't, that he was slow in going to bed anyway.

He introduced himself as Kyle Biedron. He was a short, stout man I judged to be about fifty or so. Like Becky, he had a very low opinion of Randall Stegner. "I leave for work around midnight each night," he said. "Randall was just pulling out of his driveway in that obnoxiously loud truck of his when I backed out of my garage last night. I'm sure he woke my wife. If we'd still had kids at home, he'd for sure have woken them up."

"Was he alone?" I asked.

"Nope," he said running his hand across his short-cropped brown hair. "There was a woman with him. I didn't get a very good look at her, but when he backed under the streetlamp over there, I'd have sworn it was his ex-wife. Or maybe it was just someone who resembled her. My wife and I talked about it after I got home from work this morning. Neither of us can imagine why she would have been with him. Maybe it wasn't her, but it sure looked like her. Do you know her?" he asked me.

His question hit me like a punch in the gut. It took me a moment to answer, but I finally was able to say, trying to keep my face from showing my concern, "I do. She's the reason I'm here. She didn't show up to work yesterday morning and hasn't been seen or heard from since."

"That doesn't sound good," Kyle said. "I heard she was abused by Randall before she finally left. And I heard him cursing loudly at her a lot of times. I would never have expected to see the two of them back together."

CHAPTER THREE

I COULDN'T THINK OF ANYTHING else to do right then about Denadene. So, sick at heart, I drove back to St. George. I tried to keep busy by working on the murder case. I ran a criminal history on Alvin Melville. He had a long record involving burglaries, assaults, sale of illegal drugs, and a number of other things. I also found he was connected to a criminal gang in Las Vegas. He had served two stints in prison. His brother, on the other hand, had only a few misdemeanor convictions.

Next I contacted everyone I could think of about Brea Burr. No one could give me so much as a hint as to where she had gone or why. From what they all told me, she had simply vanished. My inquiries regarding her fear of retaliation by someone close to Bronson Melville met with mixed reactions.

Those closest to her said she had feared for her life, that they wouldn't be at all surprised if she had simply run away without telling anyone, reasoning it was the most likely way she could stay safe. But others said she was only minimally worried. I tended to side with the *fearful for her life* camp.

I called her cell phone several times, and each time I got no answer. I then went the more complicated route and attempted to locate it with its GPS feature. I hit pay dirt with that. The GPS indicated her phone was in the house she rented. My next move that evening was to get a search warrant for her home in case she was not there to give me permission to search. Detective Sergeant Jon Hanks, who had returned from the city hours before, assisted me in executing the warrant.

The house, a very small older one, had an attached one-car garage with no windows. We knocked first, hoping, rather than expecting, for her to open the door when she saw who was there, but there was no answer. Once we were able to get into the house, the first thing I did was check the garage from the door inside. To my dismay, her silver Honda Accord was parked there. If she'd fled, it had to have been using public transportation, and that didn't make sense, as I would have expected to find her car at the airport or the bus terminal.

I was relieved when we didn't find Brea's dead body in the house. But neither did we find her alive. My concern escalated when I found her purse in her bedroom with her cell phone in it. Sergeant Hanks and I looked at each other. His face mirrored the unease I was feeling.

He said, "This doesn't look good, Gage. She wouldn't have gone without her ID. The phone I can see her leaving because of the GPS; she might not have wanted to be found."

I pointed out the wad of cash we had found in her purse, along with a checkbook and her credit and debit cards. "If she had planned to leave, surely she would have taken all this cash. And she wouldn't be able to use an ATM without her cards."

Sergeant Hanks was thoughtful for a moment, and then he said, "You need to check with all her neighbors and see if anyone can recall seeing a vehicle matching the description of the van Randall Stegner's neighbors saw."

"I'll get right on it," I said.

Sergeant Hanks stole a glance at his watch. "It's almost too late tonight to be knocking on doors. Go home and get some rest," he suggested. "You can come back first thing in the morning to see what you can learn. But keep me informed."

I went home and popped a frozen pizza into the oven. I hadn't eaten since morning, and I was famished. I could have eaten out, even though it was late, but I didn't want to do that. I was afraid I'd meet someone who would ask me about Denadene or about the murder case. I didn't want to deal with those things right now, especially Denadene's having gone missing. The privacy and quiet of my apartment suited me fine. Well, not *quite* fine. I couldn't stop thinking about Denadene. I hadn't thought about her this much since we'd started dating. I finally put on some country music and played it loudly enough to be distracting.

Early the next morning, before a lot of folks would have left for work, I drove back to Brea's neighborhood. Once again I made progress, but it wasn't what I had hoped for. I had hoped no one had seen Alvin Melville's black van in the neighborhood, but three people remembered seeing it Wednesday evening. First it had circled the block several times, and then it had stopped in front of Brea's home, where it had sat for several minutes. With its darkened windows, no one could tell me much about the driver. It was probably a man, I was told, but I could get no further description, and no one had taken note of the license plate number. Finally the van had left the area. That was late in the evening, near sunset.

A couple of neighbors told me they had observed Brea pulling into her garage about an hour after the van left. The fact that the driver of the black van had repeatedly circled the block and then parked in front of her house didn't mean he had abducted her sometime after that. But I'm not a big fan of coincidences, so I was afraid Alvin, or whoever was driving at the time, was responsible for her disappearance. I was unable to locate anyone who'd seen the van during the night, but that was to be expected. People would have been sleeping. If the driver had it in mind to abduct her to keep her from testifying, that person would have been very careful not to be seen in the act.

That thought worried me a great deal. I had been taught there were several likely reasons people vanished. The worst were when they were abducted and or murdered or had met with an accident that prevented them from coming home or communicating with loved ones. Another reason was to avoid arrest or to avoid someone they were in fear of. The final reason I considered was something we in law enforcement refer to as *malicious missing*, when someone fled to avoid responsibilities they simply didn't want to face anymore or had stolen something they could use only in some other area. The malicious missing would also include persons who fled to escape a bad situation such as an abusive marriage or someone who had left to meet up with a secret lover.

There could be other reasons, but those were by far the most common. As I sat in my Explorer thinking about Brea and Denadene, I tried to fit each of them into one of the categories. Denadene, as far as I knew, was not unhappy. I was reasonably sure she was not wanted for a crime. She was not a witness in the murder case her employer was defending, and I could think of no reason anyone would abduct her. Her ex-husband could have done it. But why would he? The marriage was over and had been for a long time. He had gotten most of the property in the divorce. I couldn't think she would have fled in fear of him this long after the divorce. Surely she would have told me something if she was afraid. I had given it a lot of thought. She had hardly ever mentioned her ex to me, so although I knew he had been abusive during their marriage, she had not seemed to still be afraid of him.

As for Brea, I feared the worst. She was a witness to a murder. Her testimony would be crushing to Hass's defense. And Bronson's brother could be acting on his behalf. Of course, she might have simply fled to avoid being silenced in some way. Her car had been at home, along with her money and her purse, and Alvin Melville's van had been seen in Brea's neighborhood. I was afraid reality would eventually prove she had been abducted and then, what? Killed? I prayed not, but it didn't look good for Brea. I thought for a moment about Randall Stegner's diving equipment. That disturbed me, but I managed to shove it from my mind before my imagination ran away with itself.

I finally started my vehicle and drove away. Earlier I had created a list of Brea's family members and friends. I had spoken to a lot of them the previous evening, so I spent the morning locating and speaking to as many of the others as I could find. No one, including those I'd spoken to the day before, seemed to believe she would have run away. Had she mentioned to anyone that she had feared for her life? It had come up in various conversations, but she had told a number of people that since Bronson was in jail, she didn't think she was in danger. She had told me the same thing when she'd agreed to testify as our key witness. But like me, her family and closest friends knew she was afraid of what Bronson's friends could do if he wanted them to. I feared someone had taken steps to silence her.

As I finally drove back to the office that afternoon, I considered both missing women and their circumstances. I couldn't help but believe Alvin Melville and Randall Stegner were somehow involved in the disappearance of both women. After parking my Explorer, I went inside and sat at my desk.

Unbidden, the face of JC Hass came to mind, and it was not a pretty picture. I felt my skin crawl as I considered him. I wondered at that point if he might be involved in some way. He had certainly gone out of his way to malign me, despite the overwhelming evidence against his client. I wondered if he had lied to me about Denadene. Perhaps, despite his denial, he had known of our relationship before I had met with him the day before.

I smacked my head with my hand. Just because I didn't like the guy and he was defending a scummy killer while badmouthing me did not mean he was a criminal. I determined then to keep him in mind but not to mention my thoughts to anyone else, either inside or outside the police department. I did run a quick criminal check on him. There were some minor traffic violations and a domestic violence case involving one of his ex-wives, but that case had ultimately been dismissed. Other than that, his record was clear, as I'd expected.

I looked at my watch, and then I found Isaac Sparks's address. Denadene had mentioned going out with Isaac a few times. I drove there and knocked on his door. "Can I help you with something, sir?" he asked with a smile when he opened it.

"Hi, I'm Detective Gage Tipton," I said. "Have you got a minute so I can speak with you?"

He held the door open and chuckled. "Are you here to ask me not to date Denadene Stegner?" he asked. "I guess you and I and some other guy are sort of competing. I think you have the upper hand."

"I don't know about that," I said. "Have you heard from her in the past couple of days?"

He suddenly became very serious. "No, is something wrong?"

"She's missing, and no one, including her parents, has heard from her since Wednesday evening," I said. "I found her car at Randall Stegner's house in Hurricane."

"That's crazy. She would never go back to him. He was horrible to her," he said.

"Yes, he was," I agreed. I chatted with him for a moment longer, and as I was preparing to step out the door, I said, "Will you call me if you hear from her?" I handed him my card.

"I don't think she will call me, but if she does, I'll let you know," he said, looking worried.

Isaac seemed like a really nice guy. Perhaps he was serious competition. But right now, all I wanted was to find Denadene, safe and sound. I drove back to the station.

I was trying to decide what to do next when I got a call at my desk. I picked the handset up and said, "Detective Tipton."

"Detective, I am calling you to do you a favor," a slightly muffled and unrecognizable male voice said. It did not sound like a voice distorting device was being used. It sounded more like the caller was holding a cloth of some kind over the phone.

"What kind of favor?" I asked, instinctively knowing this was not going to be a good call.

"You'd probably like to know Denadene is all right, wouldn't you?" the voice said.

"Of course I would." Chills ran up my spine and created goose bumps on my skin.

"She'll be just fine if you do me a favor," the caller told me.

I said nothing.

"All you have to do is lose the evidence you have against Bronson Melville and quit investigating the death of Duane Trahan."

"I can't do that," I said hotly. "Duane was murdered."

"He was a worthless, disgusting man. His death is no loss to anyone."

"It was to Brea Burr," I countered.

"Listen to me, you idiot. I called to ask you for a favor, not to argue with you. Forget the case, and Denadene will be fine. Keep pursuing it, and she will not."

"Where is she?" I asked as the line clicked dead.

I wanted to throw the handset into the wall, but instead I replaced it and then slammed one hand into the other so hard it stung. Someone had taken Denadene against her will. She was a kidnap victim. And her life was in my hands. What I had already suspected I now knew to be true. Denadene's disappearance and the murder case against Bronson Melville were directly related. I put my head in my hands, trying to get the leering face of JC Hass from my mind.

Hass had everything to gain and nothing to lose by my throwing the case against his client. I, on the other hand, had my job and my reputation to lose. And what did I have to gain? Something more important than my job or my reputation—the life of Denadene Stegner.

I considered what the caller had said, and I realized that even if I tried to quit investigating the case, someone else in the department would be required to take over. As I sat with my head in my hands, I thought about the problem I faced. I was the loser no matter what course I took. Denadene was the loser if I didn't do as the caller had instructed, and I couldn't convince the rest of the department to do as I was told and drop the murder case.

I thought long and hard about Denadene. Would it be the end of her if I didn't meet the caller's demand? Very likely. Would it be my fault if something terrible happened to her? Not directly. Bronson Melville would be at fault, as would whoever was helping him. But indirectly, it would be very much my fault. What should I do? I had no idea.

I needed the Lord's help. I left the office and drove to the privacy of my apartment without uttering a word about the call to anyone else. Once in my apartment, I dropped to my knees and began to pray. I asked the Lord for wisdom. I asked Him that, whatever I did about the call, He would watch over Denadene. I also asked Him to help me find Brea or that someone else would find her. And I prayed that when she was found, she would be okay. She would be scared, maybe, but I prayed she would not be hurt. I prayed long and hard.

After getting off my knees, I pondered my situation. Perhaps I could simply disappear myself—flee from a difficult situation I could not control. If I did that, I reasoned, Denadene would be safe. Maybe. Melville's cohorts might never let her go, no matter what I did. And I wasn't the only one who could handle the case. It was that thought that brought me to a decision. This was my case. I was a cop. I had a job to do. I was not a coward. I could not, and I would not, flee to save myself from having to do what I should do and leave someone else to do it—leave Denadene in danger despite my cowardice.

I had to have faith. I had to work harder than I ever had in my life. If I did that, I reasoned, I could call on the Lord with greater faith to take care of Denadene. I had always been taught that when praying for a blessing, we should do all we can to achieve it and that the Lord would take it from there.

I returned to the department and asked to see the chief of police. He knew nothing of my friendship with Denadene, but he was enraged about the threatening call. "That's nothing short of blackmail," he said. He called my lieutenant and asked him to join us. After repeating my story to him, we had a discussion about what to do. Both of my bosses felt as I did—we had to proceed with the case—but Bronson Melville needed to have some pressure applied to him.

I figured it would be my job to meet with Bronson, but the chief and the lieutenant decided to do it themselves. "JC Hass will throw a fit," I reminded them.

They chuckled and told me he was welcome to have at it. Hass was clearly not a favorite of my superiors.

"I wouldn't rule him out as being behind this threat," I added a moment later, but then I wished I hadn't said it. I had no basis on which to accuse Hass of such a thing. But I got no resistance from them. In fact, they both nodded, so maybe I wasn't so far off.

After I left the chief's office, I drove back to Hurricane. I wanted to check once more whether Randall Stegner had returned home. What I found at his residence was what I *didn't find*. Denadene's car was gone.

I began knocking on the neighbors' doors again. I wasn't surprised no one had seen the car leaving. However, Becky said, "I heard that obnoxious truck of Randall's during the night. It woke me up. I should have gotten up and looked out the window. Maybe I would have seen who drove off in it."

"Are you telling me you heard the truck arrive and leave?" I asked.

"Oh yes. It was only a couple of minutes later that it left," she responded. "Randall must have had someone with him who then drove the Jetta away."

I finished canvasing the neighborhood and then returned to St. George. On a whim, I drove to Denadene's place. I couldn't park in her spot this time. It was occupied by her dark-blue Volkswagen Jetta. My heart spiked, and I found the nearest empty spot, parked in it, and ran to Denadene's door.

I suppose I should have expected to get no answer, but seeing her Jetta had raised my hopes. Those hopes were dashed though. I tried her phone. There was no response there either. It went directly to voicemail, just as it had been doing. Then I called the department and had someone sent out to open the car door and then process the car for fingerprints. The effort was a waste of energy. There were no prints. It had been wiped so clean even Denadene's prints, which should have been plentiful, were gone.

There was nothing in the car to indicate it was owned by a woman. The only things I found were the registration and owner's manual. The registration was in Denadene's name. Discouraged, I called her parents to see if they had heard anything from her. They still hadn't and were distressed to learn her car had returned but she was still not at home. I didn't tell them about the threatening call I had received. They had enough to worry about.

I spoke to as many other residents of the apartment complex as I could. No one had seen the car when it was returned to Denadene's parking space nor did anyone remember hearing a vehicle with a loud exhaust.

It was late afternoon by the time I finished in the complex. I drove back to the station to catch up on my reports. Lieutenant Dollison buzzed me and asked me to come to his office. "I thought you'd want to know how it went with the chief and me when we went to the jail to speak with Melville."

"I can sort of imagine," I said. "Did Hass come?"

"Oh yes. He's an even bigger jerk than he used to be," he said. "He basically shut us down right off the bat. Since he wouldn't let us attempt to get any information from his client, we only spent a few minutes with him."

"That was probably productive," I said sarcastically.

Lieutenant Dollison chuckled. "You can say that again. He told us he was sure you were lying, just like you had lied about Brea witnessing the murder and pretty much everything else you've reported for the Melville case."

"He's really got it in for me, hasn't he?" I said.

"Yes, but I don't think it's personal. He'd treat any other officer who was lead on the case the exact same way," he said. He chuckled mirthlessly again before continuing. "He told us it was ridiculous to think anyone would make a threat like the one you received regarding Denadene's well-being when the judge would be dropping the charges against his client Monday morning anyway."

"Like that's going to happen," I said. "Mark Stansel let me read the motion Hass wrote. It's pure garbage—mostly an attack on me."

"I can believe it," the lieutenant said. "But he may be delusional enough to think he might actually prevail. He did tell us one useful thing though. He says Denadene Stegner quit her job with him, that he has a letter from her to that effect in her file."

"Yeah, he told me that too. Did he happen to tell you what she gave as her reasons for quitting?" I asked.

"No, I'm afraid not." Lieutenant Dollison leaned across his desk toward me and slowly shook his head. "Frankly, Gage, I don't think there is a letter. But if there is, I don't believe for a minute it was written or signed by Denadene."

"Lieutenant," I began as an idea bounced around in my head. "Since we have an active missing person case on Ms. Stegner, do you think we could have the prosecutor ask a judge to force Hass to produce the letter for us?"

He sat back again. "That's a good idea. Why don't you go talk to Mark Stansel now."

CHAPTER FOUR

I HAD A COURT ORDER in my hand the following morning. Sergeant Hanks and I delivered it to Hass's office and handed it to Ms. Kwick. "What's this?" she growled as she more or less jerked it from my hand.

"It's an order from the district court. You are to hand over the resignation letter from Denadene Stegner," I said. She slowly scanned the document and said nothing.

She took her time looking at it before holding it back out to me. "This is no good, Detectives," she said, looking down as she spoke. "There is no such letter."

I peered closely at her, and she finally looked up. There was fear in her eyes, but I was not sure who or what she was afraid of. Us, perhaps? "Your boss says there is, and he told me you personally opened the letter and gave it to him, Ms. Kwick. Please get it right now."

"I told you, there isn't one," she said. Her hands were shaking. "Take this. It's no good."

I took the order back as Sergeant Hanks made a call. I listened as he said, "This is Detective Sergeant Jon Hanks. I need to speak with Mark Stansel." He waited. I waited. Ms. Kwick nervously twisted on her chair, her eyes darting back and forth. Finally Jon said, "Mark, this is Sergeant Hanks. Detective Tipton and I are at JC Hass's office. His legal secretary tells us there is no letter of resignation from Denadene Stegner."

He listened for a minute, and then he said to Ms. Kwick, "Have your boss come out here."

"He's not in," she said, her eyes failing to meet mine or his.

"That's what you told me before," I reminded her as I started back toward his private office.

"Don't go back there," she begged. "Please."

I disregarded her protest. I knocked on Hass's office door. There was no response. I tried the handle. The door was locked. I rejoined my sergeant. "I think, for once, she's telling the truth," I said.

"Too bad she's chosen to lie about the resignation letter," he countered. "I'm waiting for a call back from Mark."

The call came in a couple of minutes. By then Ms. Kwick was not only squirming and shifting her eyes but was sweating. I stared at her as Sergeant Hanks spoke on the phone. "The judge wants Ms. Kwick brought to his chambers right now?" he asked. He listened again and then said, "We'll bring her in." He ended the call. "You heard that, Ms. Kwick. I have a feeling you're going to find yourself in contempt of court for disobeying a court order."

"You can't do this," she said, shaking visibly. The fear I was sure I'd seen before was even more evident in her eyes.

"Let's go," Sergeant Hanks said.

She refused to stand up. "Mr. Hass will have your jobs for this," she threatened, but her voice held no conviction and her eyes still did not meet ours.

My sergeant already had his phone out again. He had a short conversation with the prosecutor. When he'd finished his call, he said, "You and I are to stay here and secure this office, Detective. In the meantime, a search warrant is being prepared. The judge will sign it. He and the prosecutor already had that conversation." He turned to Ms. Kwick. "And after we find the letter, he still wants you brought to his chambers. You need to think about what you're doing."

Ms. Kwick was becoming increasingly agitated. "You can't search this office. These files are confidential. You'll get me in so much trouble." She was so upset her voice was squeaking.

"If a judge says we can search, then we can search," Sergeant Hanks said angrily. "The only way to avoid that is to produce the letter you've been ordered to hand over to us."

"There isn't one," she insisted again, but her squeaky voice sounded like she was thinking seriously about reconsidering her answer. She blew her nose, and her eyes filled with moisture.

"We'll see. You might want to call Mr. Hass. He might find it would make a lot of sense to produce the letter rather than have us search his office," Hanks said.

Ms. Kwick looked like she was about to collapse and fall right off her chair. But she did pick up the phone and dial a number. She apparently got no answer. She tried another number and a third. Finally she said, "I can't reach him. I'm sorry, but there is nothing more I can do. You will have to come back tomorrow when he's in."

"No," I said. "We will not be leaving today without that letter, Ms. Kwick."

For a long time, she said nothing. Then she finally forced herself to her feet. "Mr. Hass will kill me for this," she said. I couldn't help but wonder if she meant that literally. Hopefully not, but I was getting the sense she was far more afraid of JC Hass than she was of us.

We followed as she went into a separate room filled with filing cabinets. She opened the top drawer of one of the cabinets, reached in, and pulled out a sheet of paper.

"And the envelope," I said as she handed it to me.

"We threw that away," she said.

I shook my head. "Why would you do that?" I asked.

"I just did what Mr. Hass said to do," she responded. She was as white as a sheet. I took the paper from her and once again handed her the court order. Then I glanced at the paper to make sure it was what we were after.

"Is that it?" Sergeant Hanks asked.

"It is," I said. A minute later Ms. Kwick was back at her desk, blowing her nose again and rubbing her eyes. "I'll need a signed statement from you certifying this is in fact the letter that was in the envelope Ms. Stegner sent to this office."

"I don't have to do that, do I?" She was less sure of herself now. And there was no question she was afraid of something or someone.

Sergeant Hanks once again pulled out his phone. "This is Sergeant Hanks again," he said. "I need to speak with Mark once more."

"All right, I'll type you a letter," Ms. Kwick said. "But you're getting me in so much trouble with Mr. Hass."

"Just a handwritten note is sufficient," I said.

She scowled, but she pulled out a piece of paper, wrote the statement I requested, and held it out to me. I took it; Jon and I weren't so much interested in what she wrote. It was a sample of her handwriting we were after. It was our intention to have the handwriting on the note compared by an expert to the handwritten letter she had just turned over to us.

Hanks stepped to the door and turned his back to us as he spoke with the prosecutor. As soon as I had the statement in my hand, along with the letter of resignation, he turned back to me and said, "The judge has changed his mind. Since we have the letter, Ms. Kwick won't have to go see him."

She heaved what was clearly a sigh of relief, but the fear in her eyes had not diminished. Sergeant Hanks and I left. As we walked to our vehicles, he said, "At least we didn't have to go through with obtaining a search warrant." He looked at me. "Did she seem relieved to you?"

"Yes and no," I said. "I'm sure she's not happy we have the letter, but I would imagine if Hass came back and found we had searched his office, she would have caught his wrath. I think she's scared of him for some reason, a reason that didn't seem to exist when he first hired her to fill in. And frankly, I never knew Denadene to be afraid of him."

"I think you're right. And I don't blame her." He switched topics. "Now we need to get a sample of Ms. Stegner's handwriting for the comparison."

"I'll take care of that," I said. "I'll drive to Cedar City now and get something from Denadene's parents. But first I want to look closer at this letter."

We went to the office and made copies of both documents. By then I had read the letter two or three times. It was very short and to the point. Denadene had purportedly written,

> *Mr. Hass:*
>
> *I don't feel like I can work here anymore. My relationship with Detective Gage Tipton has put me in a difficult position since you are representing a man he arrested. Please don't take this personally, as I think very highly of you and have enjoyed our time together. But I feel I have no choice at this point. I resign, effective immediately.*
>
> *Denadene Stegner*

The signature was a little shaky. I was fairly certain we would find the letter was forged by Ms. Kwick.

I had dinner before I drove to Cedar City. At Denadene's parents' home a short while later, they gave me a couple of different samples of

Denadene's handwriting. I had just put them in my pocket and was about to thank them when my cell phone rang. "Detective Tipton," I answered.

The voice on the other end of the line was hauntingly familiar, and it was muffled. "I am not someone to be trifled with. You will regret not following my instructions."

I stepped away from the Garfords before I responded. "Mr. Melville's attorney told us the case was going to be dismissed on Monday when he submits a motion," I said.

"You had your instructions, Mr. Tipton. Don't put this on Mr. Hass. You alone are responsible for what is about to happen to Ms. Stegner. She will suffer the consequences of your bullheadedness." Before I could make any further response, the call was terminated. I felt sick at heart. I stepped back to Denadene's parents and said, "I have to run. Something important just came up. Thanks for the handwriting samples." I touched the pocket where I had stored the papers they had just given me and hurriedly left their home.

I called Sergeant Hanks once I was back in my vehicle and had somewhat settled myself down. "Jon," I said. "I got another call from the person who threatened me earlier."

"What did he say?" Jon asked, concerned.

"He said I was responsible for what was about to happen to Denadene," I choked out. "I think I've made a terrible mistake."

"You did your job, Detective. You had no choice. Let's hope this is a bluff."

"He sounded dead serious," I said.

"Do you have any idea, after hearing the voice twice, whose it was?" he asked.

"I have no idea. All I could tell was that it was a deep voice, likely a man's, but it was effectively muffled. It was the same one as before. I don't believe the caller was using a voice-modulating device. I think he just had something over his phone."

We talked for a moment longer. I didn't catch a lot of what Jon had to say because I was so upset. I was sure he was trying to calm me down and ease my conscience. The call only ended when I got a call from Denadene's father. I switched calls.

"I'm sorry I didn't bring this up earlier, Gage. I was going to ask if it's okay if my wife and I go pick up Denadene's car. We have a key," Ed informed me.

"Sure, that's a good idea," I said. "When did you want to do that?"

"Tonight," he said. "We can leave right now."

"That sounds good," I said, trying desperately to keep the emotion I was experiencing from my voice.

When he ended the call, it was a relief. I was afraid that if Denadene had not already been killed, she soon would be, and I dreaded the day I was going to have to face Ed and his wife with the news of their daughter's murder. Even though I could reason in my mind that it wasn't my fault, my heart and my conscience wouldn't accept that. I staggered under the weight of guilt as I got out of the Explorer at my apartment. I knew a long sleepless night was ahead of me.

The next morning I didn't get out of bed until after eight, still tired and unrested. I stumbled to my shower, hoping the water beating on my body would give me some energy, but it didn't. It took me an eternity to dress and eat a few bites of cold cereal. I was just putting the bowl in the sink for later attention when my landline rang.

Since it was Saturday, I hoped I wasn't being called into the office on a new case. But when I looked at the screen, I didn't recognize the number. I finally answered. What I heard next shook me to the core. It was an operator asking if I would accept a collect call from Denadene Stegner.

Could this be real? Was she really alive?

"Yes, of course," I said and waited with my hands and knees trembling so badly I had to retreat to the kitchen table and sit down.

A moment later a voice I'd thought I'd never hear again said, "Gage, I'm sorry I haven't called before now."

"Denadene, where are you?" I asked. "There are a lot of people worried about you."

"I'm sorry to bother you now," she said, her voice emotional. "But I didn't know who else to call."

"It's no bother," I said. "I'm just so relieved to hear from you. You can't imagine how worried I've been. Thanks for calling."

She didn't say anything about having caused me to worry. "Gage, I need help. I'm in jail," she said and then erupted in sobs.

I didn't think anything could shock me more than to discover Denadene was alive, but I was just as shocked to hear this news. "Where?" I asked as I tamped my own emotions back and tried to be all business. I felt she needed me to be strong.

"In Las Vegas," she said. "Clark County Detention Center."

"I'll come and bail you out," I promised.

"They won't let me make bond," she said.

"What? They have to!" I exclaimed. "What are they accusing you of?"

"Murder," she said so softly I could barely make out what she said. Sobbing, she didn't seem to be able to go on.

"Murder! That's insane. Who do they say you murdered?" I was blown away by the accusation.

There was a pause as she struggled to regain her voice. "My husband," she said. "But I have to get off the phone. There are other ladies in line, and they're getting pretty worked up. Please come."

"I'll be there as soon as I can," I promised.

"Thank you," she said and hung up.

Only after the call ended did it register in my mind that she had used the word husband, not ex-husband. Then, like a punch in the gut, it hit me. Denadene was in Las Vegas, the marriage capital of the nation. I wondered if she'd remarried Randall Stegner. That could explain her car at his place, but it couldn't explain it being returned to her apartment.

I forced myself to think calmly, rationally. I replayed in my mind the conversation I had just had with Denadene. I could think of no other explanation. Sometime after I last saw her on Monday, she had married someone. I could only assume it had been Randall. But why would she do that? I could only come up with one answer: she had to have been forced to do it.

The mystery caller from before had told me I was responsible for what was about to happen to Denadene. I had assumed it had been a death threat against her, but I had been wrong. Apparently she was being framed for a murder I did not for one second believe she could have committed. I ran two scenarios through my mind. Someone else could have murdered her *husband* and then made it look like she had done it. Or she could have killed him in self-defense, and it was now being twisted to look like murder. Her marriage to Randall had ended badly. He had abused her then, and if she had remarried him, there was no reason to think he wouldn't have picked up right where he had left off. Denadene killing him in self-defense was a very real possibility.

After a couple more minutes, I was in control of my emotions. I was ready to do whatever I had to do to help her. I was a detective. Perhaps I could get with the officers in Las Vegas who had arrested her and help them figure this out. But first I needed to know exactly whom she was accused of murdering and how she allegedly did it.

I called Sergeant Hanks. "Gage? What's happening?" he asked.

"I just talked to Denadene Stegner," I said.

"You found her?" he asked, sounding incredulous.

"She found me is more like it. She called me collect from the Clark County Detention Center."

Before I could explain, he broke in with, "What in the world is she doing there?"

"She was arrested for murdering her husband," I responded.

"I thought she was divorced," he said, sounding as perplexed as I felt.

I then explained my theories. He responded with, "You'd better go to Vegas right now. Call me when you know exactly what's going on. And, Gage, could this have anything to do with Bronson's brother?"

"That's what I was wondering," I said. "I know he has gang connections in Vegas. This makes no sense though. I can't see how he could be involved."

"I'll have a BOLO put out in the Vegas area for Alvin and Randall. And I'll list all their known vehicles, though they could be driving something different by now. I wouldn't think they would still be using Melville's van, but you never know," he said. "They also could have switched license plates."

"Thanks, Sergeant. I'll be on my way."

"I'll call the lieutenant and the chief. They need to know."

"I'll call you." The phrase hit me as I said it. That was what Denadene had promised me. *That phrase could jinx me.* It certainly seemed like it had jinxed Denadene.

CHAPTER FIVE

When I arrived in Las Vegas, I went directly to the Clark County Detention Center and requested a visit with Denadene, but I was told that unless I was her lawyer, I would have to come back on regular visiting hours. I asked when that would be and was told I could visit beginning at twelve thirty that afternoon. I had just missed the morning visiting time. I was also told I had to register in order to visit and that I would be allowed fifty minutes—less if there were a lot of other visitors there to see other inmates.

I registered and left to grab something to eat while I waited. I wasn't very hungry, but I forced a burger down and returned to the jail at twelve thirty. A few minutes later I was directed to one of the booths in the lobby area. The visit would be over closed-circuit TV. Even though I was an officer and was working on a case related to Denadene, they would not let me visit her face to face. Only lawyers were allowed to visit with inmates in person.

I sat down, and the video feed began. I looked around. Anyone in the lobby could hear what I was saying if they stepped close enough. But I didn't see anyone who seemed interested in me. I sat there for fifteen or twenty minutes while I waited for them to get Denadene on camera. I was sure the time I was sitting there was being clocked against my fifty minutes. Other visitors were sitting on either side of me—I could hear their conversations—and other people stood nearby, visiting and mingling with one another.

When I finally saw Denadene on the video feed, she looked terrified. She had lost weight just since Monday night. Her eyes were red, her hair was unkempt, and she was trembling as if she was cold, but I was sure it wasn't that.

"Hi," I said. "It's good to see you. I'm sorry for what you're going through."

When she spoke, her voice was as broken as she looked. "It isn't your fault," she said.

"Actually it is," I countered. "I was called and told if I didn't drop the murder case against Bronson Melville, you would suffer the consequences. I didn't drop it, and now here you are."

"Don't blame yourself," she said as a spark lit her eyes. "You couldn't do something like that anyway, could you?"

"Even if I could back out of the case, it would only be assigned to someone else and get me fired. Not that I was worried about my job. I was worried about you. At any rate, it's because I didn't do as I was ordered that you're in here."

For a long time she was silent. Her emotions were right at the surface. She sobbed some, and it appeared she was trying to get her emotions under control. Our time was ticking away, but I didn't try to rush her. I was afraid that would only upset her more and she wouldn't be able to say what she needed to say. Finally she appeared to have taken control of her emotions and spoke. "We don't have a lot of time to talk," she said. "They wasted a lot of time getting me to the camera. I asked them to hurry, but they only slowed down. Gage, make sure no one listens in on us. I know this video thing is probably being recorded, but I mean, someone in the lobby there with you."

I looked around again. I spoke very softly. "There are a couple of people fairly close, but no one seems interested in me. There's a guy a few feet away, but his back is toward me." The guy who was turned away from me made me nervous.

Her eyes grew wide, and she touched a hand to her mouth. "Is he alone?" she asked.

"There's no one right next to him, if that's what you mean."

"How is he dressed?" she asked. I could hear fear in her voice. I shivered.

"He's wearing blue jeans, a blue polo shirt, and black leather shoes, and he has thin brown hair," I said. "It's long on the sides. I think he has tattoos on both forearms, but I can't see them clearly from this angle."

She gasped. "It's him," she said softly, but her face filled with fear. She was shaking worse than ever now.

"Who?" I said, keeping an eye on the man.

"JC's brother," she said, once again having to fight with her emotions.

"You mean Bronson's brother?" I asked.

"No, not Alvin. But he could be here somewhere too. I mean JC's brother. I'd never met him until Tuesday night outside the office," she said.

"You mean when Hass told you that you could have Friday off?" I asked.

"JC told you that?" she asked, a little louder and with anger overpowering the emotion in her voice.

"He did, but he didn't mention anyone besides the two of you being there."

"He's lying, Gage. He told me I could *not* have the day off. He said he needed me to work. Just then this guy I'd never seen before walked up to us. We were standing by my car. JC told me it was his younger brother, Dwight. He's shorter than JC and kind of scrawny, but I could see a resemblance. He has a nasty-looking scar on his right cheek and all those tattoos. He gave me the creeps," she said.

I kept an eye on the man who could be Dwight Hass. He glanced at me and turned away quickly, but not before I saw his cheek. I turned back to Denadene. "It's him," I said quietly. "I just saw the scar."

"Oh, Gage, I was afraid of that."

"What's he doing here?" I asked.

She hesitated. I waited. "Spying on us, I guess," she said when she spoke again. "He was probably watching for someone to visit me."

"We'll just have to try to be really quiet," I whispered. "Did this Dwight guy say anything to you?"

"No, he didn't say anything after JC introduced us, but his eyes—they were scary. He kept watching me while JC and I talked, and then, if you can imagine this, he came by my apartment right after I got home."

"And you talked to him then?" I asked. I glanced at my watch. I hadn't even gotten around to asking about her dead husband. I didn't have as much time left as I would have liked. We had been cheated on the time, both by Denadene's emotions and the jail staff. *Maybe that's the way some correctional officers treat murder suspects,* I thought.

Denadene rubbed a hand over her eyes before she said, "He came to the door. I asked him what he wanted, and he told me Randall wanted to see me. That really surprised me. I didn't have any idea he knew Randall. I told him I had nothing to talk to Randall about, but he said it was important. He handed me a note and said, 'You'd better go up there tonight.' He wouldn't say what was important about it, but his voice was very threatening. I tried not to show my fear, but I'm sure he could sense it. He said a few more things about how I should do what I was told and treat Randall nicely."

"What did the note say?" I asked.

"I don't recall word for word, but it was something about how Randall had a problem he thought I could help him with. It said he was desperate and to please let past bad feelings not stop me from helping him just that one time," she said.

"Could you tell if Randall wrote the note?"

"I know his handwriting, and it looked like his. And it looked like his signature."

"Did Randall say in the note what the problem was?" I asked, glancing at my watch again. The time was flying by.

"He didn't," she said.

"So what did you do?" I asked.

"I told Dwight I would go. I mean, I felt like I needed to. I know I didn't owe Randall anything, but it isn't in my nature to refuse to help people if I can," she answered.

I knew that was true. She had a soft heart. "When did you go see him?"

"I left right after Dwight did, but before I got there, Randall called me on my cell phone—I had changed my number after the divorce, so I don't know how he got it—and asked if I could just meet him somewhere else and said I didn't need to go clear to his house."

"Where did you meet him?"

"Since he was leaving his house, I told him to come to my apartment."

"Did he have your address?" I asked.

"I hadn't spoken with him since the divorce was finalized, but I figured he must have had it, or he wouldn't have been able to send Dwight Hass there."

"He probably got it from your boss," I guessed.

"I think so. Or Dwight could have gotten it from him and given it to Randall. Anyway, he did come to my apartment. He was acting really nice, but I knew that's all it was—an act. I was married to him long enough to know that when he was nice, it wasn't real. But I invited him in, and we talked for a few minutes." She hesitated. I waited, wondering what was going through her mind.

Finally she said, "He . . . ah . . . he gave me a box of chocolates he'd been holding. It was already open, but I didn't think anything of it. I figured he'd sampled them on the way to my apartment. He said it was a peace offering. He took the lid off and held it out to me. I ate one, and then I started feeling dizzy, and . . . and . . . I, ah . . . don't remember anything after that." Her eyes strayed from the camera as she spoke.

"He doped you," I said through gritted teeth. "Where were you when you woke up?"

"I was in Randall's house, on his sofa," she said after a short hesitation, still keeping her eyes averted.

I glanced at my watch again and then at Dwight. A couple of other people were as close to me now as he was, and he said something to one of them, something about hating this place. The other people agreed.

"We don't have a lot of time, Denadene," I said. "We can talk more another time about what happened after that. But right now, I need you to tell me why you're in jail."

I glanced over. Dwight Hass was still facing the other two people, but they were not conversing now. I had been speaking very quietly, and so had Denadene, and I feared he might have overheard at least a few words here and there, but I needed to learn more about why she was accused of killing her husband. If I didn't talk to her about it now, I didn't know when I'd be able to. Visits here were restrictive, and as I had already learned, officers could cheat us on the time we were supposedly allowed. I turned to face Denadene again. "You told me you were accused of killing your husband. I didn't know you were married."

She didn't answer for a good minute or so, and once again she kept putting her hand to her mouth, stifling sobs. She also kept looking around like she was afraid someone was listening to her. "I . . . ah . . . didn't either," she said nervously, puzzling me, but I didn't respond. In a moment she went on, staring at her hands as she spoke. "Apparently, even though I have no recollection of it, Randall and I were married in some little wedding chapel here in Las Vegas on Thursday." She shook her head, and tears flooded her eyes. "How could I not know?" She paused and stared at the camera, at me over the video feed. "You've got to believe me, Gage. I have no idea how I got to Las Vegas. I don't even remember much about what happened at Randall's house. He kept saying he really needed me to do something for him, but I don't remember him ever saying what it was. I guess it was that he wanted me to marry him again, but he knew I would never agree to that." As she spoke, her eyes again were averted from the camera. I supposed she hated having to tell me all this. Not once did it occur to me that she might be lying.

She stopped talking. I was acutely aware of the time ticking away. She rubbed her head and continued looking off to the side, away from the camera. "He . . . ah . . . he offered me some, ah, some water. I guess I drank a glass of it. It must have been drugged too because the next thing I remember is . . . ah . . . was, ah . . . waking up in a room in a casino here."

"When did you wake up?"

She spoke quickly now, none of the nervous or emotional hesitation I had been witnessing evident any longer. "Friday. Yesterday. I think it was late afternoon or evening."

"What happened after you woke up?" I asked.

"A pair of detectives came to my room and arrested me. They said they had proof I had murdered Randall—that I'd shot him." She gave me a blank look for a moment, and then her eyes drifted off to the side again. When she finally looked back at the camera, she said, "I don't own a gun, Gage. I've never even shot one." She hesitated again, once more seeming unsure of herself and looking away. "But . . . ah . . . I, ah, I guess maybe I did shoot him. I mean, if I, ah . . . I, you know, if I can't remember how I got down here or ah . . . even marrying Randall again, then, ah . . . how could I expect to remember if I . . . if I . . . ah . . . killed him or not?"

"Who were the detectives?" I asked, worrying and wondering why she was speaking so differently than I'd ever known her to speak before. She appeared to be scared and very nervous.

When she spoke again, it was as if she was surer about what she was saying. There was no hesitation. She stared directly into the camera. "The one who seemed to be in charge said his name was Marcel Butler. The other one was Juan Garcia. Detective Butler did most of the talking, and when they took me in, he was the one who interviewed me."

"What did you tell them?" I asked.

"Are you kidding me, Gage? I work for a defense attorney. Well, *worked* for one. I don't know that I would go back to work for JC even if he would take me." She slapped her forehead. "What am I saying? I'm charged with murder. My life as I've known it is finished." She was silent for a long moment as she seemed to be fighting to control her emotions once more.

She finally spoke again. "I worked for JC long enough to know that if I ever got in trouble, I should tell the officers nothing. I told them I wanted an attorney."

"Did you get one?"

"Not yet. Detective Butler told me that would be taken care of on Monday morning at my arraignment if I couldn't find one for myself."

"So I assume they asked you no more questions. Did they talk to you after that, and if so, what did they tell you?" I asked.

"Just that they could prove I shot Randall—that I, ah . . . had . . . ah, married him on Thursday. I don't even know where they found his body, if he's really dead. This is all such a nightmare. I'm so scared. Surely I didn't kill Randall," she said. "But they think I did. Maybe I did."

We were informed our time was up, and just like that, the video feed went down. For a moment I just sat there, aware that Dwight Hass was still standing in the same place. Other people were milling around near him. I got up quickly, and before Dwight could get away, I was standing in front of him. My first impulse was to bash his face in, but I was in a jail. If I touched him, I would be back there with Denadene. So I did the next best thing.

I spoke to him in a quiet voice filled with as much menace as I could manage. And right then, I could manage quite a lot. "Dwight Hass. I will find out what you had to do with Denadene being in jail, and when I do, I'll come after you. I won't forget you. And I won't let you forget me. That's a promise."

He didn't respond. I hadn't expected he would. I turned and walked away. I was aware of him following me out of the facility, but when I headed for my Explorer, he went another way. I stopped and watched him. He began to jog. I jogged after him. But a minute later, a black van pulled up and squealed to a stop, and he jumped in. Then it tore out of there, and I had to jump behind a car to keep from getting hit. I managed to read the license plate though.

I didn't bother to try to get back to my Explorer in time to chase them. I knew it would do no good. So after reaching my vehicle, I got on my phone, called my department, and had them run a records check on Dwight Hass. I was not surprised to find he also had a long criminal record and had spent time in prison. I made a couple of other phone calls and learned that he, like his buddy Alvin Melville, may have had ties with at least one Las

Vegas gang. I rubbed my hand through my hair. JC Hass, defense attorney, sure had some shady connections, not that it surprised me at that point. But worse than that, it appeared Denadene's former husband shared those shady acquaintances.

I finally drove to the Las Vegas Metropolitan Police Department headquarters. Since it was a Saturday, I wasn't sure if I'd find either of the detectives Denadene had named, but both of them were in. When I identified myself, I was escorted to meet them.

I introduced myself to them.

"What brings a St. George detective to our fair city?" Detective Butler asked me. He was a burly man in his early forties with a ruddy complexion and a shaved head. He stood around six feet tall and spoke with a deep voice.

I informed them I had just come from the jail and told them I knew they had arrested a woman the day before for killing her husband.

"Oh yeah, the Stegner woman," Detective Butler said. "Not the kind of gal I would have expected to arrest for such a crime. But the evidence is pretty strong."

"Are you sure she was married to Randall? The last I knew, they had been divorced for a couple of years," I said, trying to keep my voice calm and not accusatory. I did add, "It was a contentious divorce. She had been abused for a long time, so I find it hard to believe she would marry him again."

"That's what our informant told us, and he produced a marriage license to prove it," he said.

Butler's partner, Detective Juan Garcia, was a lot smaller than Butler and looked to be around thirty. He spoke then. "The guy told us he'd seen her shoot him and then run. He guessed she was probably back in her hotel room in the casino by then but couldn't be sure."

"Who is your informant?" I asked.

The two looked at one another. Then Detective Butler said, "I don't know that we should divulge that at this point."

"I see," I said. "Then, let me guess. It was a guy by the name of Alvin Melville or Dwight Hass, or perhaps it was someone claiming to be some sort of relative of Randall's."

The two of them looked at each other with surprise. Butler said, "Why don't you sit down. I think we need to talk."

I took a seat in the crowded cubicle and said, "Which was it? Hass or Melville?"

"He told us he was Jim Stegner, a brother of the victim," Detective Butler admitted. "He had ID to prove it."

"What did he look like?" I asked.

Butler described him. I shook my head. "No, that's Alvin Melville, from the description," I said. "He's been in trouble a lot—in prison twice. We believe he has connections with a gang here in Vegas. I don't think it would be too much of a stretch for him to have a fake ID."

"Who is Melville?" Butler asked.

I explained, and he and Garcia nodded.

"Was he driving a black van with darkened windows?" I asked. They again nodded. I asked them about the license plate number, but the one they told me was different from the one I had just seen.

"Our records check showed the van as being registered to this Jim Stegner guy," Garcia said.

"That doesn't surprise me," I said. "But I saw a van a few minutes ago with Alvin Melville's plates on it. He must switch them back and forth. Who knows? He may have more. Anyway, he and his friend Dwight Hass both have long records," I informed them.

"You seem to know a lot about these guys. How do you know all this?" Detective Garcia asked.

"A few weeks ago I arrested Alvin Melville's brother, Bronson, for the murder of a man by the name of Duane Trahan. The woman who witnessed the murder was covered with the victim's blood and was holding him in her arms when I got there within a few minutes of the shooting. Bronson Melville is a local radio personality who is fairly well-known in my area, liked by some and disliked by others. He's currently being held without bond."

"That's interesting, but what does that have to do with our murder?" Detective Butler asked.

"Bronson hired an attorney by the name of JC Hass. His little brother, Dwight, whom we just talked about, was watching and trying to eavesdrop on my conversation with Ms. Stegner at the jail a few minutes ago. I spoke to him afterward, but he didn't say a word to me and took off. Guess who picked him up in a black van?"

"That would probably be Mr. Melville, with his own plates on the vehicle," Butler said, his voice a deep rumble and his face deadpan.

"That's right," I said. "JC Hass, counselor at law, has been all over TV in my area, running me down and claiming I had fabricated the evidence against his client. Then his legal secretary suddenly disappeared. I happen to be a friend of hers. Her name is Denadene Stegner. She was apparently abducted by her ex-husband on Tuesday night, but it gets worse," I said. "The witness in the murder of my victim in the Melville case is also missing. I suspect foul play."

The two detectives seemed to be tongue-tied, so I went on. "I got a phone call at my desk at the St. George Police Department a couple of days ago by someone whose voice was muffled. I was unable to recognize it. The caller told me that unless I made sure all the charges against Bronson Melville went away and he was released from jail, Denadene Stegner would suffer. I think you both realize that to comply would be virtually impossible and certainly professional suicide."

Detective Butler found his voice again. "Yeah, I'd say so. What happened when you didn't do as you were instructed?"

"I got a call back yesterday afternoon telling me I was responsible for what was now going to happen to Denadene, that she was going to suffer the consequences of my stupidity. Of course, I thought the worst. I assumed she would be killed, but then she called me collect from the jail this morning, telling me she had been arrested for Randall Stegner's murder."

The two men squirmed in their chairs and looked at each other. It was the younger detective who spoke first. "I think we have some work to do," he said to his partner.

CHAPTER SIX

"Would you go over the evidence that you have against Ms. Stegner with me?" I asked.

"Under the circumstances, I think maybe it would be okay," Detective Butler agreed. He reached into his desk, brought out a file, and turned it toward me. Typed at the top was Denadene's name. He opened it and said, "Take a look."

There were pictures of the victim. It didn't take an autopsy to determine the cause of death. He'd been shot at close range. I didn't see an autopsy report—hadn't expected to. I looked at Detective Butler. "I suppose he's being autopsied now?"

"Should be done by tonight," Butler said.

I looked back at the file and picked up a copy of the marriage license. It looked legitimate, but I still had serious doubts about its authenticity. "Have you talked to the person who performed the wedding?" I asked.

"I didn't think it was necessary," Detective Butler said. "But in light of what you've told me, I suppose we should."

"I feel it's imperative you do," I said. "And talk to the person who issued the license as well. Since it's Saturday, you may need to call some people at their homes."

Butler turned to his partner. "Detective, why don't you work on this while Detective Tipton and I continue here," he said as he held out the marriage license.

Garcia took the license and left. I began once again to look at items in the file. "This is the statement of Jim Stegner, who is really Alvin Melville," I noted. "I suppose you recorded him and then typed this up?"

"Of course," Butler said. "And, as you can see, he signed it."

I read through the statement. It was straightforward. In a nutshell, Alvin, who had claimed to be Jim Stegner, had written that he was the best man at the wedding. He claimed to have thought everything was cozy with Denadene and Randall until an argument began after the two had too much to drink a short while later. He and his friend Dwight had followed them toward an alley, which they'd entered just as Denadene had shot Randall. Then she had run. He stated he'd called 911 at that point and waited for the cops to come.

"This is all a lie," I said flatly. "I know for a fact Denadene would never drink alcohol. Tell me about the room where you found Ms. Stegner."

"Melville knew which room it was. We went there directly, but it was empty. It wasn't until last night that we got a call from Melville telling us she had returned, that he'd seen her going into her room. We went there again and found her. She seemed to be a bit hungover," the detective said.

"Did you do any blood tests on her?" I asked as I shook my head.

"Didn't think we needed to. We tried to question her, but she wanted an attorney," Detective Butler said. "So we locked her up."

"Denadene told me she doesn't remember anything from the time she drank a glass of water at her ex-husband's house until you guys came and arrested her. I suspect she was doped. I think you should get blood drawn; you'll likely find stuff in her system that shouldn't be. And I don't think you'll find any alcohol."

"We can do that right after we're done here," the officer agreed.

I looked through the file some more. "I don't see anything here about the weapon," I noted.

"It's at the very end of that report. It hasn't been found," Butler said.

"I gather you searched her room. Did you do that the first time you went there or after you were told by Dwight that she had returned?" I asked.

Detective Butler hesitated. Finally he said, "Both times."

"I take it Denadene didn't say anything about the weapon when you arrested her?" I asked.

"No," he said. "She denies using a gun at all. But when we didn't find her in her room the first time, our witness told us she would probably be coming back to it at some point in time. He also told us he would ask around and see if anyone could tell him where she might have gone. We hadn't quite finished searching her room the first time when we got a call from Dwight that he had seen our suspect in Henderson at a convenience store. He said she was still there and we could catch her if we hurried. We told him to stay there, and we took off right then without finishing. But we instructed the manager that no one was to enter that room until we gave the okay. That was probably a mistake on our part, although we couldn't have missed much. It's not a huge room."

"So Dwight saw her in Henderson?" I asked.

"That's what he claimed. We went to the convenience store Dwight had mentioned. He was gone when we got there. We spoke to one person there who told us that a guy said a woman who was wanted for murder had just left the store and that he was going to follow her. He asked them to tell us that when we got there," he said.

"I see," I said as serious doubt entered my mind. "Didn't that bother you? I mean, wouldn't Dwight have called you back when she left?"

"He called us the first time from a payphone. He said he didn't have a cell phone with him, so we thought nothing of it."

I decided to drop that for now. "At any rate, you finished the search later, after she returned to her room?"

Admittedly, I might have assumed the same thing Butler and Garcia had—that Dwight and Denadene both could have left the convenience store by the time they arrived—but I would have thought a completion of the search might have been in order before following the lead from Dwight. But, of course, I was looking at this case of theirs through a much different lens than they were. I knew Dwight was an unsavory character, but they hadn't known that at the time. "Did you find anything besides the lack of a weapon when you searched the room more thoroughly?" I asked.

"We sure did," he said.

"Why don't you tell me about that while we drive to the jail," I said. "We need Denadene's blood drawn as soon as possible."

I thought he might cut me off at some point, but instead he stood and said, "We'll take my car. I think maybe you need to work with us on this, if you don't mind. Honestly, I still think we've got the killer, but we can possibly rule things out with your help if we need to."

I stood to follow him. "All right. I'd like that. Let's go." My hope, of course, was that Denadene would be ruled out, and they could begin a new investigation looking for the actual killer.

Detective Butler put the file away, and we went to his car. On the way to the jail, I asked, "What did you find in the searches of her room?"

"There were some women's clothes there—a couple of changes worth in a small suitcase. Ms. Stegner was dressed in a pair of blue jeans and a blouse when we arrested her. And we found some pants, shirts, underclothes, and socks the guy you say is Melville identified as being her husband's," Detective Butler told me.

"Were there any nightgowns or pajamas?" I asked.

For a moment, the officer didn't respond. Finally he said, "Come to think of it, there weren't any."

"And that didn't strike you as odd?" I asked.

"It does now," he agreed.

"Were there any dirty clothes there, either hers or his, or were they all clean?"

Once again, the officer was deep in thought. "They must have been sent down to the laundry," he said.

"You think so?" I asked. I tried not to sound angry or too pushy, but the detectives clearly hadn't considered that enough to check. "We can find out easily enough," I added.

"After we get the blood drawn, I'll take you to the room. It's sealed off, as we were planning to go back again. We've been really busy."

"I can see that," I agreed. "Did you find any books or other personal items such as a cell phone?"

"Nothing like that," he reported.

I realized I should have searched Denadene's apartment to see if her cell phone was there. I knew she had a tablet too, so I would check for both, I decided, as soon as I got back to St. George. I was sure Denadene would give me permission when Detective Butler and I spoke with her. At least, since I had been invited into the investigation of Randall's murder, I'd be able to see and speak with her again.

"From what I understand, Ms. Stegner is an avid reader of the Book of Mormon and the Bible. You know what the Book of Mormon is, don't you?" I asked after a couple of minutes.

"Yes, but there wasn't one there," he said. "And there was no Bible other than the Gideon one in a drawer."

"Maybe we can ask her about that when we see her."

"She won't talk to us without an attorney," he said.

"Maybe with me there she will," I told him. "We'll know soon enough."

Denadene was not happy about the idea of having blood drawn. "I hate needles," she protested.

"It will prove you were drugged," I told her. She still hesitated, and Butler looked at her sternly. "Either let us do it voluntarily, or I'll have to get a warrant," he said.

She finally agreed, but she had me wondering what was really going on with her. Her behavior made me nervous. When the blood draw was done, Detective Butler took the vials, marked them, and promised to get them to a lab as soon as we left the jail. I said to Denadene, "Do you know where your tablet and phone are?"

"They could be in my apartment," she said.

"May I look when I get back to St. George?" I asked.

"Please do," she said. "The manager will let in you. She has a master key."

I tore a page from my small notebook and had her write a note to the manager stating that I was to be allowed in the apartment. She then signed it. When that was done, I said, "Denadene, I'm assisting Detectives Butler and Garcia on the investigation into Randall's death. I know you invoked the right to an attorney, but would you be willing to waive that and answer a few questions for me?"

Her face clouded over. She looked down. Then she finally mumbled, "I don't think I'd better. I want to talk to an attorney first."

I was more than a little surprised, but I simply said, "Then I'll see you Monday."

"Thanks, Detective," she said formally.

She was led away, and Detective Butler and I left. Back in his car, he looked at me with a bit of a smirk on his face. "That went well, didn't it?"

"I really thought she'd talk to me, but I guess we'll see what Monday brings."

"You'll be there for her arraignment, then?" he asked.

"We have a preliminary hearing on the Bronson Melville case that morning, but I'm sure my sergeant will handle it."

"Sounds good. Let's get this blood to the lab."

As we drove, I got a call from Sergeant Hanks. "Have you talked to Denadene?" he asked.

I gave him a brief rundown of what I'd done since coming to Las Vegas and, with Butler's permission, shared the information about the evidence Butler and Garcia had collected. After my update and answering a few questions from Hanks, he said, "I just got the results on the handwriting from the note of resignation. It was written and signed by Ms. Kwick."

"That's not unexpected," I said. "I'll be interested to hear what she has to say about that."

"I think you can deal with her when you get back here," he suggested.

"I can do that," I said. I looked forward to it.

After the call, Detective Butler and I left the blood at a lab to be analyzed. Then Detective Butler received a call from his partner saying he'd returned to the office and was waiting for us, so we went back there to join him before going to the room where Denadene had been found.

"Did you find the person who performed the wedding?" Detective Butler asked.

Garcia shook his head a bit sheepishly. "This certificate is forged," he said. "There's no record of it being issued by the clerk's office or of a person by this name performing weddings at all, let alone this specific one." He touched the officiator's name on the certificate. It was my turn to smirk, but I diplomatically resisted.

Detective Butler looked at me. "Okay, so that just shot a hole in our case," he admitted. "Too bad Ms. Stegner won't talk to us. Would you still like to see her hotel room?"

"I would. Then I think I'll head back to St. George. I want to see if her tablet and phone are at her apartment," I said.

"Will you call me and let me know?" Detective Butler asked. "I'll probably need to get a warrant and go through them."

"Of course," I promised. I was confident there would be nothing on them that would incriminate Denadene.

A few minutes later, at the hotel, we entered the room where she had been arrested, where I suspected she'd been held while drugged. While Butler and I checked the room, he sent Garcia to check on the laundry to determine whether any clothes had been sent down for cleaning. I felt a depression settle over me as we looked through the room. There was no odor of the perfume she usually wore. There were definitely no scriptures. This had been nothing less than a makeshift jail cell, but I didn't mention that conclusion to Detective Butler.

When Detective Garcia rejoined us, he reported, "No laundry was taken from this room."

"Oh boy. I wish Ms. Stegner would speak to us," Detective Butler said.

"So do I," I agreed. It bothered me that she wouldn't. As much as I hated to admit it, my faith in her had taken a hit when she'd refused to speak to us and because of the way she'd acted when I'd spoken to her earlier. But despite all of that, I still didn't believe she had killed her ex-husband. It looked to me like a setup, but I didn't know what was and wasn't true about how she'd come to be with Randall in the first place. Her evasiveness hurt me, but I couldn't brush my thoughts about it away. I now had to look at her case through the same lens as Butler and Garcia. I hated myself for it, but I was a cop. I had to follow where the evidence led, and her refusal to talk to me further had led me to question the reason for her behavior. At length I said, "I think I'll head back to St. George."

"All right. In the meantime, Detective Garcia and I need to see if we can locate our witness," Butler said.

"Good luck on that," I told him facetiously. "He'll probably be with Melville in his black van, but I'll be surprised if you can find it. I don't have any idea what Hass drives, and Melville may have another vehicle. I wouldn't be too surprised if he hid the black van after I saw him in it. I suppose one of them could be driving Randall Stegner's pickup. If you can't find Alvin or Dwight, then maybe the two of them will show up on Monday. I'll check in St. George tonight and tomorrow, just in case. He and Dwight Hass might both be back there."

"Thanks for your help, Detective," Butler told me. "I hope you're right and Ms. Stegner is innocent. She *seems* like a nice lady." He hesitated before adding, "But I doubt it."

I made no comment about that last bit, nor was I going to tell him my faith in her had been shaken. I had to work on that.

The first thing I did when I got back to St. George two hours later was go to Denadene's apartment complex. I showed the note to the apartment manager, who said she'd been wondering where Denadene was. I told her it was a police matter and that I couldn't talk about it.

I was almost elated when I found her cell phone and her tablet in the apartment. Why Randall or one of his buddies hadn't taken them was beyond me. I also found her purse in her bedroom. Her car keys were missing, but her apartment keys were there, along with a small amount of cash, a couple of credit cards, a debit card, her driver's license, and her temple recommend. Seeing that last item gave me pause. I shouldn't doubt her like I was, but the fact that she wouldn't speak with me after she'd learned I was working with the Las Vegas detectives still bothered me. After all, she had called me for help, and help was all I wanted to give her. But

I also wanted to find out who killed Randall. The lens I was now looking through was blurry. If I could, I needed to make it blurry for Detectives Garcia and Butler as well so they wouldn't overlook anything because they thought Denadene was guilty.

I drove back to the police department after finishing at her apartment. I had taken the items I found and wanted to make sure they were where no one else, such as her former boss or his brother, could find them. I placed them in the evidence room, properly marked and dated.

It was getting late by then, and I was surprised when Sergeant Hanks and Lieutenant Dollison rushed into the building.

"Gage, I'm glad you're back. We have a problem," Sergeant Hanks said.

From the look on my supervisors' faces, I had a feeling I may not want to know what the problem was.

"What's happened?" I asked.

"Your murder suspect has escaped," Lieutenant Dollison said.

"What? That can't be! The jail is secure, and the officers there knew what he was in for. They would have been extra cautious."

"He didn't escape from the jail," Hanks said. "He claimed to be really sick, and they decided they needed to take him to the hospital, that the medical staff at the jail might not be able to handle it, and they didn't want to give Bronson a reason to sue them if he got sicker. He got away while he was being transported."

"How did that happen?" I asked with a mixture of anger and concern.

"His escape was well planned. Let me give you a number where you can reach one of the officers, and he can tell you exactly what happened. His name is Deputy Charlie Lockridge," he said and gave me the number. "Get back with us after you talk to him."

As soon as I'd introduced myself on the phone, Deputy Lockridge said, "I'm sorry we lost your suspect. It happened so fast we didn't have time to react."

"Tell me what happened," I said.

"We were taking Melville to the hospital in the jail van. I was driving. My partner was watching the back, where we had Melville trussed up. Melville was moaning and crying for us to hurry because he thought he was dying. All of a sudden a pickup truck pulled in front of us and blocked the road. I slammed on the brakes, barely avoiding a collision. By the time the van came to a stop, there was a guy on the road with a rifle. He fired, and the windshield blew out."

"I suppose that got your attention," I said blandly.

"I'll say. It scared the daylights out of us. We were lucky neither of us were hit. Anyway, the gunman and the pickup driver were both armed and wearing masks and stocking caps. They made us get out of the van and drop onto our bellies on the road with our arms outstretched. Neither of us had a chance to pull our firearms. They caught us completely by surprise. The same guy who shot the windshield out fired his rifle right in front of my face and told us if we moved, we would be killed. The other guy took our pistols. I kept hoping someone would come along and call 911, but no one came. There were some houses in the area, but most people would have probably been at work."

"What did they do to you after that?" I asked.

"They handcuffed us, and one of them held a gun on us while the other took our keys and freed Bronson. They kept looking up and down the road and at the houses in the area, but they made quick work of it. Then they made us get into the back of the van after they took our radios and weapons. Bronson was laughing and making threats. He said we were lucky they didn't just shoot us and that no one would ever find him. And he said to tell you if you go looking for him, he and his friends would take care of that girl of yours permanently," the officer said. "I guess you've been warned."

"Thanks," I said, trying to keep my voice level. For now, Denadene was safe, but I had to find Melville and his cronies before he could make good on his threat. "When did this happen?" I asked.

"It was probably about three hours ago," Deputy Lockridge said.

"What happened next?"

"They locked us in the back of the van, and one of them drove it while the other one drove the pickup. They left us locked in it behind an old warehouse a couple of miles from where they'd stopped us. The jail got worried when they couldn't get ahold of us and had some officers start looking for us, and someone had called in about shots being fired in the area where they'd stopped us. Anyway, a big search was started, and they finally found us."

"Are you two okay?" I asked.

"Other than my face being cut up a bit when the rifle bullet hit so close and sprayed me with chunks of pavement, we're both fine."

"What kind of pickup did they take Melville away in?" I asked. "I assume you got a good look at it."

"Oh yes. It was a jacked-up silver Dodge Ram with a very loud exhaust."

"Did you get a license number?" I asked.

"No, there was too much going on," Lockridge answered. "We were just hoping to get out of the situation alive."

"I think I can give it to you," I said. "That sounds like Randall Stegner's truck, and I know the license number."

"Stegner?" he asked.

"Yes," I said and quickly explained who Randall was. "Were there only two of them?"

"The truck had dark windows, so I suppose there could have been someone else in it, but if so, we didn't see him."

"Okay, thanks," I said. "Sorry you had to go through that. I'm going to get the information about the truck on the air to every police officer in the area."

I did that and then met with my lieutenant and sergeant. After I briefed them, Lieutenant Dollison said, "The chief is coming to the station shortly, and I'll need to report what we know to him."

After he had hurried away, I said to Sergeant Hanks, "I wonder if we should put Alvin Melville's black van on the air as well," I said.

"Do you have the license number?"

"I do. Two of them, actually." I explained my suspicions about the false set of plates. "Alvin was in it when I left the jail after talking to Denadene the first time. It was shortly after one. He was driving it. JC Hass's brother, Dwight, jumped in as I was chasing him on foot. I have no idea what Dwight drives, or we could have an ATL put out on that as well."

"We'll figure it out," Hanks said.

After we had finished with the ATLs, Sergeant Hanks and I sat down in his office, and he said to me, "Okay, so give me a complete rundown on your day." After I recounted what had happened in Vegas, he said, "So she shut you out when you went back with the Las Vegas officers?" Hanks looked concerned. "That surprises me."

"Me too," I admitted. "I thought she'd be willing to talk since she'd called me for help, but I guess she didn't want me working with the guys who arrested her."

"That doesn't look good for her," Hanks said. "She could have been set up, but on the other hand, if her ex tried to force her to marry him again, it would give her motive. You can't ignore that."

As much as I hated the thought, I knew my sergeant was right.

CHAPTER SEVEN

I WAS IN THE COURTROOM in Las Vegas on Monday before court was due to begin. Detectives Butler and Garcia walked in and joined me there. We sat near the front of the large courtroom. After the officers told me they had not been able to locate either Alvin Melville or Dwight Hass, I told them about the escape of my homicide suspect. I then told them about finding Denadene's tablet and phone in her apartment. Butler reminded me he would need to search them. I promised I would make them available to him.

"Any idea who the two men were?" Detective Butler asked, reverting back to the escape.

"I have my suspicions, but they both wore masks and had their heads covered with stocking caps, so I can't be sure. The pickup they whisked Bronson off in was a jacked-up and very loud silver Dodge Ram," I revealed.

The two officers looked at each other for a moment, and Detective Butler said, "That sounds like our victim's truck."

"My thoughts exactly."

"And do you think it was either Alvin Melville or Hass driving it?" he asked.

"What do you think?" I asked.

He shook his head. "I suppose it could be."

Just then the bailiff called court into session and introduced Judge Lathelia Morvent as we all rose to our feet. The judge sat down before saying, "You may all be seated."

Judge Morvent was a large woman with gray hair that she wore in a tight bun. She stared down at us with a certain disdain in her eyes. At least, that's how I interpreted it. She called a case, and a defendant and his lawyer moved to the podium. Denadene was one of several defendants being arraigned that morning. I hoped her case would be called soon.

The attorney at the podium had barely begun to speak when a very attractive woman who looked to be in her mid-twenties entered the courtroom, hurried to the front, and sat on the counsel bench in the well in front of the bar not far from us but to one side.

"That's Miss Ashley Webler, attorney at law," Detective Butler said quietly as he leaned toward me. "She's with the public defender's office. She's a feisty one and smart as a whip. I've gone up against her a few times. We got a conviction each time, but it was a battle."

I took a closer look at her. Her dark-blonde hair was long and wavy, and when she looked toward us, I could see striking green eyes, almond-shaped. Her face was slightly angular. To say she was attractive would be an understatement. She was medium height, maybe five-six, I thought. She fixed her eyes on Detective Butler, raised one hand, and wiggled her fingers. She smiled then—a pretty smile, but one that could be intimidating in a courtroom. He smiled back.

When she looked forward again so all I could see was her profile, Butler again leaned toward me and whispered, "She's easy on the eyes, am I right?"

"You could say that," I whispered back.

"I wonder if she'll get assigned a case today," he said softly as a door at the side of the courtroom opened and Denadene was brought in. She was in her jail clothes, handcuffs, and shackles, and her hair was a mess. The corrections officer escorting her led her to one of the jury chairs and had her sit down.

For a moment, she looked at the floor in front of her. Then she lifted her head and looked around. She saw me, and I smiled at her. She didn't smile back—just looked at me with a frown on her face and then looked away. I was stung. Had I misjudged her on our dates? It was like she was a different woman than the one I thought I knew. But then, I was seated beside the detectives who had arrested her. Maybe she felt like she didn't know me, that I had joined the enemy, so to speak.

I watched Denadene as she continued looking around the courtroom like she was trying to find someone, like she expected someone she knew besides me to be there. She showed no recognition on her face, though, and finally looked down at the floor in front of her again.

I remembered our kiss on the doorstep, so sweet and full of promise, and I could almost hear her saying, "I'll call you." She had called me, but it hadn't been the call I had hoped for.

The judge finished with the previous defendant and called Denadene's name, and the officer helped her to her feet and then pointed at the podium, whispering something to her. She shuffled over, lifted her head, and looked toward the judge. My heart ached.

Judge Morvent looked hard at Denadene for a moment and then told her what her charges were. Murder, as we already knew, and illegally possessing a firearm. "Do you understand the charges?" the judge asked.

"Yes," Denadene said very softly.

"Speak up; these proceedings are being recorded," the judge said rather harshly.

"Yes," Denadene repeated, louder now.

"Thank you, Ms. Stegner," the judge said, and for a moment her face seemed to soften. I sincerely hoped she was human.

The judge then spent a few minutes explaining to Denadene what her rights were and how the procedure would work that morning. Finally she said, "Do you have an attorney?"

"No, Your Honor," Denadene said very clearly now. "And I don't have a job, so I hope you will appoint an attorney for me."

The judge asked a few questions about her financial state and then finally said, "So do I understand, then, that you would like me to appoint you an attorney?"

"Please," Denadene said.

"Miss Webler," Judge Morvent said.

"Yes, Your Honor," the young defense attorney responded as she rose to her feet.

"You are appointed," the judge said. "Please join your client at the podium."

Miss Webler moved up beside Denadene and smiled at her. She was probably two inches shorter than Denadene, but with Denadene only in jail slippers and Miss Webler in heels, they looked fairly close to the same height.

"Ms. Stegner, the young woman standing beside you is Ashley Webler. She is from the public defender's office. She will represent you in this matter." She then addressed Miss Webler. "Counselor, I suppose you would like to speak with your client before entering a plea?"

I expected Miss Webler to say she would, but she surprised me when she said, "No, Your Honor. We will enter a plea of not guilty to both charges."

"Do you agree with that, Ms. Stegner?" the judge asked.

"Yes, Your Honor. I'm not guilty," Denadene said with some spunk. I was glad to see that.

"Your Honor, I would like to request that bond be set," Miss Webler said.

A middle-aged man rose to his feet at one of the counsel tables and informed the court no bail would be appropriate in this case. Miss Webler then said, "I request a chance to speak with my client and review the evidence, and then I will be back for a bond hearing, if you will agree to that."

"Granted," Judge Morvent barked. She looked down for a moment and then back up. She set a date for two days away, Wednesday morning.

"Thank you, Your Honor," Miss Webler said.

A moment later Denadene was led from the courtroom, her leg irons and handcuffs jangling. She looked at me one more time as she passed near where we were seated. She shook her head, frowned, and then looked away. A moment later she was gone. Miss Webler strode quickly to the back of the courtroom and went out the door. I noticed she moved with a slight limp, but I gave it no serious thought.

I followed quickly and caught up with her in the corridor. "Miss Webler," I said. "Do you have a moment?"

She stopped and turned toward me, eyeing me quickly from top to bottom. "And you are?" she said after she seemed to have completed her assessment of me.

I pulled out my credentials. "Detective Gage Tipton," I said. "I'm with the St. George Police Department."

She looked up at my face for a moment and then said, "You were sitting with Detectives Garcia and Butler," she said. "I think they might be the arresting officers on this case. Are you working with them?"

"I'm assisting," I admitted. "But I'm also a friend of the defendant. She's also from St. George. She's accused of killing her ex-husband, but you'll soon learn all about that. Until the middle of last week, she was a legal secretary for a St. George defense attorney by the name of JC Hass."

Miss Webler frowned. "I take it he fired her," she said.

"He claimed she quit, but her letter of resignation was forged by the woman he hired to fill in for Denadene," I informed her. "Denadene denies quitting. She was declared a missing person when her parents couldn't make contact with her. I'm the case officer."

"Maybe we should sit down for a moment," Miss Webler said as the two detectives joined us. "Detectives, I will of course need some information. I suppose you have given what you have to the prosecutor."

"We have," Detective Butler said. Then he looked at me. "Would you meet us back at the department when you finish speaking with Miss Webler?"

"Of course," I said. "We won't be long."

"We'll see you in a few, then," he said. He smiled at Miss Webler. "And I guess we'll see you again too."

"You can count on it," she said. She smiled at both men. "I assume you will have your ducks in a row, as you usually do."

"That we will," Detective Butler said with more confidence than he had expressed to me earlier. "And you can depend on Detective Tipton to be straight with you. His interest isn't quite the same as ours, but he understands the evidence."

"Detective Tipton," she said, turning her attention back to me as my two colleagues turned away. "There is an attorney-client room right over there. Perhaps we could visit there for a moment." She pointed across the corridor.

I followed her into the room. There was a small table there. She motioned for me to sit in the chair on one side, and then she sat across from me.

"Miss Webler," I began.

"Ashley," she interjected and held a hand out.

"Ashley," I said, shaking her hand. "And you may call me Gage," I said.

"Maybe at some point," she countered. "But for now, you are Detective Tipton to me."

"That's fine," I said, feeling perplexed.

"Okay, Detective. Let's have that talk now. First, I know JC Hass. He practices in Nevada from time to time. He's the kind of attorney who gives us all a bad name. If my client worked for him, she has my sympathy. Now, with that out of the way, I want to ask you this: in your opinion, is my client guilty?"

"That's where Detectives Butler and Garcia disagree with me. They think she's guilty, although they're coming to understand their case isn't as open and shut as they first thought," I said. "In answer to your question, I don't think she's guilty."

"You don't *think?*" Ashley said as she looked me in the eyes. "Do you have doubts?"

"Very small ones," I said. "Let me tell you what I know for sure."

"Please do," she said, leaning forward, giving me the impression I had her undivided attention.

"I know her fairly well, or at least I thought I did."

"But something happened to give you doubts about her?" Ashley asked.

"Yes, but let me take this from the top. Denadene and I have dated a few times—not exclusively, but enough I felt I knew her quite well. I asked her if she would go with me on an overnight visit to Zion National Park. She said she wanted to go but she would have to clear it with Mr. Hass. On Monday of last week she told me she would call me and let me know if she would be able to go."

"And what did she say when she called?" Ashley asked.

"She didn't. At least, not until Saturday morning, when she called from the jail to tell me she had been arrested and to ask for my help. She swore she didn't kill anyone." I then recounted everything that had happened since and how my Melville case was linked to Denadene's, pausing now and then to answer Ashley's questions as best as I could.

"So why is it you now have some doubts about Denadene?" she asked.

"I went to the jail with Detective Butler to have her blood drawn to determine if she had been doped and, if so, what drug was used. We don't know anything on that yet. At that time, I tried to talk to Denadene again, and she said she wouldn't speak to me without her attorney present. That would be you." Ashley smiled and signaled for me to continue. "Denadene did give me permission in writing to search her apartment to see if her cell phone and other items were there, and they were, but she doesn't know that yet," I explained.

"I'll tell her when I meet her at the jail in a little while," Ashley said. "But first I need to know exactly what you found and what you did with it, assuming there were more than the items you already mentioned."

I recited what I had found and said, "I'm sorry. Maybe you don't know what a temple recommend is."

Ashley leaned across the table and touched my hand, smiling warmly. "I have one too," she said. "And the fact that my client does tells me a lot." She moved her hand and then asked, "So where are those items now?"

"I placed them in evidence at my department," I said.

"Excellent, Detective. What about her car? Where is it now, and has it been searched and fingerprinted?" she asked.

"Her parents have it, and yes, it was fingerprinted and searched. It was cleaned out and thoroughly wiped down before we got it in our possession. Not even Denadene's own fingerprints were found."

"That's strange," Ashley said. She looked at me thoughtfully for a moment through her bright green eyes. Then she leaned toward me again and asked, "Did anything else happen that made you wonder about Denadene?"

"Just the way she looked at me this morning. I'm no longer high on her list of friends, that's for sure," I responded. "I don't think she killed anyone—she's not that kind of person—but there's something she hasn't told me. I'm certain of that. I can't help but wonder what it is and why she's unwilling to share it with me."

Ashley stood up. "I guess I should get over to the jail and talk to my client, then." She moved around the table until we were standing next to each other near the door. "One more thing," she said. "I will want to know what's on her phone. Is there a chance Detective Butler is going to try to get the device from you and have it analyzed?"

"Yes, he wants it. He's getting a search warrant for it today." Just then my phone rang. I looked at the screen. It was Sergeant Hanks. "Sergeant," I said as I lifted a finger to Ashley to convey that I needed another minute before she left. "How did it go in court?"

"Just like we expected. The judge was angry with Hass for filing such a frivolous motion and denied it, of course. He also told Hass that when he heard from his client, he was to immediately inform the court. The pretrial, of course, was not held since we have no defendant in custody. That's the main reason the prosecutor didn't think you needed to be here. He had it in mind to delay the preliminary hearing until Melville is back behind bars."

"That makes sense," I said. "So Hass got a stern rebuke, did he?"

"That's right," Sergeant Hanks said with a snicker. "But I doubt he'll admit to hearing from Bronson, since his own brother, probably with his knowledge and maybe on his orders, likely broke him free. Oh, and one more thing. I have an arrest warrant for Ms. Kwick. Would you like me to serve it, or do you want to?"

"I'd like to make that arrest and see if she'll talk to me. Maybe she'll implicate Hass," I said. "I should be home this evening. I'm with Denadene's attorney right now, but we're about finished here."

I ended the call a moment later and said, "That was my sergeant." I told her what I had learned.

"Detective, I appreciate you telling me all of this. I'll go meet with my client now. If I need something, may I call you?"

I gave her my card, which had my cell number, my landline number, and the department number with my extension there. I watched her as she walked down the hallway, noticing again her slight limp. I was impressed with her and knew Denadene's future was in good hands. My budding relationship with Denadene might be over, but at least I could be confident that with Ashley's help, she would have her name cleared.

CHAPTER EIGHT

I MET WITH BUTLER AND Garcia after leaving the courthouse. We talked briefly and then Butler said, "I think I'll have Detective Garcia go to St. George this afternoon, since you're headed back there, and take possession of Ms. Stegner's cell phone. I don't think I'll need the tablet, but please hang onto it in case I decide I need it later. I'll have a warrant ready so we can see what calls she made and received prior to her disappearing."

"Sounds good. I'll keep the tablet and other items in my evidence room. Is there anything else I can help you guys with before I go?"

They assured me there wasn't, and I left Las Vegas with Detective Garcia following me. As I drove, I thought about Denadene's purse and the items it contained. I thought perhaps I should take them with me to Las Vegas and give them to her in case she was released or have the jailers keep them in her property at the jail for later. That was the course of action I finally decided on.

I went directly to the police department in St. George. When I got there I transferred custody of Denadene's cell phone to Detective Garcia. I mentioned to him that I would keep the tablet in the evidence room but that I would bring her purse and its contents with me, explaining that she might need them at some point.

After Garcia left, I talked to my sergeant, who said with a bit of a chuckle, "Ms. Kwick is a stubborn woman. She could have made it much easier on herself if she'd simply given us the letter when we first asked and explained why she wrote it. Surely she had a reason."

"I wonder what Hass has on this woman that makes her so stubborn," I said. "There has to be something. And whatever it is could be the reason."

"That's a good point," Hanks responded.

He handed me the arrest warrant for Lily Kwick. "Too bad we can't get one on Hass as well," I said. "I don't for one minute believe he didn't order her to write that letter."

"If he did, maybe you and I can get Ms. Kwick to rat him out. I'll give the prosecutor a call while you're picking her up. If he'll agree to some kind of deal we can offer her if she will agree to testify against Hass, then maybe we can take him into custody before the day is over," Sergeant Hanks said.

I had a uniformed officer accompany me to make the arrest. I didn't want Ms. Kwick to be able to make any allegations of impropriety against me. That wasn't likely to happen if I had a witness who was wearing a body cam. We arrived at Hass's office a few minutes later. "What do you want?" Ms. Kwick asked the moment she saw me.

"I have a warrant here for your arrest for forging the letter of resignation of Denadene Stegner. Please stand up and come around the desk," I said.

The color drained from her face, but she did as I instructed. I had the uniformed officer put the handcuffs on her. Then I showed her the warrant, advised her of her rights, and said, "Let's go."

"I need to call JC," she said.

"Later, if you want him to represent you," I said. "I take it he's not here."

"No, he's a busy man," she said. She was shaking visibly and appeared to be on the verge of tears.

"Do you have a purse here?"

"I do," she said in a very subdued voice.

"Get it, and then you can lock up behind you, or we'll help you do it," I instructed her.

A little while later she was seated at a small table in an interrogation room. I had removed the handcuffs, and she sat there wringing her hands and occasionally wiping perspiration from her forehead. Sergeant Hanks and I watched through a one-way glass window. "She's obviously very nervous," he said. "We have Mark Stansel's permission to offer her immunity if she'll agree to testify against Hass. We'll just have to hope she'll turn on him when we tell her we need to know exactly what happened and why she wrote it."

"That's great," I said as the sergeant looked at his watch.

"Mark said if he could get away, he'd meet us here. That way it will be very clear what she's being offered. Let's give him a few more minutes," he suggested.

After the prosecutor appeared, he and I went into the interrogation room while Sergeant Hanks observed through the one-way glass. I brought a form with me that I hoped I would need before we were through. After the preliminaries were out of the way and the recorder was running, I said, "Ms. Kwick, this is Deputy County Attorney Mark Stansel. He is here to speak with you about the letter we believe you forged."

"I want my lawyer," she said stubbornly.

"Whom would you like us to call?" Mark asked kindly.

"JC Hass, I guess. But he's in court in Fillmore right now," she said.

"In that case, Detective," he said, looking at me, "book her. We can do this tomorrow or the next day."

Ms. Kwick looked like she might pass out. I almost felt sorry for her—almost. "Let's go then, Ms. Kwick," I said.

"You'll actually put me in jail?" she stammered, her eyes wide with shock.

"That's what we do," I said. "Of course, if you can make bail, you will be released until the next court date."

"How much is bail?" she asked.

"I can't tell you that. The jailers will know. It'll be according to the Uniform Bail Schedule," I said. "Stand up, please."

"But can't I talk to JC first?" she begged.

"Not if he's not available," I said.

"This isn't fair," she protested.

"And forging the resignation of someone you barely knew was?" I asked a little peevishly.

"I didn't—" she began.

"No, no," I interrupted hastily. "You must not say anything more to us about the case at this time since you have invoked your right to counsel."

"But—"

"Not another word," I broke in again. "Now, please, I've got work to do. I need to take you to the jail so you can be booked, and so I can get back to it."

I'd kept hoping Mark would interrupt me. He finally spoke as Ms. Kwick reluctantly got to her feet. "There is something you can be thinking about between now and when we meet again with Mr. Hass present," he said.

"What is that?" she asked weakly.

"I will offer you immunity if you tell us why you wrote the letter and at whose direction," he said. "Of course, that doesn't mean you'll get immunity if it was your idea and done because you wanted to do it."

"You mean I wouldn't have to go to jail?"

"No, it does not mean that," he said. "You have already asked for an attorney. I'm just saying that when you and your attorney meet with us, that will be the deal."

"I can't take the deal right now?" she practically begged.

"As Detective Tipton explained, you invoked the right to counsel, as you are entitled to do," he said.

Ms. Kwick sat back down, almost collapsing into the chair. "Hey, what are you doing? I am taking you to jail," I said with feigned anger.

"I don't want an attorney after all," she said. "I'll answer your questions if you really will let me go when I've done that."

"Are you saying you've changed your mind?" Mark asked. "You don't have to do that. The deal will still be in place when your attorney is with you."

"I can't say what I need to say if he's here. I don't want an attorney. I'll sign something to that effect if you want me to," she said.

I produced the form I had brought into the room on the off chance that she would sign it and handed it to Mark, who laid it in front of her. He pulled a pen from his pocket and held it out to her. She held the pen over the paper, but Mark said, "Just a moment, Ms. Kwick. Read the form first, and make sure this is what you want to do."

Without a word she read the form and then affixed her signature. "There. Now we can talk?" she said.

"Ms. Kwick," I said after taking a seat next to the prosecutor, "was it your idea to write the letter and forge the signature of Denadene Stegner to a letter of resignation?"

"It was not my idea," she said. "Are you sure you'll drop the charges against me if I tell you who told me to do it?"

"That's what I said," Mark replied. "And it's recorded. I can't and I won't go back on my word."

"Okay. I was ordered by JC Hass to write the letter. He dictated it to me and then told me to sign Ms. Stegner's signature."

I could have shouted with glee, but I kept my composure and asked, "Ms. Kwick, did he tell you why he ordered you to do that? You knew it was illegal, and so did he."

"He was angry with Ms. Stegner because she wanted time off to go out with you, Detective. He told me you were a crooked cop, that you were framing his client, and that he couldn't have your girlfriend working for him anymore," she said.

"Didn't you fear you might get into trouble?" I asked. "At some point, you should have known Denadene would deny it."

She shook her head. "He promised me I wouldn't get into any trouble. He even said Denadene was going to be in enough trouble of her own that she wouldn't even think about the letter."

"Did he say what kind of trouble?" I asked.

She shook her head once more. "Not exactly. He just told me he had a feeling she was off somewhere getting herself into trouble."

"What would make him think that?" I asked. "Denadene had never been in trouble before. He knew that."

Ms. Kwick looked at me with her brow furrowed. "Is she in trouble now?" she asked.

I looked to Mark for guidance. He took over and said, "She has been arrested in Las Vegas for murder."

Lily went as white as a ghost. "Surely JC couldn't have known that would happen, could he?"

"You tell us," he said.

Slowly she shook her head. "I only know he seemed to think she would get into trouble. Maybe she'd threatened someone in his presence," she speculated. "Who did she kill?"

"She didn't kill anyone," I said quickly. "She has been framed for killing her ex-husband. Someone else planned the crime and carried it out. JC Hass's brother was in Vegas, along with Alvin Melville, and they claim she did it."

I thought for a moment that Ms. Kwick was about to pass out. "Are you okay?" I asked with concern. "Could I get you a bottle of water?"

"Please do, Detective," she nearly whispered. The shock was evident in her face.

After providing her with the drink, we resumed our interview. "Did you at any time see either Dwight Hass or Alvin Melville with your boss?" I asked.

"He's not my boss anymore," Ms. Kwick said angrily. "And I don't want him to ever represent me. I quit as of this moment. I have a few personal items at his office. Will someone take me back there to get my stuff and make sure I get home safely?"

"Why would you not get home safely on your own?" I asked. I didn't ask her what stuff she had there. She had her purse, but perhaps she'd left something else.

She began to tremble violently. "Both of those men you mentioned were at the office. I don't know what they talked to JC about, but now I'm afraid I could be in serious danger. Alvin and Dwight frighten me."

"Ms. Kwick," Mark began. "Did you overhear anything the three of them might have said that would have given you the idea Denadene was going to get arrested for murder?"

"Goodness no," she said, flailing her hands above the little table that separated us. Then she stared at those hands for a moment and clasped them together in front of her. Mark and I waited to see if she had anything more to say. She finally looked up. "I did hear Dwight say something about Brea Burr. And Alvin said, 'We won't need to worry about her anymore.'"

"Did he say why?" I asked.

"No, because he looked up and saw me, but I was pretending to type, and I think he didn't realize I had heard him. They were just leaving JC's office. Is Ms. Stegner okay?"

"You typed the motion to dismiss, the one that the judge denied this morning, didn't you?" I asked, sidestepping her question.

"Do you mean the one on Bronson Melville?" she asked. But before we could answer, she said, "Yes, I did. And I remember wondering why JC had me write that the state didn't have an eyewitness."

"Are you not aware that Brea Burr is missing, as was Denadene Stegner until Saturday morning?" I asked.

She shook her head. "It hasn't been on the news, has it?"

"No, it has not," I confirmed. "But surely JC said something to you about it."

"I asked him what happened to the witness, and he told me she had recanted her statement," she said. "He lied, didn't he?"

"Yes, he lied." I said. "Are you aware that JC's client, Bronson Melville, escaped custody?" I asked.

"I saw it on the news. It said two masked men in a silver pickup held up the jail van and freed him," she said.

"Do you remember what kind of pickup it was?" I asked.

"A silver Dodge Ram? I think that's what they said."

"Were you aware that Denadene's ex-husband, Randall Stegner, who is now in the morgue in Las Vegas, drove a silver Dodge Ram?" I asked.

"I didn't know anything about her personal life, except that she's your girlfriend," she said to me.

"She is not my girlfriend, but I did take her out a few times," I corrected. "Ms. Kwick, did Hass say anything about Bronson's escape?"

"He mentioned it this morning just before he told me he had to go to court in Fillmore."

"What did he say about it?" I asked.

"Only that Bronson Melville had escaped and that there would probably not be a murder trial now since he imagined Melville would not stick around to be arrested again," she responded. "He did say it was too bad because now he wouldn't collect the money for Melville's defense."

This was new ground she was plowing. I had not planned on speaking with Ms. Kwick about anything but the forgery, but since the opportunity had presented itself, I felt like I should press forward. I looked at Mark, and he nodded his agreement. "Ms. Kwick," I said. "From what your boss said when he had you type the motion, do you think he had any idea that Bronson might escape?"

"Not exactly," she said as she pressed her hands against the sides of her head. "But he did say Melville would get out of jail soon, and I wondered how that could be since he was being held without bail. I assumed he must have meant the motion he had me type was going to be granted. I figured he must have known more about the case you had against Bronson than he had mentioned to me because other than his saying your witness had changed her mind about what she had seen, it seemed to me you had a pretty strong case."

"We do, even without Miss Burr," Mark said.

"I thought so," she said.

"The preliminary hearing has been continued until Bronson is back in custody," Mark added.

"I see," she said, nervously licking her lips for a moment. "But now that Bronson is loose, I wonder if JC did know something about what was going to happen."

"Or planned something?" I said, hoping Hass might have said something to or in the presence of Ms. Kwick that would indicate he'd had something to do with Melville's escape.

She looked at me shrewdly. She was thinking very clearly now that she was sure she was about to be released and the charges against her dropped. "No, but now that I think about it, I can't help but wonder if he instructed

Dwight and Alvin to do it. I mean, I don't have any proof of that, but after the way he made me break the law for him, I can believe he would be capable of it. Who knows? Maybe he won't be losing a lot of money not defending him. Maybe he got paid to, well, you know, figure out a way to get Bronson free besides just badmouthing you, Detective. Because he sure was doing a lot of that."

"Ms. Kwick, while you were working with Hass the past few days, did he say or do anything that would make you think he had something against Denadene Stegner?" I asked.

She was very quiet for nearly a minute. She closed her eyes and kept working her hands against each other. She licked her lips again. I sat silently and waited. Finally, without opening her eyes, she said, "He hated you because you arrested Bronson Melville. At first I thought the fact that you were friends with Denadene was the reason he didn't like her, and I definitely came to believe he wanted her gone from his office."

"Did Hass say he wanted her gone?" I asked after she had again resumed silence.

She finally opened her eyes and looked into mine with sadness. "He wanted her to be more than his secretary. He told me just before he asked me—no, ordered me—to write the letter of resignation and sign her name that he had given her a great opportunity to be truly happy, but she had messed it up."

"Are you suggesting that opportunity had to do with something other than her job working for him?"

She snickered then. "Yes, Detective, that's exactly what I'm saying. I can't say he told me that, but I could see it in his eyes. I'm pretty sure he was in love with her. I didn't realize what a beautiful young lady she was until I looked at her social media page. That was when I realized he probably wanted more from her than just to do secretarial work for him."

"Is there anything else that would have given you the idea that he was, shall we say, obsessed with her?" I asked, sick at the very thought.

"No," she said slowly, and then she suddenly gasped. "Oh, Detective, I just remembered something he said. I think he wanted her to be more than gone from his office after she had rejected him. It wasn't something he said to me; it was to his brother. I was in the restroom, and Alvin and Dwight had been with JC back in his office. I heard them come out. But then I heard JC practically shout, 'I don't ever want to see her again.' I didn't know who they were talking about at the time, but now I think it was Denadene," she said as she began to rub her eyes. "I couldn't hear Dwight as well through the bathroom door because he didn't shout, but I'm pretty sure he said he'd take care of *it* or *her* or something like that. I was through in the restroom, but I waited until I heard the front door close and gave JC enough time to get back to his office before I came out and went back to my desk."

She was silent for a long moment after that, and so was I. I was stunned. I finally asked, "Could he have been referring to anyone else?"

"At the time, I figured it had to do with some former wife or girlfriend of JC's. But it made me think I would try to never get on his bad side," she said. She looked directly at me and said, "I'm sorry for the way I treated you, Detective. But he spoke so harshly about you I didn't dare treat you the way I normally would have. I wish now I had never accepted that temporary appointment. It's turned into a nightmare."

The interview lasted a short while longer, but it appeared she had told us everything she could, which was more than I had expected or even wanted to hear. "Well, I guess you'll need a ride back to the office," I said after I had turned the recorder off.

She suddenly began to tremble again. "Officers, I don't dare work for him anymore. I know you'll be charging him with making me write the letter, and he'll know I told you what he did. I know I said I quit, but if I do, will he send those two guys after me next?"

I supposed that was a possibility, but I didn't want to frighten her worse, so I said, "It's up to you what you do at this point."

Mark Stansel broke in before I could say more. "I will be pressing charges against JC Hass, and furthermore, I will be reporting him to the Office of Professional Conduct of the Utah State Bar. This will more than likely get his law license revoked. But if you decide to leave town for a while to keep safe, just remember that you must keep Detective Tipton and me informed of your location, as we will need you to return at some point in the not too distant future to testify about what you told us today."

She started to bawl. "I wish I'd never gone to work for him," she said again. "I thought he was nice, and he's a very successful attorney. But now I learn that he's evil." She sobbed. "I should have known you guys would figure out I wrote the letter. I should have just quit right then, but he paid me a nice bonus for doing it for him, and I guess I got greedy, which is stupid. I don't even need the money."

"He bribed you to forge that letter?" I asked in surprise.

"Yes, he gave me a thousand dollars, in cash, nontaxable," she said. "And then he said if I ever told anyone, I would wish I hadn't. At that point I got really worried, but it was too late to change things then. Oh, I've been such a fool."

"Ms. Kwick, are you sure he's in Fillmore today?" I asked.

Her eyes popped wide at the suggestion. "No, I guess I don't know that for sure. He didn't mention a specific case to me, nor did I prepare any documents for him to take with him."

Now I was left to wonder where Hass was and what he was up to. Although he had not specifically named Denadene in the conversation Ms. Kwick had overheard, I was very suspicious that he was behind her disappearance and may have even ordered that she be framed for murder. There was much more to JC Hass, I feared, than his being a difficult and dislikable attorney.

After returning Ms. Kwick to her office and making sure she got the few things she had taken there from her home and left safely, I called the courts in Fillmore. Hass didn't have any cases up there in any court. So where was he, and what was he doing?

I worried as I thought about it. I wondered if Alvin and Dwight would return to Vegas or if they would simply disappear and let the case against Denadene fall apart. That would be a good thing, but would she be in further danger when she did get out of jail? I was worried about Ms. Kwick too and how she might decide to keep herself out of harm's way.

My cell phone rang shortly after I had returned to the office. It was Ashley Webler.

CHAPTER NINE

"DENADENE IS INNOCENT," ASHLEY STARTED. "I'm totally convinced of that after meeting with her today, but she's also very frightened."

"What is she afraid of?" I asked, wondering if she'd been threatened in jail. That certainly was not uncommon.

"Her former boss, his brother, and the Melville brothers. And her fear is justified," she said.

"You're right about that," I agreed. "The woman who took her place at Hass's office, the woman who forged the letter of resignation, confirmed that. JC Hass is in a lot of trouble now." I explained what he had done and what Lily Kwick had told us after her arrest.

"Goodness, Detective. I'm sure he was referring to Denadene when he told his brother what he did. It fits with what Denadene told me. I asked her if she would waive client privilege so I could tell you some of what she said, and I have her permission."

"What did she tell you?" I asked.

"She had just recently become terrified of JC Hass and wanted to find a way to quit working for him, but she feared if she did, he'd cause her serious trouble. She said making people believe she liked working for him was an act to protect herself. She said she didn't even tell you the truth. She wasn't more specific than that, but after what you just told me, I think we both know she feared what Hass might do and why," Ashley said.

My heart was pounding, and I was sweating. Danger in the jail either Ashley or I could probably deal with by making a couple of phone calls. But this? I felt quite inadequate. We still had a long way to go to get Denadene cleared and to get Hass behind bars. "I'm afraid he would have hurt her had she told him she was quitting," I said. "I wish I'd had any idea she was under such a shadow of fear. I wonder now what exactly he said when he told her she couldn't have the day off to go on that weekend trip with me."

"She didn't say anything to me about that beyond what you told me," Ashley said.

I thought for a moment as I brought my emotions under control. Then I asked Ashley, "Is there anything specific you need me to do or anything else I should know as a result of your visit with Denadene?"

"I hate to say this, Detective, but I'm afraid there is. You're not going to like it, but I promised I'd tell you. First, she says she's sorry for the way she acted with you in the jail when you were with Detective Butler."

"It was strange, but knowing what I know now, I'm not terribly surprised. What else did she say?" I asked.

"She made it clear she thought it would be best if the two of you didn't date anymore when she gets out of jail."

That hit me like a baseball in the face, even though I had to admit to myself I was not in love with her. "She said that?" I asked stupidly.

"I'm afraid so, but she asked me to tell you she would like you to visit her again; she wants to explain to you why she feels this way. When she gets out of jail, and she will, she'll probably move from St. George and find work somewhere else, possibly near her folks in Cedar City or even in the Salt Lake area."

"She doesn't need to do that. I mean, we were only dating," I said as I felt emotion rise in my throat.

"I think it's not so much about you as it is about JC Hass. Maybe she'll open up to you more if you do visit her. But what you do is up to you. As for me, I am going to do everything I can to get these charges against her dismissed. She doesn't deserve to be locked up the way she is. She's innocent." In a sudden departure from speaking about Denadene, Ashley said, "Any word on your escaped killer?"

"I'm afraid not, but I think JC Hass may have had something to do with it. I'd sure like to know if he was paid off to get Melville out of custody."

"At this point, I think anything is possible," Ashley said.

"I'm afraid that's true."

"Do you have any idea where Hass is?"

"I don't. He wasn't where he told Ms. Kwick he would be today, so I don't know what he's up to," I told Ashley. "I was planning on looking for him in a few minutes, but first I need to call Detective Butler."

"Please do. He needs to know what you've learned about Hass." She paused for just a moment, and then, with anger in her voice, she said, "Hass will lose his license to practice law over this, as he should, and when he does, no one will be shedding tears over it. I assume you're going to arrest him when you locate him."

"You'd better believe it," I said. "And I will visit Denadene, if you think I should."

"I do," she said. "The sooner the better. Maybe with what you've learned now, she'll tell you more about her relationship with Hass. And you're more than welcome to tell Detective Butler what Denadene told me. I think he needs to hear it too, and she's okay with it."

I could only hope Denadene would soon be cleared and that what I had to tell Butler might help. "I'll do that," I said.

Then Ashley said, "If you need to speak with me tonight, I'll be unavailable. I'm going scuba diving tonight at Lake Powell. My friends and I left Vegas early this morning. We are almost there."

"You're kidding. You're a diver too? That's one of my favorite hobbies," I said. Maybe I'd found a kindred spirit. "Maybe we can get together sometime and do some dives."

"I'd like that," she said. "I'll talk to you later. My friends are already waiting for me."

After ending the call with Denadene's defense attorney, I dialed Detective Butler's number, my mind on the fact that Randall Stegner had also been a diver and had loaded his gear into Dwight Hass's van. There had to be some significance in that.

Butler answered almost immediately. I said, "Detective Butler, this is Detective Tipton. Have you got a minute?"

"Sure do," he said. "I was actually planning on calling you in a little while. What have you got?"

"JC Hass, Denadene's former boss, is going to be arrested as soon as I can find him. I already arrested his temporary secretary and released her. I think you need to hear what she had to tell me."

"Fire away," he said. "And then I'll tell you what my partner and I have been doing."

I then told him all about the interview and that, from what Ms. Kwick had told me coupled with what Denadene had told her attorney, I thought he should review his case. "But there's more than that," I revealed. "I have good reason to believe your star witness and his pal won't be coming around to help you with your case and testify to what they claim they saw. They're probably the ones who broke my murder suspect out of custody, and if so, they're long gone."

Detective Butler groaned. "After Melville lying to me about being Stegner's brother and Hass supporting him in the lie, I'm not too surprised. I take it you think my suspect's former boss may be involved."

"That's right," I said. "More reason to review your case."

"I already am," he told me. "That's why I was thinking about calling you. Detective Garcia and I have been busy with another murder today, one that occurred during the early-morning hours. It was in the same general area where Randall Stegner was shot. The victim in this case was a well-known gang member in Las Vegas. His name was Bobby Drummond, and he was a really dangerous man. We caught Drummond's killer, and we have the gun he used. It's the same caliber of the one used by Stegner's killer. The cartridge we found at the murder site is what made me think we needed to have the bullet from Stegner's body compared at the lab with the one in Drummond's body."

"Are you thinking your victim from this morning might possibly be Randall Stegner's real killer?" I asked. "Are you saying Drummond killed Stegner?"

"Either him or *his* killer. We'll know soon. I'm waiting for ballistics testing to come back," he said. "But there's more. The new killer in custody tried to make a deal with us a little while ago. His name is Axel Walters. Walters said he'd tell us who killed Stegner if we'd cut him a break."

"I see," I said. "So where does that stand?"

"We haven't run it by the prosecutor yet, but we will in a little while. It has me thinking maybe my witness saw what happened to Stegner, met Alvin Melville or Jim Stegner—whoever he is—and Dwight Hass and worked out a deal with them to frame Ms. Stegner for it. You mentioned the two of them have ties with one or more of our gangs. I'm wondering if my latest killer and victim, Drummond and Walters, are friends or at least acquaintances of Dwight Hass and Alvin Melville. As near as we can tell, the falling out between Walters and Drummond only occurred last night some time. We're told they were friends and members of the same gang."

"Makes sense," I said. "Have you checked in the area for surveillance cameras?"

"Detective Garcia is doing that as we speak. Another pair of detectives is assisting us now. They're currently questioning folks in the casino closest to where both murders occurred. I'm hoping someone saw or heard something. Customers are so fluid I doubt we would find many there tonight who were also there on Friday night other than staff."

"I hope this all pans out," I said with a great deal of relief—relief I hoped wouldn't be dashed later. "By the way, Denadene wants to speak with me again. I'm hoping she'll tell me more of what was happening with her and her boss. I'm afraid I won't be able to visit very soon since I already had that visit on Saturday."

"Don't worry about that. I'll get you in to see her," Butler said confidently. "But it can't be tonight. I'm too busy on this other case right now."

"And I'm going to be spending the evening trying to find JC Hass and hopefully arresting him," I said.

"Why don't you plan on going in the morning," he suggested. "If you could be at the jail by ten o'clock, we'll go have a visit with her."

"That'll work," I said. "Although I would like to have a couple of minutes with her alone if that's possible."

"I'll make sure it is," he assured me. "Thanks for the call. Tomorrow I'll bring you up to date on what's going on with my case—or I guess I should say *cases.*"

I thanked him and turned my attention to finding JC Hass. I was itching to put him behind bars. But I failed to find him, nor could I locate anyone—neighbors or anyone else—who had seen him since he left his house early that morning. It appeared Ms. Kwick was the last person to have seen him, before he'd told her he was going to Fillmore.

I checked on Ms. Kwick, both to make sure she was okay and to ask her if by any chance Hass had contacted her. She told me he hadn't and she hoped he didn't. She also told me she was going to go on a trip, that she wanted to get away for a while. I encouraged her to do that but again asked her to keep in touch with me, which she promised to do. I certainly preferred dealing with the new and improved Lily Kwick as compared to the former one.

I finally gave up on searching for JC Hass and went to bed after eating a cold sandwich I'd purchased at a convenience store. My diet had suffered since I'd started working the Melville case, and I wasn't getting nearly as much sleep as I needed.

I was up and on the road early Tuesday morning and arrived at the jail in Las Vegas at twenty minutes to ten. Detective Butler joined me in the parking lot a few minutes later. He was walking from the direction of the jail and had a long face. "What's up?" I asked, wondering if I really wanted to know.

"I would have called you, but I only found out myself a couple of minutes ago. Denadene Stegner has been released," he said.

For a moment I wasn't sure what to say, but finally I responded to the news. "I guess that's a good thing, from her point of view," I said. "But unless she's hanging out around here, I may not get to talk to her. What happened that she got released?"

"My case against her fell apart when I got the ballistics test back. The weapon used to kill Drummond was the same one used to kill Randall Stegner. His killer, Walters, claims the gun was not his but Drummond's. He told us he'd wrestled it away from him and killed him in self-defense," Detective Butler said.

"Likely story," I said. "But I like it better than having Denadene accused."

"I get you, Gage," he said with half a grin. "We questioned Walters again early this morning. He had counsel, but we were able to ask a few questions. I more or less accused him of killing Stegner too, but he quickly said the man he killed, Drummond, did it. He didn't even ask for a deal before he said that. Anyway, with that and what you told me last night, the prosecutor told me he was going to ask the judge to dismiss the charges against Denadene."

"He must have got right on it," I said glumly.

He nodded. "He told me he was going to call the jail and have her released as quickly as they could do it. I tried to get over here before she got out, but my lieutenant insisted on a few minutes of my time, which turned into a lot more than a few minutes. By the time I got here, she was gone," he said.

"How did she leave?" I asked.

"Maybe she got a cab."

"Without money?" I asked. "I have her purse with me. It has money in it, as well as her driver's license and some credit and debit cards. I was going to give it to her or at least have it put in her property at the jail."

"Good point. Maybe a friend picked her up."

"That's very unlikely. I think most of her friends are in St. George, so they can't have gotten here that fast."

"Let's go inside and see if we can figure out who she went with," Detective Butler suggested. "I have her cell phone with me, and I had planned to give it back to her before she left, but that didn't happen, so we can't even call her. So she is free but has no money, no cards, no phone, and no driver's license. That's not good."

As it turned out, Denadene and another woman were released at the same time. A correctional officer told us he'd heard the two of them talking and that the other woman had offered Denadene a ride with her mother. We found out the name and address of the other freed inmate, and I left Butler to his work and drove to the address in Henderson.

I prayed I would find Denadene there, but I was told she had borrowed some money from the other woman's parents, promising to repay it soon, and caught a cab to an unknown destination.

I was frustrated, to say the least. I checked at the airport, but I was pretty sure Denadene wouldn't be able to get a flight anywhere without ID, and I doubted her new friend's parents would have been willing to lend her very much money. After all, they didn't know her from Eve. She had not, as near as I could learn, been to the airport. And she had not rented a car. She had vanished into thin air, which might be exactly what she'd wanted, not that I could blame her. In her shoes, I would have probably done the same thing.

I decided it was time to head back to St. George. Maybe with some luck I'd find her back at her apartment. I called Ashley Webler. "Hi, Detective," she said.

"I think you can call me Gage now, Ashley," I said, amused.

"Why is that? Is there something I don't know?" she asked. "I just got back from my diving trip, a short one, I'm afraid, and was going to shower and head right over to the jail. I was hoping to be there by one o'clock or so. Are you in Vegas? Have you seen Denadene yet?"

"That's a lot of questions," I said. "I'm not sure which to answer first, so I'll go with the most important one: Denadene was released this morning before I arrived here. All the charges have been dismissed. I have no idea where she's gone. I've been trying unsuccessfully to figure that out for the past couple of hours. Have you heard from her?"

"Oh my goodness," she said. "No, I haven't heard from her, and no one called to tell me she was released. Where can I meet you?"

"I'm hungry. I'll buy you a late lunch if you'll tell me where you'd like to meet," I said.

She named a restaurant, gave me the location, and then said, "I'll see you there in about forty-five minutes if that works for you."

I drove there and parked and saw Ashley get out of her light-blue Camry and look around for me. I got out of my Explorer, sorry to give up the air-conditioning for the oven-like air, and called out, "I'm right here, Ashley."

She looked my way, smiled, and waved. She strode toward me, and I noticed again that she was limping a little. I met her halfway between our cars and held out a hand for her to shake, but she bypassed it, to my surprise, and hugged me tightly. It was not an unpleasant experience, and my blood pressure spiked.

"I'm sorry I'm out of the loop, but a couple of other girls and I had this trip planned weeks ago," she said as she stood back and looked at me for a moment. "I didn't want to let them down. We dove for several hours last night and then took turns driving this morning. We all had to be back, but I'm exhausted. I'm afraid we didn't get as much diving in as we would have liked. But we had fun anyway."

I knew what she was seeing when she looked at me: a six-foot-two man of 220 solid pounds with short brown hair and a less-than-average face—a very tired and worried one. "It's okay," I said. "I love to dive when I can, so I don't blame you for one minute."

"Let's go inside," she said. "I think I'm as hungry as you are." She smiled again, a little brighter than she had a moment ago, but she did look worn out. A hurried diving trip could do that to a person. She continued. "Then we can brainstorm. I guess, technically, I'm no longer Denadene's attorney since she's free of the murder charge, but I still feel obligated to help locate her. Unlike most of the people I represent, I think I forged a friendship with Denadene, and like you, I'm worried about her."

CHAPTER TEN

THE FOOD WAS GOOD, BUT the company was better. Ashley and I talked about our mutual interest in scuba diving. She reiterated my earlier suggestion. "We'll have to go sometime."

"I'd like that." I looked into her astonishingly green eyes. I had never seen eyes so green. They were beautiful. Yes, I would like that a lot.

"Let's set a date. Is Lake Powell okay with you?" she asked. "And if it is, we'll give ourselves a lot more time than my friends and I did."

"That's where I do most of my diving," I told her. "I have a couple of friends who dive with me most of the time."

"You don't ever dive alone, do you?" she asked with a worried look on her face.

"Of course not, but sometimes only one of the guys I dive with can go, so it's often just two of us," I explained. "We just drop anchor from our boat, and into the water we go."

We talked a little more as we waited for our lunch to be served. But our conversation kept coming back to diving. When I saw she really was serious about diving with me, we looked at our calendars and set a date for a couple of weeks away. "Now hopefully our jobs won't interfere," she said with a little pout on her face.

"That's always a risk," I agreed. I hoped there wouldn't be any obstacles. I really wanted to get to know Ashley better. I still felt the sting of Denadene's rejection, but I was determined not to let that get me down.

"I'll call you in a few days, and we can set a time and place to meet to go diving," she said with a smile.

I'll call you. I didn't consider myself to be superstitious, but those three words sent a chill through me. After what had happened with Denadene after she'd said that same thing, I hoped nothing would happen to Ashley.

She seemed really nice. Spending some time with her would be enjoyable. "Okay," I said. "It'll be good to have a new diving partner."

She agreed, and we finished our lunch with discussion about how to go about finding Denadene. I told her what I had already done, and we talked about maybe checking more at the airport. She also suggested a bus depot. I'd missed that one and I told her I'd get right on it. Other than that, we didn't come up with a lot of ideas. Afterward, she went her way, and I went mine.

I made a few more phone calls and stops to try to find Denadene, including the bus depots and airport, but I finally gave up, called Ashley to tell her of my lack of success, and then left Las Vegas and headed back to Denadene's apartment in St. George. I arrived in the early evening, but she wasn't there. I then drove up to Cedar City and stopped at her parents' home.

Andrea Garford yanked the door open, her eyebrows knitted with worry. "Gage," she said. "Have you found Denadene?"

I hadn't told them she was in jail, and it appeared that Denadene hadn't called them about her situation. "Yes," I said, "but it's complicated."

"Is she okay?" she asked, wringing her hands. Concern of a loving parent was etched into her face, and she seemed to hold her breath for my response.

"She is, more or less," I said. "Is your husband at home?"

"Oh yes. Come in," she said. She hastily stepped back and waved me in, the worry lines in her forehead deepening.

She led me to their living room and called for her husband to join us. We sat down, and Edward Garford, his voice stern, said, "You found our daughter? Where is she, and why isn't she with you?"

"She was in Las Vegas," I began.

"Was?" her mother asked quickly. "Where is she now?"

"I don't know," I said. "I was in Vegas much of the—"

"You said you found her, and now you say you didn't?" Edward interrupted angrily.

"As I said to your wife a moment ago, this is complicated. Let me explain." For the next few minutes, I summarized what had happened to Denadene, beginning with her being abducted from her apartment by their former son-in-law and ending with her being released from jail.

Before I could say anything more, her father said, "Why would anyone want to frame Denadene for murder? She's a sweet and wonderful girl."

I had left out the part about the demand I had received to make the murder case on Bronson Melville go away, but I gave a general explanation. "This whole thing involves the murder I arrested Bronson Melville for."

"We heard he escaped," Edward said. He clenched his fist, and I could see the worry in his face.

I nodded. "I have reason to believe that JC Hass had something to do with that," I said bitterly. I had already mentioned Dwight Hass and Alvin Melville and the parts they had played in the Las Vegas fiasco, so I expounded on it. "I believe Dwight and Alvin helped Bronson escape, and I can't help but think JC Hass may have been paid off to see to it that those two men made it happen. There's no way he'd ever be able to get Bronson off the murder charge. Despite all the noise he made in the media to the contrary, I suspect that Hass could see he had a losing case. And when he couldn't bluff his way into getting the judge to drop the charges, he found another way to beat the system."

"So you think Bronson's family or someone paid JC Hass to help him escape?" Edward asked.

"I don't know it for a fact, but that's what I think. This way, Hass doesn't have to face us in court and be embarrassed after all the public statements he's made against me and the case we have on his client. He still gets paid, and he can go on claiming I was only trying to make a name for myself without having to prove his client is a murderer."

"But what if Melville is located and arrested?" Andrea asked.

"I believe we will find him, given time," I said. "And when we do, we will convict him."

The Garfords looked at each other. "This is unbelievable," Edward said.

"Denadene's ex is really dead?" Andrea asked.

"He was killed by a gang member. What I don't know is what part Dwight and Alvin played in the killing. I'm almost certain they somehow were involved," I said. I couldn't very well tell them why I was so certain Dwight and Alvin were involved in Randall's murder. He must have become a liability to them in some way I didn't yet understand. Perhaps he threatened to turn them in to the authorities. I honestly didn't know. But I believed they wanted him dead but weren't willing to dirty their own hands.

Denadene's parents were frustrated. "Gage," her father said, "what I want to know is what's being done to find her again. And what are you doing to find whether there really is a connection between the Melville murder and them doing to Denadene what they did?"

"I already told you what I've done. I will continue to check back at her apartment. As far as JC Hass's friends, both myself and several detectives in Las Vegas are working on that. I wish I could tell you more," I said.

"So do we," Denadene's mother said. "I'm sorry if we seem frustrated. We know none of this is your fault and we appreciate your taking the time to tell us what has happened. Please, keep us informed."

"I will do that," I promised. They asked a few questions about the murder, which I had very few answers for, and finally, Mrs. Garford said, "What matters to us is that Denadene has been cleared and is out of jail. And we hope, wherever she is, that she's safe."

"Denadene is a smart girl," I said. "She's taking care of herself. Of that I'm certain."

"We pray that's the case. Is there anything else you can tell us?" Mrs. Garford asked.

I hesitated, but finally I said, "She made it clear to her court-appointed attorney that she didn't want to continue dating me."

"Really?" Mrs. Garford said in disbelief. "She's very fond of you, Gage."

"I'm afraid that's not how she feels. But dating or not, I'm deeply concerned about her. I have reason to believe she fears for her life since her old boss is likely involved with the men who broke Bronson Melville out of jail. She told her attorney that JC Hass wanted more from her than an attorney-secretary relationship. She rejected him, and I think that had something to do with her ex-husband becoming involved and kidnapping her. I came here hoping she had contacted you."

They both shook their heads, and Edward said, "If those men find her before you do, they may do something far worse to her than land her in jail. But I'm sure she'll get ahold of us soon. And like you just said, she's very smart. I'm sure she's being very careful. But I can't imagine she'll want to be without her car for very long. It's parked in our garage now."

I tried to assure them. "I'm sure you're right. Please let me know when you hear from her."

"We will," Denadene's mother said. "Thank you for everything you're doing to find her, Gage. Please keep us informed too."

"I will," I said. "And I'll keep looking."

I politely declined an invitation to stay for dinner with them—it was such an awkward situation with Denadene missing again and us no longer dating—and returned to my vehicle. I headed south on I-15.

On a whim I exited the freeway, drove to Hurricane, and stopped at Randall Stegner's house. I didn't expect anyone to be there, but I wanted to make sure his friends weren't using it as a convenient location to hole up.

Becky Currier from next door saw me and walked over, her baby in her arms. "I haven't seen Randall since you were here last," she said. "It's been kind of nice to not have the noise of his truck in the neighborhood. Have you found Denadene yet?"

"Yes and no," I said. "I saw her the other day, and she was okay but very upset. She was accused of killing Randall, which of course she didn't."

Becky gasped and turned pale. "That's terrible," she said. "Why was Denadene accused?"

I gave her a short version of the nightmare Denadene was facing and said, "I don't know where she is now, but I'm pretty sure she's safe for the time being. I'm sure she's doing everything she can to avoid Randall's friends, including her former boss."

"I can't believe Randall is dead. I mean, I didn't like the guy, but I hate to think of anyone getting murdered. It's so sad," Becky said. "I hope they catch whoever did this to him." She was silent for a moment and looked in the direction of Randall's empty house, slowly shaking her head.

After the initial shock had worn off over hearing all her friend had been forced to endure, Becky's expression turned to worry as she glanced at her baby and asked, "So why did you come here tonight, Detective?"

"I just wanted to make sure his buddies weren't using his place as a hideout, but I don't think anyone is here."

"There haven't been any lights on over there. And I haven't seen the black van again, but I can let you know if I do," she offered.

"Please do," I said. "And, specifically, watch for Randall's truck. If it comes here, I need to know. And if you or your husband see anyone prowling around his house, regardless of what they're driving, call me and give me a description of whatever vehicle they're in. And a license plate number, if you can see one."

She agreed she would, and I headed for my Explorer. I looked back at her as I opened my door. She waved with a couple of fingers and attempted a smile, but I could tell from the color of her face and the fear in her eyes that she was still badly shaken.

As I drove back to St. George, I got a call from Lily Kwick. She sounded frantic. "Detective Tipton," she said. "JC called me a few hours ago."

"Good. What did he want?" I said.

"It's not good! He's angry I wasn't at work and he had to call me at home. He said I needed to make sure things were taken care of at the office."

"Did he say when he was coming back?" I asked hopefully.

"I'm afraid not, but he did tell me he would be gone for a few days. He didn't specify how many," she responded.

I knew there was more she needed to tell me, because so far there was nothing that should have made her as frantic as she sounded. "Did you ask him anything about what specifically he wanted you to do?"

"I asked him what I should tell clients who called for him and whether I should have them call his cell phone."

"And what did he say?"

"He shouted and cursed at me. He said no one was to call his cell phone. He also said I should tell people he was out of state attending to the illness and impending death of his grandmother," she said. "But I don't believe that's where he is."

"So I guess you didn't ask him what state he was in."

"I didn't dare."

"What did you tell him?"

"I told him I wasn't feeling well and couldn't go in today, that he might have to hire another temp from the agency."

"Did he graciously accept that?" I asked facetiously.

"It just made him angrier than ever. He was in a really foul mood when he called, and it kept getting worse."

"I don't like the sound of this. What are you going to do?" I asked.

"What should I do? I've been stewing about this for several hours now. That's why I finally called you," she said, her voice beginning to break. "I need advice."

"Did he threaten you?" I asked.

"He said if I didn't take care of the office and do what he'd asked, I would wish I had," she answered. "I don't know if that's exactly a threat, but the way he said it terrified me."

"Did he say anything that would give you any idea of where he's at?" I asked.

"No, he didn't. I suppose he could have been calling from right here in town, but I don't think he was."

"Was the phone he used to call you the one he usually uses?" I asked.

"Now that I think of it, it was a blocked number, so maybe it wasn't."

"A burner phone," I mumbled to myself.

"What did you say?" she asked.

"I think he's changed phones. I'd like you to try calling his cell phone and call me back with the results. If he answers, which I don't think he will, based on what he said about not wanting any calls, make up something to ask him," I suggested.

"I don't think I can do that," she said. "I'm so rattled I can hardly think."

"Okay, then, give me the number and I'll try."

She recited the number, and I pulled off the freeway, put the Explorer in park, and called the number. As expected, the call went directly to voicemail. I called Ms. Kwick back. "It went to voicemail," I told her.

"I was sure it would," she said. "I've been thinking. Wouldn't he be afraid of you tracking him through the GPS in his phone? Or does that just happen on TV and in movies?"

"No, it happens all the time. I think I'll try just in case he hasn't disabled his phone. I'll go back to the office and see what I can do. In the meantime, what are your plans? Are you going into Hass's office in the morning?"

"Of course not!" she said. "I'm scared to death of him now. I was just packing for my vacation when he called me. I would appreciate it if you would call me when JC is found, and then I'll think about returning home."

"Ms. Kwick," I said. "Are you planning on keeping the same cell phone?"

I heard her gasp on the phone, and then she said, "He could track me too, couldn't he? Oh no! What should I do?"

"I seriously doubt he would go to that kind of effort to find you," I told her. "Still, I think if I were in your shoes, I would change phones just to be on the safe side."

"You didn't hear his voice on the phone," she said. "I'm going to get a new phone. I'll call you with my new number so you can call me if you need to. No one else will have it yet except my sister in Florida."

I was relieved at her decision. "Be safe, Ms. Kwick, and I'll stay in touch and let you know if there are any developments."

Even though it was getting quite late, I drove to Ms. Kwick's house instead of going straight home that evening. She had finished packing her suitcases, and I helped her carry them to her car. "Thank you, Detective," she said after she was loaded up and ready to go. "I'm sorry again for treating you so badly when we first met. JC seemed like a nice man, but he had such a vendetta against you I felt I had to follow his lead to stay on his good side while I was working for him."

"That's okay," I told her. "I feel like I've found a friend now."

"Indeed you have," she said. "I don't have many friends. I've never been much of a social creature, but it's nice to know there's someone I can call if I need to. I was wondering if you would mind keeping an eye on my house while I'm gone."

"I'd be glad to," I said. Then I asked her, "Will you be okay financially, taking off like this tonight?"

She smiled at me. "I have money saved up. My sister and I have an inheritance from our parents, so I don't really need to work. I just like to occasionally for a change of pace. That's why I work through the temp agency. I never did intend to work more than a few days for JC. Don't you worry about me and my finances, Gage. I'll be just fine." Then she got into her car, buckled up, and gave a little wave.

After she had driven away, I went back to the office and began to work on tracing the GPS on Hass's phone. As I had feared, it had been disabled in some way, so I gave that up, completed some paperwork, and then drove home. I was hungry, but when I looked in my fridge, it was about empty. I had some cereal, but my milk was sour. I didn't feel like eating out, but as I poured the sour milk down the drain, I decided I would have to. I thought I'd get a few groceries on the way home so this wouldn't happen to me again tomorrow.

I stopped at a restaurant and tried to relax as I slowly ate my late dinner. I felt like a failure. I had found and then lost Denadene. I had arrested Bronson Melville and built a strong case against him, and then, in a way, had lost him too. At least there was no trial in the immediate future, unless he was found somewhere and arrested again. I had to get back to work first thing in the morning on attempting to locate Denadene. And I had to do it with a positive outlook I didn't feel. It wasn't like me to be so gloomy.

After eating, I drove by Denadene's apartment. I don't know why I did, and I honestly hadn't expected to find lights on there, but there were. For a moment, my heart lifted. But then I saw there was a white Chevy Malibu in her parking space. There was most assuredly someone in her apartment, but that wasn't Denadene's car. I looked more closely at it. My first thought was that Denadene could have rented it earlier that day. A rental was exactly what it was. I saw a rental car sticker on the rear bumper. Even though it was quite late, I found myself much cheered as I started toward the apartment. I wasn't sure how she'd been able to rent a car without her driver's license, but it looked like she had. I hurried toward her door just as my phone began to ring. I looked at the screen and stopped in my tracks.

CHAPTER ELEVEN

IT WAS ASHLEY. I CLICKED on the phone and started back toward my Explorer. "Hi Ashley," I said cheerfully. "I hadn't expected you to call so soon, but I'm glad you did."

"Thanks. Have you found Denadene?" she asked.

"No, but there's a rental car in her parking space and lights on in her apartment, so I think she's home," I said, standing outside my Explorer. I leaned my back against the hood so I could have a good view of Denadene's apartment.

"Let me know as soon as you find out," she said. "Sorry if I caught you at a bad time. I'll call back later."

"No, now is fine. I can check on Denadene in a minute. You must have had a reason for calling me," I said.

"I did," she responded. Her voice sounded despondent. I felt a chill pass over me.

"Tell me," I prompted, worried something was wrong.

"Actually, Gage, there are a couple of reasons. First, shortly after you left I got a call telling me I was appointed to represent the man accused of murdering Randall Stegner's alleged killer."

"Wow, I'm sorry."

She chuckled without mirth. "I'm not looking forward to it, that's for sure. But I'll do it. It's my job, after all. I met him at the jail already. His name is Axel Walters. He doesn't deny killing Bobby, his friend, but he claims he did it in self-defense. Axel says the victim, Bobby Drummond, thought he was going to rat on him for killing Stegner and was going to kill him, but he wrestled with Bobby for the gun, and it went off, killing his friend. Who knows? That could be true," she said. "Axel didn't tell me anything different from what he told Detective Butler—I wouldn't be able to tell you if he had. For now, as his counsel, I'll have to go with what he told the officers and confirmed with me."

"You'll do fine on the case," I said. "Was there something else?"

"Hang on, I'm getting another call. Can I put you on hold? I'll make this short if I can," Ashley said.

"I'll wait. Whoever's in Denadene's apartment can't leave without me seeing." And frankly, I was nervous about what to say if it was Denadene.

"Okay, I'll get back with you in a minute," Ashley said and then clicked off. I waited for a minute, then another one, and finally for five minutes. I was wondering if Ashley had forgotten about me when she finally came back on the line, sounding breathless. "I'm sorry, Gage. I didn't mean to be so long, but I can tell you it isn't Denadene who's in her apartment."

"How do you know?" I asked.

"Because that was Denadene on the other line," Ashley revealed.

"Where is she? Is she okay?" I asked anxiously.

"She wouldn't tell me where she is," Ashley responded. "She said she's safe for now."

"Did she know who's in her apartment?" I asked.

"I didn't ask, but what she did say has me shaking my head."

"What's that?"

"She says she doesn't think Randall is actually dead. She thinks the body the cops found is someone else and that Alvin and Dwight identified him as Randall. And since Dwight had ID showing he was Randall's brother, there would be no reason for anyone to question him," she said. "I'd better call Detective Butler and let him know. Maybe by now they have proof other than Dwight's and Alvin's say-so that it's Randall." It seemed the medical examiner as well as the detectives had no reason to believe the victim was anyone other than Randall. If they hadn't already done so, then it would be time to start comparing fingerprints, DNA, dental records, and whatever else might prove who the victim really was. Dwight and Alvin may have hoped the victim's identity would never come into question and that their identification was enough. That would no longer work.

"Will you let me know what you find out?" I asked, after thinking about this for a moment and shaking my head at this new development. Could Denadene be right? And how would she have come to suspect such a thing?

"Of course," she said. "But there's more. Denadene asked me to tell you she's sorry it ended this way but that she appreciates your help."

"I guess it's really over, then," I said, not sure how I felt about that.

"She also said to tell you that even though she thinks Randall is alive, she's not afraid of him killing her."

"Really?" I asked, not attempting to hide the skepticism in my voice.

"She says he's mean and angry, but she doesn't believe he would ever actually kill anyone. She says he was forced by Alvin and Dwight to kidnap her. When I pressed her on that point, she told me they had made threats against his sister."

"I didn't know Randall had a sister," I said. "Denadene never mentioned it."

"She's apparently younger by several years. Her name is Selena, and she lives in Grand Junction, where she works as a waitress. She'll be nineteen by the time she begins college there in the fall."

"How does Denadene know Selena was threatened?"

"When Randall came to her apartment, he told her he desperately needed her to go with him. She said she claimed if she didn't do as he asked her to, Alvin and Dwight would do something horrible to his sister. And despite how abusive he got toward Denadene in their marriage, she knows he adores Selena, and Denadene loves her like a sister too. She couldn't bear to have something happen to her."

"So you believe Denadene?" I asked.

"Honestly, I do. She told me she has Selena's number and has tried to call her several times, but she hasn't gotten an answer, and that scares her. She's going to keep trying in hopes she can reach her to warn her. She asked me to give you Selena's number, so as soon as I hang up, I'll text it to you."

"Good. I think I'll try to call her," I said. "But did Denadene give you the number she was calling from?"

"No, and it showed as blocked on my screen. She's scared and doesn't want to be found. She doesn't ever want to see Randall again, but at least she doesn't think he would actually ever kill her. He could have done that earlier if he'd wanted to."

"But she believes *someone* is after her?" I asked.

"Yes. She's afraid of Alvin and Dwight, but she's most afraid of what JC Hass would do if he found her," Ashley said.

I shook my head, reeling from all of it. Shaking my head made me dizzy, so I stopped and closed my eyes for a moment. Opening them again, I asked, "Will you please keep me posted on what you learn?"

"Of course, Gage. But there's one more thing I need to tell you. It's not about Denadene; it's about me. I'm not exactly the girl you think I am." She hesitated and then said quietly, "I'm defective."

That rocked me. "What in the world does that mean?" I asked before she could say more.

"There's something about me you need to know before you go diving with me," Ashley said.

"I'm not backing out," I said. "I'm looking forward to it."

"You might change your mind when I tell you what I need you to know about me. Don't get me wrong. I don't have a boyfriend or anything, and I try really hard to live the gospel. I'm not a bad person. It's just that I—"

I cut her off. "Whatever it is, don't tell me. I want to go diving with you, and I hope you won't change your mind either."

"It'll be up to you," she said. "But I want you to know—"

I interrupted her again. "Please, don't tell me. I like you, Ashley, and I look forward to our date, and I hope that's what you'll consider it. Now, I need to find out who's in Denadene's apartment."

"Gage, please," Ashley said.

I had to be honest with myself. I didn't want her to tell me for fear it *could* cause me to change my mind. I didn't think it would, but after what had happened with Denadene, I was worried about what Ashley might really be like.

I debated with myself for a moment. I almost decided to let her tell me, but then I changed my mind. It scared me. I didn't want to know anything bad about her. "I'll let you know what I find out," I finally told her firmly. "And I do like you, Ashley. I want to get to know you better." Now I was being forward, pushing far beyond my comfort zone. Was it because I both did and did not want to know what she meant by being defective? I was confusing myself. I didn't know if I'd meant what I said or not, but before she could say anything else, I said goodbye and ended the call. I hoped I hadn't just made a huge mistake. I had apparently done something to make Denadene end our new but somewhat budding relationship. Had I just done the same thing to Ashley? Or was her defect something I wouldn't be able to handle? Perhaps I was the one with a defect. Perhaps there was a reason I didn't recognize that was keeping me single.

I waited for a minute, thinking Ashley might try to call me back, almost hoping she would so I could go ahead and ask her to tell me what she had wanted to. But she didn't, leaving me both relieved and regretful.

I did get the promised text from her. It was short and simple—just Selena Stegner's phone number. Maybe I *had* made a mistake. I was more worried and curious by the moment about what she could possibly mean by her being defective. Surely she didn't have some terrible disease that would take her life at an early age. Maybe I should call her back and let her say what she wanted to. But, after debating with myself for a minute or two, I decided not to. If she called again, I'd let her tell me, but right now I needed to put that out of my mind and find out what was going on in Denadene's apartment.

I pushed away from my Explorer and headed toward Denadene's door again, my mind in a whirl and my stomach in knots.

I knocked on the door, standing at the very spot where we had kissed just over a week ago. It felt more like a month now, and the memory of the tingling from that kiss was gone. So much had happened in those few days. After waiting for a minute, I knocked again. Finally the door opened. I was greeted by a pretty, smiling face—one I had never seen before.

"Hi, I'm Detective Gage Tipton," I said as I wondered who this young lady was and what she was doing in Denadene's apartment.

"I know who you are," she said with a dimpled smile. She was slender and had short brunette hair. "I'm a friend of Denadene's. She told me a lot about you. Please, come in."

I stepped inside, feeling let down that Denadene really was hiding somewhere, afraid for her life. It felt very awkward seeing this stranger here in her place, but at the same time, I was hopeful I was about to learn more regarding Denadene's whereabouts.

"My name is Paige Pendergrass. Denadene and I were roommates back before she was married, and we've stayed friends." Paige gestured to the familiar sofa and said, "Please, sit down."

"Thanks," I said. "I am assuming you've heard from Denadene."

She smiled, but it was a sad one this time, I thought. "She called me just after she got out of jail this morning, from a payphone. I don't know how she found one of those. It seems like they're just about non-existent now. Needless to say, I was shocked to hear she'd been arrested. She told me what had happened and asked me if I still wanted to move to St. George— I'd told her before how much I love it here."

"Where do you live?" I asked.

"I guess I live here now. But I've been living and working in Provo. I quit my job a few days ago, and Denadene was going to help me find a place to live down here, but suddenly she vanished. I guess you know all about that," she said.

"I'll say." I waited for her to go on.

"Well, as I said, I was shocked when she called me this morning. She told me she was still in danger and that she had no intention of coming back to St. George. I asked her why, and she said it held bad memories."

"I suppose I'm one of those bad memories," I said, unable to keep the bitterness from my voice.

"Oh no, not at all. She said she liked you, that you were a good guy, but that under the circumstances, she needed to move on. She told me she feels really bad about not talking to you directly, but . . . well, I guess she treated you badly," Paige said. "I have some milk in the fridge and some cookies I bought a little while ago. Would you like some?"

I wasn't in the mood to eat, but I wanted to learn everything I could from this friend of Denadene's, so I said, "Sure. That would be nice."

She headed for Denadene's kitchen. "Why don't you come in here with me."

I followed her into the kitchen and sat at the table while she got some glasses out of the cupboard and a box of cookies from a bag on the counter. She opened the cookies and set them on the table, got the milk from the fridge, and poured us each a glassful. After returning the carton to the fridge, she sat down, smiled at me, and said, "I'm sure you can guess why I'm in Denadene's apartment."

"Yes, but I'd like to hear the details," I said, attempting to smile back but not doing so well.

"My head is still spinning over it, but Denadene insisted I take over the lease on her apartment since she isn't going to live here anymore. She told me to box up her things and that she would pick them up sometime or have her parents do it for her," she explained.

"My head is spinning too," I admitted.

"I'm sorry, Gage. Is it okay if I call you Gage?"

"Of course. That's my name, Paige. Hey, we rhyme. Paige and Gage," I said, feeling stupid for saying it. But Paige laughed, so I chuckled too.

"Denadene told me what a nice guy you are. I think she's making a big mistake dumping you like this," Paige said.

"She really didn't dump me. We weren't exclusive yet," I said. "And I believe one of the other guys she was dating likes her a lot."

"She did mention one other guy, but I don't remember his name," Paige said, shaking her head. "Denadene and I talk a lot and still get together once in a while, although it was hard to stay in touch while she was with Randall. He was so controlling. But she tells me he's dead now. I guess I don't feel too bad about that. Shame on me."

"She told you Randall was dead?" I asked, thinking about what Denadene had told Ashley.

"Not exactly. She said she'd been accused of murdering him and they dropped the charges, but she wasn't convinced Randall was dead. I think he is. For her sake, it would be better if he is," she said, a dark look crossing her face.

"Did she tell you why she thinks he's still alive?" I asked.

"No. I told her I thought she needed to accept that he was dead. She argued, but she finally let it drop. He kidnapped her from this apartment," Paige said. "He was an awful man."

"I see," I said, deciding not to tell her what Ashley had told me. Denadene apparently hadn't confided as much to her roommate as she had to her attorney—former attorney, actually.

"Denadene, on the other hand, is a great person," Paige said. "I wish she'd never met Randall. He was such a creep, but I guess he was a good actor in the beginning." It was pretty clear Denadene hadn't convinced Paige the dead man she had been accused of killing wasn't Randall. On the other hand, I had a feeling it could be true. The medical examiner had some work to do since there was now a question about the friends who'd identified the body and what their motive was. There was reason to believe they might have lied.

"So you'll be living here?" I asked, directing the conversation back to where we'd started.

"That's the plan," Paige said. "I sort of have a job lined up, but I won't know until after tomorrow if I'll actually get it. I've talked to my prospective employer on the phone several times, but he said he wouldn't tell me for sure I had the job until he'd met with me."

"I hope it works out for you."

"I think it will, but if it doesn't, I'll look for something else," Paige said. "I think I'll like living in St. George."

We ate cookies and drank milk in silence for a moment. I felt antsy. I hadn't learned anything that had brought me any closer to discovering where Denadene was hiding. So I finally asked directly, "Do you know where Denadene is now?"

"No," she said, looking hurt. "She wouldn't tell me. She said it wasn't safe right now for anyone to know where she was. She told me she's afraid her former boss would come looking for her if he had any idea where she was. But I would never tell him."

"Denadene's an intelligent woman," I said. "She knows someone like Hass or one of his cronies might try to force you to tell him. Although, at this point, I can't imagine why they would care. I mean, they've done her a lot of damage. But, Paige, they may want to do more."

"That's exactly what she thinks. She's afraid they might. After what they put her through, I guess I can't blame her."

My phone rang. "I'm sorry," I said. "I should answer this." I pulled it from my pocket and looked at the screen. It was Denadene's father. "Hello, Mr. Garford," I said. I glanced at Paige, and her face showed recognition of the name.

"Gage, Denadene called a minute ago. She won't tell us where she is, but she says she's safe for now. She doesn't want to put us in danger by telling us where she is. But she asked me to tell you she's okay and she's watching out for danger," he said.

"I'm glad to hear that," I responded. Denadene seemed busy calling everyone but me. I wondered again what I had done wrong. To Edward I said, "I'm actually at Denadene's apartment right now. I came to see if she might have returned, but obviously she hasn't. A friend of hers is here though."

"Yes, she told us about Paige taking over her apartment. She wants me to go pick up her things in a few days and store them in the garage with her car."

"Did she say when she'll come get them or what her plans are?" I asked after a moment of silence.

"No, but she said she told Paige to keep the furniture and some dishes and other things. She only wants her personal things and a few cooking and eating utensils so she can start over somewhere else. That's all I know of her plans." Edward stopped talking, and I could tell that he was fighting his emotions. When he was able to speak again, he said, "We're worried about Denadene. Don't forget about her, Gage, despite what she's said. She has gone through a very traumatic experience."

"She's kind of hard to forget," I acknowledged. "Let me know when you plan to come get Denadene's belongings and I'll help you load them." I glanced at Paige and raised my eyebrows in question to see if that was okay with her, and she nodded.

"Oh, there won't be much since she's giving most of her things to Paige, but if it turns out to be more than I think, I'll give you a call. Thanks, Gage." A moment later, he ended the call.

"Sorry about that," I said to Paige as I put my phone away.

"Denadene told me she would call her parents," Paige said. "I'm glad she did. I know they're worried about her, and so am I. She doesn't deserve what she's going through. But I know you could help keep her safe; I sure wish she would call you."

"You and me both," I said, once again unable to keep a touch of bitterness from my voice.

I didn't spend much more time with Paige. It seemed so strange to visit with someone else in Denadene's home. It just didn't seem right—not that there was anything wrong with Paige. She seemed like a nice person. It was just that Denadene still should've been living there. But she'd been run out of her own home. And more than anything in this world, I wanted to bring Denadene's tormenters to justice for everything they were doing to her.

CHAPTER TWELVE

THE NEXT MORNING I WENT to work early despite having had a restless night. For the first three hours, I worked on my report on the case. I got a call shortly after I finished the report. It was Detective Marcel Butler from Las Vegas. He asked, "Have you heard from Denadene Stegner?"

"I haven't, but I've talked to several people who have," I said. "She called Ashley Webler. She also contacted her parents and a friend she asked to take over the lease of her apartment, but she wouldn't tell any of them where she is. She insisted she's safe. Why do you ask?"

"Miss Webler called me. She told me what Denadene was thinking about the possibility that the identification of Randall Stegner was incorrect, and as strange as it is, she was right. Alvin Melville, under the alias Jim Stegner, and Dwight Hass lied when they identified the body for us."

I broke in and asked, "Are you telling me the dead man is not Randall?" At that point I was not surprised. In fact it was good to hear this.

"That's exactly what I'm saying. The dead man is about the right age, size, and build, but the medical examiner informed me after I spoke to him a little while ago that the blood type is wrong," Butler told me. "The examiner had accepted the identification given by Alvin and Dwight, especially since the dead guy had Randall's marriage certificate on him and he thought Alvin was a brother, but we now know the marriage license was planted there. When the examiner discovered the blood type was wrong, he did further examination and found that the fingerprints were also wrong. He has now identified the actual victim as a local man who spent a lot of time gambling and who, by the way, was reported missing by his wife just yesterday. She says she would have reported it sooner but that he often went a couple of days without going home when he was on a gambling binge, so she wasn't worried at first. Now she has a lot to worry about."

I was confused. "Let me get this straight. First, you told me Axel Walters claimed his victim Bobby Drummond murdered Stegner. Now you tell me this Drummond guy didn't kill Stegner, that he killed someone else. What's the name of the man we thought was Randall Stegner?"

"That would be Niko Munion," Butler said.

"Okay, so Walters told you Drummond killed Stegner, as if Munion and Drummond knew each other."

"We've talked to Walters again at the jail. It was Alvin Melville who told Walters the first victim was Stegner. Walters didn't know Munion, and he had no reason to believe it wasn't Stegner," the detective told me. "It turns out our second victim, Drummond, thought Walters was going to rat him out to us for killing Munion and went to shoot Walters, but they wrestled for the gun and Walters won. So Walters shot Drummond but claims it was in self-defense. Drummond only knew who he had killed when Melville told him, but of course, we now know Melville lied. Melville didn't know the victim, but he looked a lot like Randall Stegner, so apparently Alvin and Dwight turned that to their advantage in order to accuse Denadene."

"But sooner or later the true identity would have come out," I said. "Or Randall would have turned up somewhere very much alive."

"Probably, but Dwight and Alvin didn't know that. They probably thought when they identified the body that the medical examiner would simply believe them, especially since we'd found that fake marriage certificate," Detective Butler said. "And he did believe them, until I called him about Denadene's call to Miss Webler."

"I'm glad it's you guys who have to sort this mess out. For me, the question is where is Randall Stegner? I know it was Randall who kidnapped Denadene and put diving equipment in the back of the black van Alvin was driving at Randall's house. And, of course, as I'm sure Ashley told you, Denadene claims Randall had only taken her in order to save his little sister from being harmed by Dwight Hass and Alvin Melville."

"She did," Detective Butler said.

"So where is Randall now, and what is he doing? Others might have been fooled, but Randall certainly knew he wasn't dead."

"That's a good question," Butler agreed. "Although I'm not sure we should even care."

At that moment, a terrible thought struck me. I voiced it to Butler. "I don't like to even think this, but could Randall have taken Denadene again? What if he's using some kind of threat to make her say what she did to her parents, to her friend Paige Pendergrass and to Ashley Webler?"

"Is Paige Pendergrass the young lady moving into Denadene's apartment?" Butler asked.

"Yes. And she's convinced she's doing exactly what Denadene wants her to do, but now I have to wonder."

"Didn't you say Randall Stegner's truck was used to break Bronson Melville out of the jail van there in St. George?" he asked.

"Yes, that's what I think," I agreed. "And I still believe that, but could one of the two men who broke him free be Stegner? Or could there have been a third man helping to break him out that the officers didn't see?" I had a lot of questions but precious few answers. "I would rather think that than to think that Stegner has kidnapped Denadene again," I said. "Of course, I suppose he could have done both."

"It sounds like we have more work to do, Gage. We'll see if we can learn anything more about Randall here in Vegas. Maybe someone has seen him," Butler said. "We also need to investigate our gang killing further. We still aren't sure if Drummond killed the Randall lookalike or if Walters killed both of them. The same gun was used in both killings. This is a very strange case, to say the least."

"You guys will figure it out. I just pray Stegner hasn't taken Denadene again. The fact that he's out there somewhere puts her in danger, despite Denadene telling Ashley she wasn't afraid Randall would kill her."

"I guess we care about where Stegner is after all," Butler confessed.

"I'll let Paige and Denadene's parents know Randall Stegner is alive and on the loose," I told Butler. "I won't tell them that I fear he might have somehow taken her again—just that he's alive and out there somewhere."

After ending my call with Butler, I called Ashley.

"Hello?"

"Hi, Ashley. I just spoke with Detective Butler," I said. "So Randall Stegner is still very much alive."

"It would appear that way," she responded. "I haven't heard from Denadene again yet. I keep hoping she'll call me."

"I have a theory about why she hasn't, and it's not a pleasant one," I said.

I heard a sharp intake of breath, as though Ashley was bracing herself. "What is it?" she asked.

"I wonder if Randall has taken her again and is coercing her to say whatever he wants her to say to you and everyone else she's spoken with since being out of jail. As you know, I stopped by Denadene's apartment to see if she might have returned and spoke with a friend of hers named Paige. Denadene told Paige the same thing she told you." I then told Ashley about Paige moving into Denadene's apartment on a permanent basis.

"Did this Paige tell you if she knew where Denadene is?" Ashley asked.

"She said Denadene wouldn't tell her because it could put Paige in danger. Denadene told her parents the same thing, but Paige is convinced Randall is dead. I suppose, with what we now know, I'd better visit her again and break the news to her. She'll need to watch for him. Who knows what he's capable of doing at this point?"

Ashley and I discussed the situation for a while longer. Then I finally said to her, "Ashley, I'm sorry I was so rude to you last night. If anyone has a defect, it's me. If you have something to tell me, I'll listen, although I'm sure it won't make any difference in our friendship."

Ashley chuckled, a very pleasant sound. Then she said, "No, I've decided not to worry you about it. It's not that big of a deal."

"Aw, come on, Ashley. Now you have me really curious."

"Too bad, mister. I still have to check on some things with my court schedule; I know the date we discussed works for me, but I'm just not sure about the time. I'll call you."

I'll call you. There was that fateful phrase again. I tried to shake it off. I had never considered myself a superstitious guy, but those three little words gave me the chills now.

Ashley and I talked for a couple more minutes. Too soon she said she needed to go, and the call ended. For a moment, I simply sat at my desk, relishing the memory of the sound of Ashley's voice. If I wasn't careful, I could allow myself to be smitten. But would that be so bad? It could be. *I had been smitten with Denadene and look how that turned out.*

I was still sitting there doing absolutely nothing when Sergeant Hanks came in. "Gage, it looks like you need a new case to work on since Bronson Melville has escaped. I think we can arrange something for you."

"Hi, Sergeant," I said. I was embarrassed he had caught me daydreaming, but I was quick to make an excuse. "There's a lot going on I need to bring you up to date on."

Sergeant Hanks gave me a sober look and then said, "I take it things aren't good."

"You can say that again. I have more work to do on the Melville case." I told him what I'd learned from Detective Butler and about Randall Stegner.

"You're sure Randall is alive?" he asked as he sat down in front of my desk, shaking his head.

"Detective Butler confirmed it," I informed him. "But he doesn't know where Randall is or whether he was working with the guys who broke Bronson Melville loose. He could be anywhere, doing anything."

"You'd better keep working on this case, then," Sergeant Hanks said. "And tell me what's going on with JC Hass's former temp, Mrs. Fast, or whatever her name is."

"Ms. Kwick," I said with a chuckle. "She left last evening on an extended vacation. I'm still waiting for her to call me with her new phone number." As I said it, I remembered Ashley had texted me the number for Randall's sister. I needed to call her right away; I should have already done that.

"So she'll keep in touch with you?" Sergeant Hanks said, referring to Ms. Kwick.

"She said she would," I told him. "She asked me to keep an eye on her house while she's gone."

"I think maybe that lady has a crush on you, Gage."

"Ms. Kwick?" I asked, astonished. Then I realized he was kidding, so I said, "At least she doesn't detest me anymore."

"I think it goes deeper than that," Jon said, still grinning. "She isn't *that* much older than you, is she?"

"She's as old as my mother," I said flatly. I'd had enough of this, so I directed the conversation back to business. "I do think Ms. Kwick could be in danger. Hass threatened her on the phone if she didn't get back to work," I said. "And of course, she didn't. She left the area instead."

Jon nodded as his grin faded and he got a hard glint in his eyes. "I look forward to when we get our hands on that guy. JC's a real loser. Worse than any of us who had to contend with him in court even imagined." He paused for a moment, looking like he had something else on his mind, so I kept quiet.

Before he said whatever was on his mind, I suddenly remembered I hadn't told him about Randall's sister, Selena. So I said, "Randall Stegner has a little sister. Her name is Selena."

"Tell me more about her," he said.

I told him everything I knew about her. "Miss Webler texted me Selena's phone number," I said. "I haven't called her yet, but I plan to shortly; I hope I can reach her. According to Miss Webler, Denadene has apparently tried and Selena hasn't answered. I also need to go talk to Paige Pendergrass again. She needs to know Randall is alive so she can stay safe. And I also need to let Denadene's parents know."

"And I'd better report all of this to the lieutenant. We did have a case we were going to give you, but we'll give it to someone else." Sergeant Hanks smiled again, his face taking on a mischievous look. "I was just kidding about Miss Fast."

"Ms. Kwick," I corrected.

"Yes, her," he said, clearly amused. "But tell me about this Miss Webler over in Las Vegas. Is she another old maid?"

I chuckled, and Sergeant Hanks said, "She's not, I take it. Is she young and attractive and single?"

"You could say that," I said as I got to my feet in an effort to steer the conversation down a different path. "I think I'd better see if I can talk to Miss Pendergrass right away. Let me know if the lieutenant wants me to do something else on this case besides what I already have in mind."

Hanks also got to his feet. "This Miss Pendergrass, is she also a pretty young woman?" he asked, the grin once again in place.

"She's okay," I said noncommittally as I stepped past him and out of the cubicle.

"Wait a second," he said. I stopped and faced him. "Denadene Stegner. You like her a lot, don't you?"

"We were good friends," I said, anxious to get on my way. Every once in a while, Jon got on a roll like this. He did it in jest, but my feelings were rather raw at the moment, and I had had about enough.

He wasn't through though. He appeared quite serious now. "Gage, things aren't always as they appear. Ms. Stegner has been hurt. I wouldn't count her out. She's probably just saying what she is because she's confused and afraid. Take some advice from your sergeant: Be patient. She'll turn up again, and when she does, give her a chance to explain herself. She may surprise you."

"Maybe," I said, pretty sure that would never happen. And I was okay with it at that point. "I just hope Randall or his friends don't get to Denadene first." I headed down the hallway.

He called after me, "Keep me in the loop, Detective. Oh, one more thing." I waited for whatever else he had in mind to say to me. "Selena Stegner. Is she also—"

I couldn't help but grin as I cut him off. "She's eighteen," I said. That shut him up.

Once I was out in my Explorer, I wondered which I should do first—call Selena, see if Paige was still at Denadene's apartment, or call Denadene's parents. I decided to try Selena first. Her phone went to voicemail, so I left a message, telling her who I was and asking her to call me as soon as she could. Then I drove to Denadene's apartment. Or Paige's apartment, I supposed I should think of it now.

Paige's rental car was gone and had been replaced in the parking space by an older yellow Ford Escort. I mentioned the car to her when she answered the door a minute later.

"Come in, Gage," she said brightly. "I turned the rental car in locally. That old yellow thing is all I can afford for now. My other car was run into where I had it parked on the curb at my old apartment. The insurance company totaled it out. I rented the other car to get me here and I bought this one just a little while ago. It'll get me where I need to go until I can afford something better."

"Do you know anything about the job yet?" I asked as I followed her inside.

"Not yet, but I should by tomorrow or the next day." She invited me to sit and took the seat opposite mine.

"I hope you get the job," I said.

"Me too." For a moment, we made small talk, and just as I was about to tell her about Randall, she said, "I was just going to fix some lunch. Would you like to stay and eat with me?"

I thought briefly about refusing, and then I realized I was hungry and she wasn't bad company. I didn't want to be rude, so I accepted, even though I was anxious to call Denadene's parents. I helped her in the kitchen, and we soon had a light lunch fixed and consumed.

I had thought she would be upset over the news that Randall hadn't really been killed, but all she did was shrug her shoulders. I cautioned her to be on the lookout for him or his friends. I showed her pictures of each of them on my cell phone and told her what I could about the cars they drove, but she said, "They have no reason to bother me. I won't let myself be afraid."

As I was preparing to leave, I said, "Paige, please, if you see any of these men or any vehicles that look like theirs, let me know." I gave her my card and made sure I had her number in my phone. Finally I said, "Thanks for lunch."

"You're welcome," she said with a wide grin. "And if you hear from Denadene, will you let me know?"

"Of course I will," I said.

I headed for the office again, but before I got there, my phone rang. "Detective Tipton?" a sweet but timid voice said.

"Yes, this is Detective Tipton," I responded.

"Hi, my name is Selena Stegner. You left me a message."

CHAPTER THIRTEEN

"Thanks for returning my call," I said. "I need to talk to you about a couple of things."

"I've never talked to a detective before," she said with a tremor in her voice. "Have I done something wrong?"

"Oh no, not at all. I'm in St. George, Utah," I told her. "I work for the police department here."

"Isn't that near where my brother lives?" she asked. "His ex-wife, Denadene, lives in St. George."

"That's right," I said. "I'm a friend of Denadene's."

"She is such a sweet person. She still calls me every month or so. Wait—she mentioned she was dating a detective. Is that you?"

"That's me," I admitted. "I'm Gage Tipton. But I'm afraid we aren't dating anymore."

"Oh, I hate to hear that," she said. "Denadene deserves someone nice. Don't get me wrong. I love Randall. After all, he is my big brother. But he didn't treat Denadene like he should have."

"She is a wonderful lady, that's for sure," I said.

"What do you need from me?" Selena asked. "I don't live anywhere near there. I'm in Grand Junction."

"I know," I said. "I need to talk to you about your brother."

"What has he done now? Is this about Denadene?" she asked, her voice not quite as sweet as it had been a moment before. "He was a fool to treat her so awfully. He says he never touched her in anger, but I know he lied to me. Denadene admitted he'd hurt her several times. She was right to leave him. I was hoping she would settle down with someone nice. I did think she was pretty serious about you; I'm sorry it didn't work out."

"Me too," I said, eager to return to the reason I'd left her a message. "Selena, I need to ask: do you know any of Randall's friends from here in Utah?"

"Ugh!" she said. "He has awful friends. They scare me."

"Do you remember their names?" I asked.

"I do, but I wish I could forget them," she said, and I could have sworn I heard a shudder in her voice. "Alvin and Dwight are their names. I don't know their last names. I met them when I came to visit Randall a few months ago. I stayed at his house for a couple of days and with Denadene for three days after that. Anyway, those guys came over several times while I was there. They're a lot older than me, but they both tried to get me to go out with them. Randall told me it would be okay, but there was no way. I refused to even consider it. I mean, I'm only eighteen. Besides, they aren't my type at all. I told them both no several times, and then I could see they were getting angry with me. Ugh! They made me very uncomfortable."

"I can imagine," I said.

"I left Randall's after that and stayed with Denadene. She told me one of the guys was a younger brother of her boss, JC."

"JC Hass," I confirmed. "Dwight is his brother. Alvin's last name is Melville."

"Oh no! Don't tell me his brother is the guy who's in jail for murder," she said.

"I'm afraid so," I said.

"The last time I talked to Denadene, she told me you had arrested him. She said her boss was defending him and saying some awful things about you; it made her mad. I told her she should quit working for him, but she said she didn't dare, that he would cause her trouble if she did."

"She was right. That's exactly what he's done—him and your brother and his friends. And, by the way, Bronson Melville is no longer in jail. His friends broke him out."

"Oh no!" Selena said. "That's scary."

"It is, but right now we need to think about Denadene. She has been in a lot of trouble the past few days."

"Is she hurt?" Selena asked in alarm. "I'll never forgive Randall if he's hurt her again."

"As far as I know, she's okay, but she hasn't called you, has she?"

"No, but I keep expecting her to."

"Have you had any calls from a number that was blocked?"

There was a sharp intake of breath. "Oh," she said. "I don't ever answer calls from numbers I don't know. Has Denadene had her number changed?"

"I still have her old phone. It was in her apartment, so she must have somehow gotten another one. I don't know what her new number is, so I can't even call her."

"I have had several calls from blocked numbers in the past couple of days. Do you think they might've been from her?" she asked.

"I do," I told her. "Have you had any calls from Alvin or Dwight?"

For a moment, the line was silent. Then Selena finally said, "I don't answer calls from numbers I don't recognize because I've been afraid those guys might call me, but I have had several from two numbers I didn't recognize. I finally just blocked them."

"Do you have those numbers?" I asked.

"Yes," she said. "Do you want them?"

"I might be able to tell you who they belong to," I told her. I had several numbers in my little notebook, which I was now holding.

"Hang on while I find them," she said. Then she recited two numbers for me, and a chill ran up my spine. "Do you recognize either one of those?" she asked.

"Both," I said. "One is Alvin's and the other is Dwight's. I have reason to believe both of those numbers are no longer in use. When was the last time you got a call from one of them?"

"I don't know for sure, but it was probably close to two weeks ago. That's about when I blocked them."

"I suspect they discarded their phones to keep from being traced through the GPS features in them," I explained.

Selena sounded frightened. "What should I do?"

She hadn't heard the worst of it yet, but she needed to. That was why I had called her in the first place. "Selena," I said. "I have to tell you what has happened to Denadene."

I recited in some detail what had happened over the past few days, including Alvin's and Dwight's threats about hurting Selena if Randall didn't do what they wanted him to.

Selena was badly shaken. "They told Randall they would hurt me?" she asked, her voice wavering.

"That's right," I said. "It's them and JC Hass that Denadene is hiding from. She told her attorney she isn't afraid Randall would kill her, despite that he's hurt her in the past."

"I don't think he would either, but those other guys would," Selena said. "Do you think I should answer the next call I get from a blocked number?" she asked. "It could be one of those guys using a different phone, but what if it's Denadene?"

"It could be. I think you should answer it. And then, if it's anyone but Denadene, hang up right away," I instructed her. "And, Selena, if you do hear from Denadene, please call me immediately after you've spoken with her. Will you do that?"

"Okay," she said with a quiver in her voice. "And should I call if it isn't her?"

"Absolutely," I said.

"Oh, Gage, I'm so frightened—not just for me but for Denadene too," she said. She paused for a minute before speaking again. "I wonder what Randall is doing. I've tried to call him too, but he hasn't been answering. What if his friends are mad at him?"

"That's a good question," I said. "He did what they told him to, so it should be him who's mad at them." I didn't tell her I suspected they might be working together, that their threats against her might currently be in use to keep him in line.

We talked for several more minutes. It was as if she was afraid to end the call. I was sorry for the fright that I had given her, but she had to know. I tried to reassure her that if she was watchful, she would be okay. But I also told her she might want to change apartments if she could. I thought about telling her to get a new phone, but then Denadene wouldn't be able to reach her. If only I had a way of talking to Denadene, I could let Selena know her number so she could get a new phone. But that wasn't likely to happen, so I let it go for now, praying those guys wouldn't go looking for Selena.

The last thing Selena told me was that she was going to talk to her bishop. "Maybe he can help me decide what to do," she said.

"That's a great idea," I agreed. "And let me know what you do. Stay in touch with me."

She promised to do that, and we said goodbye.

I spent the afternoon and evening visiting friends, acquaintances, and neighbors of the Hass brothers and the Melville brothers. I was hoping to find someone who could give me a lead on their current whereabouts, but I struck out. Their friends wouldn't talk to me, their acquaintances claimed they didn't know anything, and their neighbors told me they hoped none of them ever came back.

I finally went home around eight that night. I was eating a dinner of macaroni and cheese—not my favorite meal, but easy to fix. I was in the process of cleaning up the little bit of mess I had made in my kitchen when my cell phone rang.

"Hi, Gage, it's Ashley," I heard when I answered. She didn't need to tell me who it was. I liked the sound of her voice and knew it well by now.

"Hi, Ashley," I returned. "I hope your day has been more productive than mine."

"I take it you haven't made much progress in the case," she said.

"More like no progress at all."

"I do have something to report," she said, "but it's not going to make your day any brighter, I'm afraid."

"That's okay," I said. "I don't see how it could be any worse."

"I heard from Denadene again. She says she's still safe but she's worried about Randall's little sister."

That did make my day worse. "So am I. I spoke with her for quite a while today. I filled her in on what's going on—I figured she needed to know. It turns out she's much closer to Denadene than she is to her own brother."

"I figured that out too," Ashley said. "Denadene has been trying to call her, but her calls aren't being answered. She's scared to death for the girl."

"Selena's afraid to answer calls from blocked or unrecognized numbers," I explained. "I told her to answer the next blocked-caller call and to hang up immediately if it isn't Denadene. She promised to keep me posted."

"That's good advice," Ashley said.

"She's going to talk to her bishop for advice too."

"That's good to hear. I'll tell Denadene that when I hear from her again. She promised she would call," Ashley said. "There's something else I need to tell you, and you won't like it either. Detective Butler told me the results from Denadene's blood tests came back showing only a relatively small amount of drugs in her system. Either she was never drugged as heavily as she said, or it had mostly gone from her body by the time you guys got the blood sample. The medical examiner doesn't think that's the case."

"So if she wasn't drugged as heavily as she claimed, why doesn't she remember things?" I asked.

"That's the problem, Gage. She does remember some things. I told her what the medical examiner said about her blood tests. At that point, Denadene confessed she had lied about the amount of drugs she'd been given. She said Randall did give her something, but it just made her very sleepy, so there are times she honestly couldn't remember."

"Let me guess," I said. "She did what she was told because of the threats against Selena. She must have believed they'd hurt her."

"Exactly," Ashley agreed. "She stayed in the room at the casino like they told her to. She didn't dare do anything else. Like I said, whatever she had been given made her extremely tired, so she slept a lot. Even though she was aware of what was going on when she was awake, she was dizzy and disoriented. When she was accused of killing Randall, she pretended she couldn't remember, although she was pretty sure she hadn't done it. She was afraid for Selena. Alvin and Dwight kept telling her what they would do to Selena if she didn't cooperate; they were pretty graphic. And it gets worse. They threatened similar things against Denadene and said they would give her more drugs, much stronger ones. And she believed them. After what she'd been through, who wouldn't?"

I clenched my free hand, furious. "I hope we catch them soon. I'd better call Selena back and update her so she can take precautions."

"Denadene said she'll keep trying to call her too. Now that you've talked to the girl, maybe she'll answer," Ashley said.

"Why are they doing all this?" I asked, even though I was pretty sure I knew the answer.

Ashley knew it too. "They wanted Bronson out of jail. They must have thought all the threats and the fake murder charges would get you to drop everything. Of course, they didn't know you."

"Don't think I didn't think about doing what they asked me to do," I said, feeling guilty.

"But you did what you knew you had to, and I admire you for that. Anyway, Denadene has been trying to call Randall, but he hasn't answered. I suppose he could have changed phones too," Ashley said.

"Could be," I agreed. "It could also be that he's still working with his friends in an effort to protect his sister. Although, Bronson is free now, so I'm not sure why they would still be blackmailing him."

"At least that's one good trait Randall has," Ashley said. "He cares about his sister. But that being the case, I'd think that, at some point, he'd rebel against those guys. Maybe they're somehow making sure he doesn't tell anyone what he knows."

"Possibly," I said.

"There's one more thing Denadene told me that could explain why they might still be blackmailing Randall. JC Hass began making her life miserable, and she kept rebuffing his advances. She said he hates her now, so she wonders if threats against her continue and if maybe Randall is trying to get them to stop. It's unclear, but Denadene thinks that even though she divorced Randall, he would try to keep them from hurting her or taking her life," Ashley explained.

"Poor Denadene," I said. "And to think I knew nothing about the torment Hass subjected her to."

"If she chose not to tell you, then there was no way you could have known. At any rate, you know now."

"Thanks for calling, Ashley. Too bad you aren't in St. George. I'd have invited you to dinner at my place."

"Did you cook?" she asked.

"I sure did."

"What did you have?"

"Macaroni and cheese."

The call ended with the appealing sound of Ashley's laughter.

I finished cleaning up my kitchen before sitting down and calling Selena. When she answered, she sounded less stressed than when I had last talked to her. "I just got back from the bishop's house. He and his wife asked me to come live in their basement until he can work something else out; they have plenty of room. Their kids are all grown except a sixteen-year-old daughter. She's really nice. I think we'll be good friends. They're going to help me move tomorrow, so I'm packing up tonight. Of course, I don't have much to pack. My roommates aren't very happy with me because now they need to find someone else to take my place, but when I told them about the threats, they admitted I was doing the right thing."

"I'm glad you have somewhere safe to stay." I told her about Denadene's latest call to Ashley. "She'll try again to call you, I believe," I told Selena.

"Oh good," Selena said. "What else did her attorney say?"

"I hate to have to tell you this," I said, "but you need to hear it." I explained what Ashley had told me. Then I said, "Denadene did what she was told because of the threats they kept making against you and her. She felt that she had no choice. Whatever they drugged her with made her sleepy and dizzy, so there may have been times when she honestly didn't know what she was doing. I suppose we may never know."

"What did they say they would do to us?" Selena asked.

"They threatened to drug Denadene further, but other than that, I don't know the specifics," I told her. "From what Ashley said, it sounded pretty bad."

"Worse than death?" she asked in a near-whisper. Her voice trembled.

"Yes, you could say that," I agreed. "Is there any chance you could stay someplace else tonight? Maybe your bishop could take you in sooner. I don't think you should stay in your apartment even one more night."

"I'll call him and see if he can help me. I'm sure it'll be okay, Gage. Although, I admit I'm really scared."

"Sometimes fear can help you stay safe," I told her. "But let me know if you're able to stay somewhere else tonight. It'll put my mind at ease."

An hour later, Selena called me back. "I'm at the bishop's house now. He told me to come right away. He seems worried too. I just wanted you to know."

"So he realizes how serious all this is?" I asked.

"He does. I didn't know this before, but he's a police lieutenant here in Grand Junction. He says he'll try to keep me safe, but he also told me he was thinking about putting me in a safe house," she said.

"It sounds like he's a wise and caring man; and I'm glad about his profession," I said.

"Me too. I feel safe in his house, although he isn't convinced it's good enough, as he can't be there all the time," she told me.

"I feel better too," I said. "You just do whatever he tells you to. Can you give me his name and number? I may want to talk to him at some point."

"His name is Lieutenant Anton Woodcock," she told me. She then gave me his home and cell numbers, as well as his address and shortly after ended our call.

But an hour later, a few minutes after ten o'clock, Selena called again. "I just talked to Denadene," she said. "She said to thank you for worrying about me. She's worried too, and I can tell she's scared. She said to tell you she isn't mad at you, but she says it would never work out for you and her. I feel bad."

"It's okay, Selena," I said softly. "Denadene's a smart person, and she knows what's best for her."

When that call ended, I couldn't help but remember the feel of that sweet kiss on Denadene's doorstep. The memory was not nearly as sweet as the kiss had been. She was lost to me, and I accepted that. It was okay. I hoped she would work at finding someone else, someone the opposite of Randall. She deserved a good guy in her life, a better guy than Randall and, for that matter, a better guy than me.

The next call woke me up at four o'clock in the morning.

CHAPTER FOURTEEN

"Gage, this is Lieutenant Dollison. The dispatcher just woke me up. I told her she should have woken you up instead of me." The lieutenant chuckled sleepily. "You need to go to Denver. I've cleared it with the chief. Fly up there as soon as you can and work with the police there."

"What's going on up there?" I asked.

"Randall Stegner's wrecked truck and a mangled dead body," he said. That brought me fully awake. "They're removing the body and hope to identify it before you get there. We need every bit of evidence you can find from that truck and, of course, from the driver. It could be Randall Stegner. He might really be dead this time. I called up there already and spoke with the investigating officer. He'll help you when you get there. His name is Corporal Jason Ott. I want you to call him and arrange for him to meet you at the airport when you get there."

***

Corporal Ott, a short stocky guy with dark-brown eyes and a shaved head, met me at the airport at eleven that morning as I had earlier requested. It had taken me that long to get there, but I could tell instantly that Jason Ott was a conscientious officer and would do all he could to help me, even though he had clearly had a long and difficult night.

"It was a bad wreck," he said as we headed for the police impound lot where he had stowed the truck. "The body of a man with no ID on him was removed with the help of the Jaws of Life," he said. "The truck hit a large tree. There was so much force on impact that it shoved the motor clear back into the front seat. You'll need to go to the morgue and take a look at the driver. The body was in pretty bad shape, but maybe you'll recognize him."

"I'll see what I can learn," I told Corporal Ott. "My lieutenant told me you guys would help me process the truck for prints and other evidence."

"We were just waiting for you to get here to begin," Ott said.

"I appreciate it," I told him.

The truck was as badly damaged as I had been told. "The truck had to have been really racing when it crashed," I said as I looked over the mangled wreckage.

"There were no skid marks at the scene, but there were black marks that showed the driver tried to stay on the road but was going too fast. The truck left the road and hit the tree at full speed. We think it had to have been going well in excess of a hundred miles per hour," he said.

We were joined by a couple of lab technicians, and then we began the laborious job of checking the truck out. We lifted lots of fingerprints and collected hair, fibers, blood samples, and so on from the back seat as well as the front.

What interested me the most was the diving gear that had been gathered at the scene of the accident. It included a dry suit for deeper dives, a wet suit, and three air tanks. I assumed the equipment had been in the bed of the truck, which had a black plastic cover, but the cover had been ripped off by the force of the crash, and the items in the truck's bed had scattered. The cover itself was damaged almost beyond recognition. The equipment I examined was first-rate—or had been. It was ruined now.

Corporal Ott had been up all night, and he was exhausted, but when I told him he should get some rest, he said, "I'll be fine, Detective. I'll stick with you until we finish up here. I don't mind at all."

"Thanks," I said. "At some point, I'd like to visit the scene of the crash."

We were standing back and watching the techs work at that point, so he said, "Maybe we could do it now. These guys will save everything of value, and we can go through it later."

"Let's do it," I said.

The tree at the crash site was a very large poplar forty or fifty feet from the highway, on a curve. I saw the black marks Corporal Ott had mentioned from when the driver had attempted to negotiate the curve. The scene had been pretty well cleaned up, but Corporal Ott and I went over it thoroughly again. I found some small pieces from the diving equipment that had been missed. I also spotted a small piece of paper a short way beyond where the other debris had been gathered up. It looked like it had blown there and then got caught in some brush. I could easily have missed it had I not noticed a flash of white and walked over to check it out. There was a number written on the paper. It looked like a phone number, but I couldn't be sure. I put it in an evidence bag.

"I'll call this number when we get back to the impound lot," I said to Ott. "Maybe somebody I recognize will answer it."

We had barely arrived back at the impound lot when I got a phone call. It was Selena Stegner. She sounded pretty upset.

"What's the matter, Selena? Are you okay?" I asked anxiously.

"Yes, but some guy showed up a few minutes ago and harassed two of my roommates. He was demanding to know where I was," she said. "At the bishop's direction, I hadn't told any of them where I was going, and now I'm glad I didn't because they couldn't tell him. He kept at them for several minutes and only left when they threatened to call the cops."

"Your bishop's a smart man," I said. "Is either of the other girls hurt?"

"Just scared. They could hardly talk when they called me; they were so emotional."

"Do you have any idea who the man was?"

"I'm pretty sure it was Dwight Hass," she said with conviction. "My roommates said he had dark hair that's thinning on top and long at the sides. They said he had brown eyes and a scar on his right cheek. And he had tattoos on both arms."

"That sounds like Dwight," I agreed. "Did they estimate his age?"

"Twenties, they said. And he wasn't a very big guy."

"That was almost surely Dwight. What did he say to them?" I asked.

"He said he was my brother and that he needed to talk to me," she said. "But I think my roommates knew it wasn't him. I wonder now where Randall is and why Dwight is pretending to be him."

"Selena," I began urgently, "are you in a safe place now?"

"I'm still at the bishop's house, and he has a couple of officers watching his place. He says he'll get me to a safe house as soon as it can be arranged. Right now, he's working with other policemen trying to find Dwight."

"Good," I said, relieved her bishop was looking out for her.

"I just wish Randall would call me," she said. "I need to know he's okay and isn't planning to hurt Denadene again."

"I don't want to frighten you when I tell you this, Selena, but I'm in Denver right now. Your brother's truck has been found. It's wrecked, but we don't know who was driving it." I had decided not to tell her that if Randall was driving it, he was now in the morgue.

"Did someone steal it?" she asked.

"We're working on that now."

For a moment, Selena was silent. Then she said, "Please let me know if you figure out if it was Randall who wrecked it. He's not a very nice guy anymore, but I don't want him to get hurt. He is my brother, and he loves me. And I love him. I hope he's okay. Maybe he's at a hospital."

"Of course you love him," I said. "I'll let you know when I know something. What I do know is there was scuba-diving equipment in the truck."

"Yeah, he likes to dive. So do his creepy friends. He keeps telling me he'll teach me how to dive someday, but I'm not sure I want to learn," she said. "But my friend Rodney wants to learn too. So does one of my roommates."

"If the three of you decide you want to learn, I know who else could teach you," I said. "That is, if you wanted to learn from someone besides your brother."

"Who?" she asked.

"Me," I said. "I'm a diver too. I'm a PADI-certified instructor, and I've done some rescue work. I also dive for fun when I have time."

"Really? That's cool," she said. "I can't wait to meet you sometime. I think I'd rather have you teach me and my friends than my brother. Is it just awful of me to say that?"

"I don't think it's awful at all." As soon as I finished talking to Selena, I called the cell phone number she had given me for her bishop.

"Hello, this is Lieutenant Woodcock," he said when he answered my call.

"Hello, Lieutenant, my name is Detective Gage Tipton. I'm with the St. George Police Department in Utah," I said.

"Oh, Detective. I'm glad you called. Selena told me about you," he said.

"She sounds like a good girl," I said.

"She's a sweetheart, but she's scared now, for good reason," he said. "Do you have some good news for me?"

"I wish I did, Lieutenant," I said. "I'm in Denver right now, at the police impound yard, looking at her brother's truck. It was wrecked early this morning. The driver is dead, but we don't yet know if it's her brother or someone else."

"I assume she knows about this?" he said.

"Not exactly. I told her about the truck being wrecked and that we don't know who was driving it, which is true, but I didn't tell her the driver is dead," I said. "I'll need your help on that if and when we figure out if the dead man is him."

"A man claiming to be her brother was at her apartment a while ago," Lieutenant Woodcock said. "But she thinks it was a friend of her brother's, a guy by the name of Dwight Hass. I assume she told you that when you spoke with her?"

"She did," I confirmed. "And from her description, I agree the man was likely Dwight Hass. He's a very dangerous individual. He helped his friend, a murderer, escape from custody the other day in St. George. Do you have a minute so I can tell you about it?"

"Fire away, Detective," he said. "I think I need to know since it involves a member of my ward and a resident of my city."

As quickly as I could, I told him what was going on with Dwight, JC, Bronson Melville, and his brother, Alvin. "If Dwight is in your area, the others could be there too," I said. "I have their pictures and personal information on my phone. I also have information on some of the vehicles they could be driving. Would you like me to text it all to you?"

"Please do, Detective. And I'll get it on the air down here so our officers can be on the lookout. It sounds like these guys are some pretty nasty people."

"You can say that again," I agreed.

I sent him the information and then concentrated again on the work the technicians were doing.

The techs, Corporal Ott told me, were within just a few minutes of finishing up when I got another call. The screen revealed it was a blocked caller. My heart rate sped up. Could it be Denadene? I hoped so. I accepted the call and said, "Hello?"

It was not Denadene. The caller, whose voice was distorted—the same one I'd heard before—simply said, "You don't listen so well, Detective Tipton. You had a chance to keep Denadene from getting into a lot of trouble. But you didn't do what I instructed you to. You have made me very angry. I have reason to believe you are still helping her. I will give you one last chance to stop. If you don't, you will regret it. So will Randall's little sister. You know I mean business, Detective. I can easily get my hands on that pretty little Selena. If I do, it won't be good for her. Bronson is free now, and if you simply back off, he will stay free, we will quit searching for Denadene Stegner, and we will not harm sweet little Selena." The voice sent chills through me.

I tried to respond, but the caller hung up before I could say a word. I slowly put my phone into my pocket. Then I slammed one hand into the other.

"More trouble, Detective?" Corporal Ott asked.

"I'm afraid so." I told him briefly what the call was about, and then I called Selena's bishop again. "Lieutenant," I said as soon as he answered the call, "I have reason to believe Selena is in grave danger."

"We already agreed about that," he said. "I did get the information you texted, and I'm putting it out to every agency in the area right now. Has something else happened?"

"As a matter of fact, it has," I said. I then told him about the call.

"You and I both know we don't let killers run free just because someone is trying blackmail. Thanks for your call, Detective. I'll make sure these guys don't find Selena or harm her in any way. As for her former sister-in-law, I'm afraid that's out of my hands."

"Mine too," I said dejectedly.

"Detective, I know from Selena that you're a man of faith. Pray. I'll do the same. And God will hear us. Thanks again for alerting me. I'll call the officers at my house and alert them, and as soon as I can break free here at the precinct, I'll go home and see what I can do to provide further protection for Selena. I about have it set up to move her to a safe house. I'll try to accelerate the process."

I was grateful to have someone else on my side, someone who was both very competent and also recognized our need for the Lord's help. I offered a quick, silent prayer, and then I made another call, even though I could see the techs were gathering up their equipment.

"Ashley," I said a moment later. "I just got another disturbing call."

"Oh no. What this time?" she asked.

I told her, aware my voice was trembling with anger.

"I'm sorry, Gage," Ashley said. "But you know what you have to do."

"Yes, I do," I agreed. Then I told her I was currently in Denver and why.

"So Randall could be dead this time for sure?" she said.

"If it's him in the morgue. I hope I can tell if it's Randall when I see the body."

"I assume steps are being taken to protect Selena," she said.

"There are," I said and told her about Selena's bishop. "But there's nothing I can do for Denadene. I wish she would confide in me. I would do everything in my power to keep her safe while we hunt these guys down."

"Honestly, Gage, I think she's taking pretty good care of herself right now. We just have to trust her to be careful and wise. And I think she is," Ashley assured me.

"I hope so. I have to go now," I said. "The officer I'm working with here is ready to take me down to look at the crash victim's body."

As we were heading for the morgue, I remembered the number I had found at the accident scene. I pulled the evidence bag from my pocket and smoothed it out so I could read the number through the plastic.

"Oh, that's right. You were going to call that number, but things got a little busy for you," Jason Ott said with interest.

"I guess I'll call it now," I said and punched the number into my cell phone. It rang several times before it was answered.

"Detective Tipton, how nice of you to call," the man who answered said. "But I really don't have anything more to say to you than I did before. You have your instructions. Follow them." Just that fast, he ended the call.

Ott looked over at me. "Didn't want to talk, I take it."

"No, but I know that voice," I said with a grim feeling of satisfaction. "That was Attorney JC Hass. Now I know for a fact he was involved in Denadene's kidnapping and all that has happened since."

Ott looked a little perplexed, so I explained about Hass and the rest of the gang. Then Ott said, "So he slipped up."

"I'm not sure how much this will help, but every little piece of the puzzle gets us that much closer to some answers," I said. I made another call. "Sergeant Hanks," I said. "I thought I'd bring you up to date on what's happening on our case."

"Dollison told me what you're doing in Denver. Was it Randall in the truck?" he asked.

"I don't know that yet. The body didn't have any ID on it. We're headed to the morgue to see if I can identify him. But let me tell you something else of interest. I got another of those calls telling me to back off or they would find Denadene and Randall's little sister, Selena, and that what they did to them would be terrible. I had found a phone number on a small piece of paper at the accident scene, so I just called the number, and you'll never guess who answered the phone."

"I would guess a Melville or a Hass," he said. "Did you recognize the voice?"

"The blackmailer's voice was disguised, but I did recognize the guy who answered when I dialed the number on the slip of paper. It was JC Hass," I said.

"You're sure?" he asked, sounding shocked.

"I would know his voice anywhere. It was him. But here's the kicker: he slipped and let me know he was the one who made the muffled calls threatening me." I told Hanks what Hass had said to me. "So now we know he has been involved all the way through this thing. He certainly has an odd way of defending murder suspects."

"But how do you prove it was him on the phone? Just saying you recognize his voice won't be enough," he cautioned me.

"True, but if his fingerprints are on this slip of paper I found, that would help, wouldn't it?"

"It sure would," he agreed. "That would be great."

CHAPTER FIFTEEN

THE CORPSE WAS CURRENTLY IN a refrigerated steel locker. An attendant rolled it out so I could examine it. I was told it would be sent to the medical examiner as soon as I was through, that they'd been waiting for me, hoping I could give them a possible identification.

As they pulled the sheet off, I could see that indeed the man had died a violent death. I looked closely at him. His face was messed up, but the general features could still be made out. I had never seen Randall in person, but I had been shown pictures of him. Two of them were on my iPhone. I opened it up and found the first of the two pictures and enlarged it with my fingers.

I showed the picture to Corporal Ott and the attendant. They both shook their heads. Ott said, "I don't think it's him."

"I have my doubts too," I said. "But I was told he has a small tattoo on his right shoulder. It would be of a silver fish. It could be hard to see, as there's too much blood here to be sure."

The attendant got a wet cloth and wiped the shoulder very gently. There wasn't a tattoo. "This man is not Randall Stegner," I said positively. I turned to the others. "So I wonder who he is and what he was doing in Randall's truck. The last time that truck was seen, it was being used to break an accused killer out of a jail van." I turned back to the body. "Wait a minute," I said and once again opened my phone.

"What is it?" the corporal asked.

"Look at this picture," I said, showing him one of Alvin Melville.

"This body has no beard," Ott noted. "And the hair in this picture is longer than our accident victim's."

"Suppose his hair was cut and the beard shaved," I said.

All three of us looked more closely, leaning near the mutilated body. Ott was the first to react. "It could be," he said as he straightened up.

I worked my phone for a minute, and pretty soon I had Alvin Melville's rap sheet pulled up. I looked closely at the description of him. He also has a tattoo," I said. "It's on his lower back. It's a red and blue star."

Without a word, the attendant rolled the bloody body onto its side. Once again, the attendant wiped blood off, and there, clearly visible now to all three of us, was a red and blue star in the center of his lower back. The attendant laid him back down and asked if I thought it was Alvin Melville.

"Yes, I think so," I said. "The size is right. The haircut and shaved face could have been an attempt to change his looks so he was not so likely to be recognized. There's one more thing listed here we can check. Alvin Melville is missing the little toe on his right foot."

The attendant had not pulled the sheet down that far, but he did so then. Ott said, "His legs were nearly severed, as you can see, and they're badly damaged."

We all moved to the end of the table the corpse was lying on. Once again, three heads were lowered. The attendant attempted to straighten out the body's badly crushed and nearly severed right leg. Even though I could see that his left foot was smashed so badly it would have been hard to tell anything about it, his right foot wasn't in too bad of shape. But the right little toe was missing.

"This is Melville," Corporal Ott said.

"I agree," I said, as did the attendant. "His fingers are still mostly intact. I would say a fingerprint comparison would clinch it. His fingerprints are on file."

"It's him," Ott said. "I have no doubt."

I had to agree, but absolute certainty was going to be important. "I wonder what he was doing driving so fast in Randall's truck," I said as much to myself as to the other men.

Corporal Ott grinned. "You might call that number you called earlier. Maybe JC Hass would tell you."

"That's not such a bad idea. I think I'll try that. It can't hurt," I said. "Who knows? The other guys might not have even missed him yet."

"You can send the body to the medical examiner now," Corporal Ott said to the attendant. "And they should be looking at confirming that this is in fact Alvin Melville."

I waited until we were back in the corporal's patrol car before I once again dialed the number from the scrap of paper I'd found at the scene of the wreck. It was answered more quickly this time. "I told you to drop it, Detective," the voice I knew to be that of JC Hass said.

"Sorry, JC, I just have one question. What was Alvin Melville doing driving Randall's truck so fast last night?"

I expected Hass to end the call immediately, but when he didn't, I spoke again. "He's dead, you know. I just identified his body from the star tattoo on his lower back and the missing toe on his right foot."

Now Hass ended the call, but I had a feeling I had just informed him of something he hadn't known, or if he had, that he hadn't expected to have an ID made so quickly. And I was sure he was doubly surprised when I called him by name. He couldn't be happy about that.

I put my phone away. I could call my sergeant and Selena's bishop in a few minutes. Right now, I had a question for Corporal Ott. "Were there any high-speed chases in this area last night in which the vehicle got away?"

"I'm not sure. It was a very busy night. Are you suggesting Alvin might have outrun a cop somewhere and then just kept going until he wrecked?" he asked.

"I was just wondering," I said.

"It never occurred to me to check," he said as he pulled out his phone. Three calls later, he said, "You hit it right on the money, Detective, but it was several miles from here. It was a few minutes before my shift began. It was a silver Ram, and the cops did lose it. They backed off for their own safety since it was being driven too recklessly."

I nodded. "Maybe he thought they were still after him," I said.

"And he got killed because of it," a very tired Corporal Ott replied. "Are you going to stay in Denver tonight, or would you like me to let you know whatever results the lab turns up?"

"Let me call my boss," I said. "But I think I've probably done all I can here for now. You could drop me off at the airport either way. If I decide to stay, I'll rent a car. If not, I'll catch a plane. Maybe I'll fly down to Grand Junction. Either way, you need to get home to bed before you end up like Alvin. And you can call me when you get the lab results."

I called Sergeant Hanks as we drove to the airport, hoping I'd get clearance to fly to Grand Junction. After I had briefed him on what we had learned, I asked him if it would be all right if I headed for Grand Junction.

He said he'd check with the lieutenant or the captain and get back with me soon. The captain had been on vacation out of the country, so he'd been out of the loop regarding the cases I was working on, but he had finally returned.

I next called Selena's bishop. "You can take one of the men off the wanted list," I said after we'd greeted each other. "The driver of the wrecked pickup was Alvin Melville, one of Randall Stegner's pals." I explained how I had come to that conclusion.

"I have Selena hidden away now in a secure safe house where I'm sure no one can get to her."

"She's safe from Alvin, that's for sure," I said dryly. "But the others could be down your way rather than here in Denver."

"That being the case, I'm pretty sure it was Dwight Hass who was here in Grand Junction earlier. His description matches what Selena's roommates gave, so I already thought that was the case, but I'm more certain now," Lieutenant Woodcock said. "I'll let you talk to Selena in person if you decide to come down here this evening. Otherwise, I'll talk to her myself."

"Thanks," I said. "I'll let you know what I'll be doing as soon as I figure it out."

It was only a few minutes before Sergeant Hanks called me back. "Go ahead and fly down to Grand Junction. You can spend the night there and come home tomorrow," he said. "The captain says you're doing a good job. I've brought him up to date on everything we've done so far."

"I'm trying. Tell him thanks when you talk to him again," I replied.

"I also briefed him and the chief on everything you reported so far today," Hanks said. Then his voice became lighter. "Are you sure Randall's little sister is only eighteen? You are planning on meeting her, aren't you?"

I chuckled and shook my head. You had to like Jon Hanks. "I'm sure she's eighteen," I said. "I'll talk to you later." I ended the call before he could come up with something else to kid me about.

I was starving by then. So was Jason Ott, but he told me he needed sleep worse than food. He let me off at the airport, and I arranged for the first flight I could get to Grand Junction. Then, since I had a three-hour wait, I went looking for something to eat.

I was eating a hamburger and onion rings as a late-afternoon lunch when my phone rang again. The battery was getting low, and I had it charging on a small, round portable charger I had brought with me. I looked at the screen and was glad my sergeant couldn't see who the caller was because he would surely have had something smart to say about it.

"Hi, Paige," I said. "What's up? Did you get the job?"

"I did," she said with excitement in her voice. "I want to celebrate. Would you like to come to dinner tonight? I'll fix something really nice. I don't want to celebrate alone, and you're the only friend I have here."

"I'm sorry, Paige, but I'm out of state on an investigation. I'm afraid it won't work," I said. I really had no interest in spending more time with her, and yet I hated to bruise her feelings.

"Can we celebrate tomorrow night? Will you be home by then?"

"I hope so," I said with a frown on my face. "But I can't promise anything."

"I hope you get home. If you do, please call me. I'm glad I met you," she said with so much enthusiasm it made me shudder. "By the way, I talked to Denadene a little while ago. She's really happy for me. I was glad she called."

I did not want to commit myself, and yet she was pushing it. "Paige, I appreciate the invitation, but I can't commit to anything for tomorrow night. Did Denadene say how she's doing?"

"She says she's okay. She's scared, but she says she'll get over it once you catch those guys, and she seems confident you will."

I said, "Well, if she calls again, tell her she can mark Alvin Melville off her list of enemies. He's dead. That's why I'm in Denver. And one of the other guys is in Grand Junction. At least, he was a few hours ago. He went looking for Selena Stegner and scared her roommates pretty badly."

"Was she not at her apartment?" Paige asked.

"She's in protection. Dwight Hass was looking for her, telling her roommates he was her brother and needed to talk to her. Of course, they knew she had moved because some dangerous men were looking for her and meant to do her harm."

"That's scary," Paige said. "How did Alvin Melville die?"

I filled her in, and after a few minutes ended the uncomfortable call. I finished my meal and went to wait for my flight at the gate, but my phone was not through with me. I had it charging again when I got another call. I didn't recognize the number.

"This is Selena," her sweet voice said. "I have a different phone now. The bishop insisted, but I did give the number to Denadene when she called me on my old phone a few minutes ago. I didn't disable it until she'd called. Gage, I think she's lonely. She sure calls a lot."

"That and she's worried about you," I suggested.

"Yeah, that's what she says," Selena agreed. "She's so sweet. I just hope she takes care of herself. Oh, and Gage, I'm so excited. Bishop Woodcock says I'll get to meet you tonight. I told Denadene, and she said I would like you. I wish she would change her mind, but so far, she seems like she won't. I'm sorry about that."

"Hey, Selena, it's over between me and Denadene," I said. "I hope she and I will be friends, but that's all. I'm sorry if this hurts your feelings."

"That's okay," Selena said. "I'm sure you still will be friends."

"Time will tell," I said.

Selena was silent for a moment. I assumed she was processing what I'd just told her. I really hoped she'd quit talking about Denadene. She finally said, "Bishop Woodcock says you have something you want to talk to me about. Can you tell me now?"

"Sorry," I said. "You'll have to wait."

"Can you at least tell me if my brother was driving his truck?"

"Okay, I can tell you that much. He wasn't. I'll see you in a few hours."

"Okay," she said. With a whimper, she added, "I hope you find Randall soon." But then she cheered up again. "I can't wait to meet you."

"Same here," I said. "You take care now." We said goodbye, and I tried to entertain myself while I waited for my plane. I read the news on my phone, checked my social media pages, and played a stupid little game to pass the time. Then, after having such a short night's rest and many busy hours since then, I began to nod off. I woke up to the ringing of my phone. To my delight, it was Ashley. We talked for a few minutes about nothing much. I had to admit she was growing on me.

"So have there been any other developments?" she asked.

"There have," I said, and I told her about Alvin Melville and the latest call to JC Hass.

"Do you have any idea where Randall Stegner is?" she asked. "Denadene keeps insisting she's not terrified of him, but she sure calls a lot and asks if I've heard anything. She did admit she's frightened of Randall's friends. I told her I'd keep checking with you and that when she called again, I'd let her know."

"I wish I knew where he was. He certainly wasn't in his truck. No one could have survived that wreck, but there's no evidence anyone but Alvin was in it," I said.

"I'll let Denadene know," she said. "I'm excited to go diving with you. I've done a little investigating and found out you're a PADI-certified instructor."

I chuckled. "You've been checking up on me?"

Ashley laughed too. "That's right. I've done some diving to more than three hundred feet down. I just wanted to make sure anyone I dive with really knows their stuff, and Kenny Keyes tells me you're really good."

"You talked to Kenny?" I asked, surprised. Kenny Keyes was a ranger who patrolled the waters of Lake Powell; he always said when he needed a diver, I was one of the first he would call.

"Sure. I called him to check up on you. Kenny has taken me out for dives before. I've known him for a long time."

"So have I," I told her. "He's a good friend. I've helped him out on some rescue dives."

"That's what he said. Deep-water stuff, I'm told. So I guess it is safe to dive with you."

"I've never actually dived *with* Kenny," I said.

"I know that. He doesn't dive. But he likes to associate with those of us who do," she said with a chuckle.

"That's right. And he likes to help us. He takes me out on his boat so I can do the diving," I said.

"Well, he says you're good, and that's all I needed to hear," Ashley said. Then she laughed. "I'm just teasing you," she said. "I called him for something else too—a case that reaches clear out to Lake Powell involving a man I'm defending. While I was talking to Kenny, I brought your name up. He told me I should go diving with you, that you're one of the best, and he laughed when I told him we already had a date scheduled to do just that. He said to be sure to look him up when we go."

"Then I guess we'd better," I said.

CHAPTER SIXTEEN

LIEUTENANT WOODCOCK MET ME AT the airport. He informed me I would be staying at his place that night and that we'd pick Selena up at the safe house to bring her back for a late dinner.

At the safe house, Selena flew into my arms like I was a long-lost friend. She hugged me and then stood back and looked me over. She said, "It's nice to meet you, Gage."

"Same here," I said. "I'm sorry about all the trouble you are having."

"Yeah, it's not very fun," she agreed. Then she turned to Lieutenant Woodcock and said, "Do I really have to stay here tonight, Bishop? I'd rather be at your house."

"This is the safest place for you right now," he said firmly.

"But you're there, and there's been another cop out front," she said.

"We've talked about this," he said a bit sternly but with a smile.

"I know. I understand. But thanks for having me for dinner tonight," she said, and then her bright smile returned. She chattered like any other teenager all the way to the Woodcocks' house.

I hadn't gotten around to telling Selena about Alvin dying in her brother's truck. She hadn't brought it up, so I had waited. But finally we were seated in the Woodcocks' family room—just me and her and her bishop. "Okay, Selena, let me tell you about Randall's truck. He wasn't driving it, but the guy who was is dead."

"That's terrible! Had he stolen it?" she said.

"I don't know if it was stolen or not. But the driver was Alvin Melville," I said.

For a moment, she just sat there, stunned. Finally she said, "Oh, I hope my brother's okay. Alvin was one of the guys who was after me and Denadene."

"That's right," I said. I then told her about the warning call, or rather, the blackmail call, I had received. I explained to her and Lieutenant Woodcock about the piece of paper I had found at the accident scene and my subsequent call to the number on it. "JC Hass answered the phone," I told them.

"Denadene's boss?" Selena asked, her eyes wide.

"Her former boss. He was the blackmailer."

Bishop Woodcock said facetiously, "I guess he wanted to make sure his client got off."

"A bit unorthodox, but that's right," I agreed. "Not one of the more honest attorneys, nor the smartest."

After I had eaten dinner with Selena and the Woodcock family, the bishop returned Selena to the safe house, and I finally went to bed and got some sleep. I should have shut my phone off so I could at least sleep to a decent hour the next morning, but it wasn't to be. Not that six was all that early, but I was sleep-deprived and had not planned to wake up for at least another hour.

"Hey, Gage, are you ready to go for a dive?" I recognized the cheerful voice of my friend Kenny Keyes.

"Not really," I said. "I'm still in bed."

"Well, get up and get going, Detective. I need you to help me with some underwater detecting," he said. "And I think the sooner the better."

I was interested, but I wasn't sure my superior officers would let me go diving for Keyes with all I had going on. "I don't know if I can get away," I told him honestly. "I'm working a homicide case that has me in Grand Junction at the moment."

"It wouldn't be that matter concerning that radio announcer Bronson Melville, would it?" he asked.

"It would," I said.

"I hear you lost him," Keyes said with a chuckle. "So surely you can get away for a day to help me. There are others I can get, but you're my first choice. I need more than just a great diver. I need a detective."

I took a deep breath as I swung my legs out of bed. "Tell me what you have," I said.

"I got a call late last night. I'd have called you then, but I didn't want to wake you up," he said.

"You could have called. You woke me up as it is," I said, trying to sound grumpy, although in all honesty, I wasn't. Whatever he had going on, I was hoping I could take the time to go help. Mixing diving with detecting certainly piqued my interest.

"The old fellow who called said he has worried about this for two or three days. He saw a boat leave the dock with three men on board early one morning. It was probably Monday or Tuesday. Anyway, he was just pulling out in his boat and happened to be going in the same general direction. A little later, he noticed it was sitting still about where that old houseboat wreck is at. Do you know which one I'm talking about? There was a small explosion on board, and it sunk—let's see, I think that was about four or five years ago—but all the passengers miraculously survived."

"I remember it," I told him. "I've never dived where it went down. So what about it?" I asked.

"Well, this guy wondered if they were diving there, so he pulled out a pair of binoculars and watched for a little while. He didn't see them go into the water," Keyes explained, "but he could see only one guy on the boat, so he figured two of them had gone down. Now, granted, he admitted he was quite a ways away and that even through his binoculars he couldn't be sure of what he was seeing."

"That makes sense. So what was his concern?"

"He saw only one guy come out of the water. Like I say, he was quite a ways away; he thought he could see the guys loading something, but there were only two guys then. He wondered if one of the guys got hurt or something. His wife scolded him for having a vivid imagination. And he might at that," Keyes said. "But after worrying about it for a while, he decided to call me. I've known the fellow for years, though, and he's pretty solid."

"And you want me to go down and see if I can figure out what they were doing down there?" I asked. "I wouldn't know what to look for."

"I agree," he said. "But there's more. The old fellow got back to the dock a little after they did, and they pulled away in a black van. My friend got the license plate number off the van—or I should say, he got most of it. There was one letter he couldn't be sure of. He asked another guy at the dock if he'd seen them, and he did, but he hadn't paid much attention."

"Did you run the number anyway?" I asked, more interested at the mention of the black van.

"Of course," he said. "And that's really why I'm calling you. I tried some letters for the one he couldn't make out. Several of them were legitimate plate numbers, but only one was listed to a black van, registered to a guy by the name of Alvin Melville, from St. George."

That woke me up. "Are you sure?" I asked as my heart began to race.

"Very," he said with a chuckle. "I thought it might interest you. Now, granted, the old fellow might have got one of the other numbers or letters wrong too. But I remembered reading that your escaped killer's last name is Melville. At the moment, I couldn't remember the first name, although I know it now."

"Bronson Melville," I said. "He's Alvin's brother. You sure know how to hook a guy, don't you? I'll come, but I'll need to find a buddy who can dive that deep. If I remember, that houseboat is at a hundred twenty feet or so."

"About that," he agreed. "When can you come?"

"It'll depend on when I can get someone to join me. Let me make a couple of calls, and I'll get back with you," I promised.

"I have guys here who can help you, but I didn't know if you would want one of them involved if it has something to do with your murder case."

"You're right. I want to be very selective on this," I said.

"I can send a plane to pick you and your buddy up if you need a quick way to get here. And I'll operate the boat when we go out. I'll bring one equipped with sonar so I can guide you from above if I need to. I have the GPS coordinates to where that houseboat is lying."

My first call woke my sergeant. When I explained, he agreed I should go. Then I called the guys I usually dive with. Neither of them could go. The divers at the lake had to be my last resort. I decided to make one other call before I called Keyes back.

"Gage, what in the world are you calling so early for?" Ashley asked after she'd answered the phone. "Has something happened to Denadene?"

"I hope not. But I have to make a dive today at Lake Powell. Kenny Keyes just woke me up. Neither of my normal diving partners can go with me," I said.

"And you wonder if I can?" she asked.

"Yeah. I can use divers from that area, but I want to keep this matter quiet if I can," I said.

"Why's that?" she asked.

"It may involve my murder case," I told her. I explained what Keyes had told me since, so far, she hadn't refused to go.

"I would love to," she said with enthusiasm. "I'll need to arrange for someone to handle a couple of things I have scheduled for today. I'm pretty sure I can do that, but I won't know for an hour or two."

"Okay. If you can't, I'll use someone from down there. Keyes will provide and drive the boat. Call me when you know for sure. He'll pick us up in a plane, so once we know, he can get right on it. I have to fly back to St. George first, so I'll be a while getting there. But I don't want to be too late getting to the lake."

"Okay, I'll start calling right now. I'd really like to help you," she said. "I'll bring two tanks and my other gear."

"I'll do the same. I hope you can go. I'll work on getting a flight," I said.

I got lucky and got a flight that left at eight, so I would have to hurry. I would probably need a cab. I hated to disturb the Woodcocks, even though I needed to explain about my change of plans, but I needn't have worried. The lieutenant and his wife were both up and almost already. I explained what I had going on and promised to return when I could. Lieutenant Woodcock told me he understood completely and that he would keep me apprised of any developments while I was gone. "And I'll make sure Selena is safe," he said.

He then volunteered to take me to the airport. His wife offered to fix me some breakfast, but I didn't think I could take the time.

Just before I boarded the plane, Ashley called. "I'm going with you," she said eagerly. "I can drive to St. George. That way the plane won't have to fly over here, and it'll save us a little time. I'll have my gear packed and ready to go in just a few minutes. I'm sure I can be there before you're ready to leave. Where should I meet you?"

"My vehicle is at the St. George airport. I'll need to go to my place and get my gear loaded, but I think it would be best if we just met at the airport. I'll call Keyes back and set a time."

"I'm so excited," Ashley said. "I just hope it isn't anything too serious."

"I hope not either, but it probably is; Keyes wouldn't be calling me for help if it wasn't," I told her. "I have to board now. I'll see you in a few hours."

While I was waiting for takeoff, I called Paige. She was very understanding. "This is a great job; I'm starting in a half hour. Maybe I'll see you sometime after you get back to St. George."

"Good luck on the job," I said.

I made one more quick call to arrange a time for Keyes to pick Ashley and me up. When a flight attendant gave me a stern look and gestured to my phone, I abruptly ended the call, turned my phone off, and finally settled back into my seat. Then I thought about Ashley and Paige. Ashley, I was quite drawn to. Paige, not so much. She was pushy, and that made me very uncomfortable. Yes, she was attractive and bubbly, but I wasn't in any way interested in dating her.

The flight from Grand Junction landed, and I was just getting back to my Explorer when Ashley pulled up and parked beside me. Her eyes were shining, and she had a huge smile on her face. She didn't offer to shake my hand. She just stepped close and gave me a pleasantly tight hug. "I'll ride with you to get your gear," she said. "I brought an overnight bag, just in case. Since tomorrow is Saturday, I don't have anything scheduled."

"That's a good idea," I said. "I'll take a bag as well. I keep one packed since my work often takes me out of the area."

I opened the door for her, and she climbed in. "I sure appreciate this," I said. "But you're not off the hook for our fun dive in a few days."

"Unless you decide you don't want to dive with me again," she teased, but I thought I heard a hint of real worry in her voice.

"That won't happen," I said.

"We'll see," she said as I closed the passenger door. Her comment left me wondering what in the world was wrong with her that she thought would make me want to have nothing to do with her. She had a slight limp, but that didn't bother me in the least. Surely she wasn't worried about that.

I got in the Explorer on the driver's side and headed toward my apartment, taking the opportunity to change the subject as I said, "Have you had any more calls from Denadene?"

"No, but I suppose I will pretty soon. Wherever she's hiding, she must be alone. She sounds really lonely," Ashley said, repeating her concern from earlier. "I feel so sorry for her. It's just horrible what these dreadful men have put her through."

Before I could agree with her, that doggone phone of mine went off again. I looked at the screen. It was a number I didn't recognize. I answered and heard, "Hi, Gage, it's Lily."

I had to smile. Ms. Kwick was no *lily*. "Hi, Lily," I said. "I see you have a new phone number."

"Yes, I do," she agreed. "I wanted you to have it. Have you heard or seen anything of JC?" she asked.

I mouthed to Ashley, "Lily Kwick." She smiled. She knew who Ms. Kwick was. Then, to Lily, I said, "Actually, I spoke with him three times just yesterday."

I heard her gasp, and then she asked, "Is he asking about me? I trust you didn't tell him anything." Before I could assure her I hadn't, she asked, "How did you talk to him? I thought he'd changed his phone number. Or did he answer it finally?"

"It's kind of a long story," I said. I gave her an abbreviated version, ending with, "But he hasn't said anything about you. Let me tell you, though, that man is in huge trouble when we catch up with him, and we will." *Unless he flees the country,* I thought. I supposed it could happen.

"What about the other guys?" she asked.

"Alvin Melville is out of the picture. He was killed in a wreck in Denver either late Wednesday night or early yesterday morning," I informed her. "As for the others, I don't know. We know where Dwight has been quite recently, and I think we're making progress. But as long as you stay away, you have nothing to worry about."

She thanked me and asked me to call if I learned anything about any of the others. After I hung up, Ashley said, "These men have seriously upset a lot of people's lives."

I agreed and a moment later pulled into my driveway. Ashley helped me load my equipment. We made sure we had plenty of lights, some knives, and extra tanks. We had no idea what we were going to find.

An hour later we were in the air, well on our way to Lake Powell.

CHAPTER SEVENTEEN

KENNY KEYES TOOK US STRAIGHT to where the sunken boat lay at a depth of a hundred twenty feet or so beneath the surface of Lake Powell. On the way, Ashley and I were busy getting our gear ready and putting on what we could. We were taking precautions because of the depth and the temperature of the water that deep. Another issue we planned for was how to overcome the murkiness of the water at the bottom of the lake.

We attached lights to the anchor chain as Keyes slowly lowered it so we wouldn't have trouble finding our way back when we had to come up. We talked things over as we got our equipment ready. Ashley and I attached a light to our buoyancy compensator vests so we could see each other easier. We agreed to stay close to each other as another precaution. We would take down extra lights for each of us, and we would both be carrying two long, sharp knives in case one of us became entangled in something. We each had a pouch attached to our BCD vests, and in them, we each had a small underwater camera and a bag to pack anything in that we might have to cut loose so we wouldn't add debris to the surface of the lake. What we were doing was hazardous at best.

We didn't plan to bring anything up with us if we found something alarming down there. We would go down later to accomplish that if we needed to; it would give us a chance to plan, take extra equipment, and arrange for help from local divers if we felt we needed it.

Because of the depth of the water, we would need to come up fairly often. We had brought nitrogen-enriched oxygen tanks just to make sure we didn't have problems with the depth of the dives. The necessity for short stays at the bottom was frustrating, as we needed to decompress for several minutes a couple of times on the way up to allow our bodies to adjust to lessening water pressure. That would all take extra time, and it was already getting late in the afternoon.

As we were pulling on our dry-dive suits, I saw what Ashley referred to as her defect. She had a prosthetic limb from a little below her knee on her left leg. She saw me glance at it, and her face went red. "I warned you I have a defect, but I promise it won't affect my ability to dive. If you want to call this off and get someone else to help you, I'll understand."

I had to admit I was a bit shocked, but I tried to hide it. I said, "I have every confidence in you. Don't worry about it."

Keyes said, "I thought you knew, Gage. But believe me, she does just fine. We only need to add a little more weight to her to help her go down, but it's no big deal." Then, to Ashley, he said, "I would have thought you would have talked to Gage about this before today."

She chuckled, an embarrassed sound, and said, "I told him I had a defect, but he wouldn't let me tell him what it was. So I decided he could just be surprised."

"I tried to get her to tell me later," I said in my own defense. "But she wouldn't tell me then."

"Okay, kids," he said with a stern face. "It's all good now. Let's finish gearing up and get you to the bottom as quickly as we can. That's a big boat down there, and it'll take a while to check it all out, so the sooner we get started, the more likely we'll have it completely searched before dark."

"Yes, Daddy," I said with an attempt at levity. It worked. Ashley laughed along with Keyes.

Within a few minutes, we had finished preparing, done our predive safety check, made sure we were together on hand signals so there would be no confusion when we needed to communicate, and reassured each other.

Then we went in, Ashley first and me next. We descended slowly. As soon as we got almost to the bottom of the lake, we looked around, being careful not to stir up the silt below, as that would make it doubly hard to see. We were only about twenty feet from the boat, which we could barely see through the murky water. It looked more like a hulking shadow from our position. As we'd previously discussed, I was acting as dive commander, and I led the way toward the boat.

When it had sunk, it had ended up resting on one side, so the upper deck faced us as we approached. We stopped and looked it over, and then I made a decision. We would search from the stern toward the bow. Since the houseboat was lying on its portside on the lake bottom, we would start at the top and work our way down. I signaled that I thought we should begin with the lower deck, and Ashley nodded in agreement. So, close together, we entered an opening which had been the door to a stairwell leading to the second level of the vessel.

It didn't take me long to realize this was going to be very difficult. Our lights were bright, but it was very, very dark in there, and the murkiness of the water made the visibility even worse. We stayed close to each other and began our search for who knew what. After about ten minutes, we returned to the opening, having found nothing. We swam back toward the anchor line. I was grateful for the lights we had attached to it, or we might have had a difficult time finding it. When we were close, we began our slow assent, stopping twice to decompress side by side. When we reached the surface, Keyes was leaning over the edge and helped us both aboard. "Find anything?" he asked.

"Nothing notable," I said. "A few fish did visit us from time to time. There are some big ones down there."

"Mostly we found a lot of darkness and murky water," Ashley added.

"Are you both feeling okay?" he asked.

We told him we were. I was feeling energized, and Ashley was grinning. I could tell that, like me, she was enjoying this dangerous adventure we had embarked on.

"How close to the boat are we?" Keyes asked.

"We're pretty close," I said. "About twenty feet."

We switched out our tanks, made sure all of our equipment was still attached to our vests, and discussed how to proceed once we again reached the bottom. Ashley suggested, "Gage, why don't we do the top deck first. That way if we find a body or something, we may not have to spend more time on the second deck."

"That's a good suggestion," I said. "There's no question the lower deck is the more dangerous of the two. I was thinking that if there is a body down there, it would most likely be below, but I agree with you—we should finish the top deck first. It shouldn't take as long to complete as the lower deck anyway. We can still work from the stern to the bow, starboard to portside."

After resting for a little while and double-checking our equipment, we were both ready to get back down there. We descended once again and swam back to the boat. We slowly and thoroughly checked out the starboard side of the top deck. It didn't take long, and we were able to complete the top deck. I was both disappointed and somewhat relieved we had found nothing. I hadn't expected it to be easy, if there even was anything to find. To do the kind of activity we were engaged in took a lot of energy and a toll on our bodies, but we were both in good shape and holding up well.

Back into the intense darkness of the lower deck we ventured. We swam to where we had stopped on the first dive and began searching again. We had to go in and out of rooms and watch out for floating objects like chairs, tables, and other furniture. We opened each door we came to that was not already hanging open. With the pressure of the water opposing us, that took a lot of effort, and it was made even more difficult since the boat was on its side. We either had to lift the door up or pull it down, depending on how it was hinged. Fortunately most of the doors opened out, which to us on this side of the boat was down. But some of them were jammed, and it took a lot of effort to open them. Still, somehow, we managed to open each of them.

We approached another door that was closed, and nearby, one that was open. I helped Ashley open the closed one, and then, in the interest of time, signaled to her that I would check out the next door while she checked that one out.

It had only been a moment when Ashley's light appeared in the room I had entered. I swam back to the door and out as she motioned urgently toward the room she had been checking.

I looked in and shined my light about. The room appeared to be a large closet, and floating among some old clothes, shoes, and other items was what could be a body wrapped in a large blanket of some kind; the blanket was secured with a rope or line of some sort. I snapped some pictures. Then we both moved a little closer. Due to the density of the murky water, we had both missed the second possible body wrapped in another blanket just beyond the first one. Both objects had items tied to them, which I assumed had been used as weights to get the bodies down and keep them there. I took more pictures, glanced at the time, and signaled that we needed to go up now. We had not touched anything yet, and I felt it best we go up first and then check the suspicious objects closer on our next dive.

I pulled a light from a bag and attached it the best I could to the doorknob of the door that was now gently swaying back and forth in the water. I turned the light on and again signaled to Ashley that we should go. We headed back to the opening that led us to the upper deck and swam out. When we finally reached the surface, Keyes again helped us into the boat and asked, "I can tell by the looks on your faces you found something. Was it a body?"

"Ashley found a body, and then I found a second one just beyond it," I responded.

Ashley said, "To clarify, we found two person-size objects, each wrapped in a blanket, floating in a closet with all sorts of clothing around them. We don't know yet that they're bodies. They were actually pretty hard to see in the murk."

"Did you get pictures?" he asked as we unencumbered ourselves.

I nodded, pulled out my camera, and opened it to the first picture. I looked at it for a moment and then passed it to Ashley, and then Keyes took a turn.

"I suppose those could be bodies," he said. "But that makes no sense. My friend said three people went out on that boat he was watching and only two came back. Finding one body makes sense, but that doesn't account for a second body."

Ashley spoke up then. "Your informant also said he was quite a distance away and that even through his binoculars, he couldn't see very well, didn't he?" she asked in a lawyerly voice, like she was conducting a cross examination in court.

"That's right."

"So perhaps there was a body already in the boat," Ashley suggested. "Your informant wouldn't have been able to see it, and the other men could have taken it overboard."

"Or it could have been taken there earlier," I said as I thought about my missing witness, Brea Burr. "Brea has been missing for a while," I said. "Perhaps she's one of them and was put there first. I wonder who the other could be, if they're bodies at all. I hope they are not, but we'll have to find out."

Ashley reached for Keyes to hand her my camera and scrolled through the images, studying each one for a moment. "One is quite a bit larger than the other," she said and then looked over at Keyes. "Do you have a computer on board? It would be nice if we could get a look at these pictures on a larger screen."

"I sure do," he said. "Let's go into the cabin and take a look."

He opened a large laptop and booted it up. I imported the images to it, and then, with the three of us looking at the screen, I opened the first one. The object nearest the door where we had entered was the larger of the two. The large fishline or small rope keeping the blankets in place were more visible on the screen than when I had noticed them in the murky water. "If Brea is the smaller one, then she was likely put there first and the larger one added later," I conjectured.

"I still can't tell for sure that they're bodies," Keyes said. "I suppose something shaped like that and enclosed in blankets may have been in the closet when the boat went down."

"I had that same thought," Ashley said.

I leaned down again, enlarged the photo of the closest object, and peered closer. I felt a chill go through me, even though I had warmed up since we had left the water. I touched the screen with my finger. "There's a piece of fishline or string of some kind going down to the floor here, but I can't see what's on the other end of it. I didn't notice it before."

Ashley and I looked at each other, and we both shuddered. "Are you thinking what I'm thinking?" she asked.

"If you're thinking something dangerous is attached to that line and we'd better go back down and look before we touch anything, then yes," I replied.

She nodded.

"Hey," Keyes said suddenly, "I was just wondering about fish damage. These blankets look like they're in pretty good shape."

"The door to that room was closed when we got there," Ashley said. "I assume that if those are bodies, the door was found closed by whoever put them there and then closed again when they left. At any rate, there were no fish in there like there were in rooms where the doors were hanging open, so we might be lucky in that regard and be able to identify the bodies more easily since they'll be mostly intact."

"If one of those is Brea Burr, the only thing I know for sure is that the other one could *not* be one of the Hass brothers or Alvin Melville," I added. "Unless there's someone else those guys might have been involved with, I'm guessing the other body is either Bronson Melville or, more likely, Randall Stegner."

"I hope they aren't bodies," Ashley said, shivering. "This is creepy."

"If they aren't bodies, then you and I have more searching to do down there; maybe we should be hoping we've found what we were searching for. I personally don't relish any more swimming around in there than is absolutely necessary," I said.

"I couldn't agree more," my diving partner said. "It was exciting at first, but it's not so much now. Let's go down again and take a closer look at what that line is tied to."

"You two be very careful," Keyes stressed. "I don't want anyone getting hurt. I honestly hoped this was nothing more than a wild goose chase. I feel guilty even involving you two now."

"Don't feel that way, at least not for my part," I said.

"Mine either. I came with Gage of my own free will, and even though this is turning out in what could be a very bad way, I'm glad I came."

Back in the sunken houseboat a short time later, we again entered the closet. The light I'd left there had helped us find it relatively quickly in the darkness. There wasn't a lot of room in there for both of us and our bulky equipment, but by being careful, we were okay. I moved ahead of Ashley and went to the bottom, which would have been the portside. The water was the murkiest, almost muddy, down there. It was easy to see how we had missed the second object at first.

I was very careful not to touch the line leading from the larger object that was floating against the top of the room to whatever was down at the bottom. I had to lean very close before I could finally see a small, rectangular black box. It had a glowing green light on the top. On one side was a small lever to which the line was attached. I signaled for Ashley to move out of the room as my heart thudded like thunder in my chest.

After she had disappeared, I then pulled out my camera and took several pictures from as close as I dared. There was no way I would touch the wire; it looked to me that if the lever was pulled, the room would blow to bits.

While down there, I saw another object. It had a rope tied to it that was moving lazily back and forth as I caused the water to ripple by my own movements. I looked closely at the end of the rope and could see it had been severed. I took a picture of it and the object to which it was tied, which I was sure was a weight that had been used to take one of the bodies, if that's what they were, to the bottom. When I rejoined Ashley moments later above the room, I signaled that we should go back up to where Kenny was waiting.

Once we had left the houseboat and were floating near the anchor chain, she signaled to me that she'd like to know what I'd found. I described it the only way I could think of: by bringing both hands up and spreading them out as rapidly as I could.

She nodded her head in understanding and pointed up.

CHAPTER EIGHTEEN

IT WAS FRUSTRATING TO HAVE to spend so much time decompressing as we made our way to the lake's surface, but if we hurried, it would be fatal to us. My mind was busy conjuring up all sorts of terrifying scenarios. If a large fish were to swim into the room, which had been closed to such creatures before, it could hit the line, pulling the lever and blowing Ashley and me up. Another disturbing thought that kept slamming around inside my head was that perhaps someone had seen us with a drone or a plane enter the water, could be watching us, and could detonate the bomb remotely. Or, though I thought it the least likely scenario, the bomb could be on a timer that could go off any moment.

I had a feeling Ashley was experiencing similar concerns. I chastised myself for having brought her along on such a dangerous mission. She was, I was learning, a very special person. If I was killed, so be it. I had signed up for that possibility when I'd pinned on the badge. But she had not.

When Keyes finally pulled us from the water, I knew that since we had already made three dives, there was no way we could go down again until the next morning. The first thing I said to Keyes was, "Pull the anchor up, and get us out of here."

I must have had a look about me that kept him from arguing. He did as I instructed and, after we'd gone a few hundred yards, slowed the boat back down. By then I was out of my dry suit and was helping Ashley finish getting out of hers. We were both exhausted. It wasn't until we felt the boat slowing down that either of us spoke about what was in that dark graveyard at the bottom of the lake.

"Were you telling me you found a bomb?" she finally asked.

"I'm sure that's what it is. And there was a rope tied to a weight that must have been used to get at least one of the bodies down there," I responded.

She forced a smile and then said, "You can't imagine how eager I was to get back to the boat after you did this," she said and threw her arms wide.

"I think I can," I said. Then I went on to explain in greater detail what I had found. By then, Keyes had stopped the boat, and while it bobbed in the lake, he joined us. He heard only the last of my description of what I'd discovered, but he had alarm written all over his chiseled face.

"There's a bomb down there?" he asked.

"It has to be," I said.

"What if a fish hits the line?" Ashley said. "We should have shut the door again, if we even could."

I touched Ashley's arm but looked at Keyes's worried face. "How about if we take a look at the new pictures I took." As I spoke I searched the sky above us.

"What are you looking for?" Keyes asked.

"A small plane or a drone."

Ashley shivered. "If those guys are up there, they could have blown us into little pieces," she said.

"Do you think we're far enough away to be safe now if the bomb does detonate? We're more than a mile from the houseboat now," Kenny said.

"I'm sure we're fine," I said as the three of us now searched the skies. When none of us saw anything suspicious, we went into the cabin. There we all studied the latest pictures from my camera on the laptop's screen.

Despite the murky water, my pictures were reasonably clear. We all agreed we were most likely looking at a bomb, a booby trap set by whoever had killed the people wrapped in the blankets. At that point, none of us believed for one second that the objects wrapped in the blankets were anything but bodies.

"My foot itches. That happens from time to time, especially when I get nervous. It started itching while we were coming up," Ashley suddenly said. She smiled that large, beautiful smile at me, and I returned it with my own less-than-beautiful one. There was something about this girl that I liked more and more all the time. The only question that hung in my mind was how she had lost the lower part of her leg.

"Then scratch it," I suggested stupidly to her comment of an itch.

That got me a punch on the shoulder. "Not my good foot," she said with a grin. "The one the shark bit off."

"But it's just a piece of—" I began, even as I registered the fact that I now knew how she had lost her foot.

Ashley interrupted. "A piece of very expensive material. This one is made mostly of carbon fiber. My other one is made of a titanium alloy. This one has proven best for diving. But that's not what I'm talking about. In case you don't know, it's not uncommon for people who have lost limbs to itch where the limb should be. I know it's strange, but it's true."

I remembered that fact now. I was embarrassed, but I decided I shouldn't let it show. I asked, "What happened to the part of your leg the shark bit off?"

"I hope he choked on it!" she said with venom, but then she laughed, and Keyes and I laughed with her. After we had all quieted, she said, "Does this bother you?"

"If you're referring to the bomb, yes it does," I said, pointing at the computer screen. I glanced at her, and she raised an eyebrow. She knew I had understood what she'd meant. "No, your leg doesn't bother me. But sometime, I'd like to hear how you lost it—I mean, what you were doing when you were attacked by a shark."

Ashley suddenly threw her arms around me and pulled me close. She hugged me for what seemed like a full minute, maybe longer. When she finally released me, she kissed me, right in front of Keyes and square on my lips. I did the only thing I could think of: I kissed her back. And that kiss eclipsed the one I had experienced on Denadene's doorstep just a couple of weeks before. When Ashley stepped back, her eyes were wet, but they were shining. "Thank you, Gage. I like you a lot, and I've been scared to death how you would react to my . . . ah . . . my defect."

"Let's not call it a defect," I said. "I think the term *bionic leg* would be a better fit."

That got me another hug, but then Keyes broke the spell when he cleared his throat. "Sorry, kids," he said. "I hate to break up the little celebration, but we have a serious problem on our hands, remember?"

"You mean you have one," I said, trying to keep a straight face, but it didn't work. I grinned. "It's your responsibility, you know. We're just your humble servants."

Keyes laughed. "I guess that's true. However, I still need the help of my humble servants. Those bodies need to be removed without detonating that bomb," he said, sobering. "Do either of you have any idea how we're going to accomplish that?"

I was so elated by Ashley's reception to my attitude about her missing foot that I couldn't get serious. I said, "Bring in a bomb squad, and let them deal with it."

"Okay, wise guy, I suppose we can do that, but someone is still going to have to dive, and frankly, you two are the best divers I know," Kenny said. "And besides that, I like you two the best of any I know."

Ashley got caught up in the levity too and quipped, "If you like us so well, why do you want us to go back down there and get blown up? That's what you would do if you wanted to get rid of somebody."

Keyes's face became very serious. "I do like you guys, and whatever we do, it will be with the utmost care. We do need bomb experts, but they'll need your help and advice. Let's get back to shore and go to my office. We have some calls to make."

"Are we okay leaving that, those, you know—can we leave the *things* unattended?" Ashley asked.

"I don't think anyone will disturb them, but I think it would be good to have the immediate area patrolled, as long as they keep a safe distance just in case the bomb goes off," Keyes said.

He got on his radio, and in a few minutes, an officer pulled his boat up next to ours. Keyes introduced the ranger as Sam Connor. We told him there was an area we needed him to patrol. Then Keyes ordered him to keep what he was about to learn about why the patrol was necessary to himself until told otherwise. Sam agreed, and Keyes said, "You know that houseboat that sunk about a mile back that way?" He pointed in the direction we had come from.

Sam said, "Only too well. I was on duty when it went down."

Keyes continued. "We believe there are two murder victims down there and that one of them is attached to a bomb. I don't want anyone getting closer than a quarter of a mile from that point. We've got to find a way to disarm the bomb and bring up the bodies without blowing them away."

"What are you going to do?" Sam asked. His brow furrowed in concern.

"Our plans aren't final yet, but we're going to find out which of our local law-enforcement agencies has a bomb squad that can come out here, and then we'll coordinate with them," Keyes said. "Your job is to keep all boats out of the danger area. If what my friends found is a bomb, it could explode with something as simple as a fish bumping the line that's tied to the trigger mechanism."

"Wow, this is crazy," Sam said. "Do you have any idea who the bodies are?"

"Detective Tipton here is missing a couple of folks who are part of a murder case in St. George. We think it might be them," Keyes told him, not going into specifics. Sam nodded and assured us he'd keep people away from the houseboat site, and we parted ways.

As we rode back to the marina, Ashley and I checked our cell phones. I returned a call from Sergeant Hanks and filled him in on our findings. Then I returned a call from Selena and told her very little, except that I was doing some underwater investigation at Lake Powell for a ranger friend of mine. Next I called Selena's bishop, who assured me that the wanted men had not shown up at Selena's apartment again, nor had law enforcement been able to locate them anywhere else.

Ashley also had several missed calls. Three were from blocked numbers. The others she called—none of them very important, she told me. But she was worried she had missed what were most likely calls from Denadene.

As we continued the ride to the marina, we had a little time to talk about how she lost her lower left leg. As I had suspected, she had been diving, but it was in the ocean, and she had been unlucky enough to encounter a shark. She had lost her foot and a bit of her leg above the ankle, but thanks to quick action by others, she had not lost her life. She thanked me again for being so understanding. "I promised myself I wouldn't let it keep me from doing any of the things in my life I want to do," she told me.

"I admire your courage," I said.

Very sternly she replied, "That's fine; just don't ever pity me, Gage. I hate when people pity me."

I made up my mind then and there to honor her request. She was growing on me very quickly, and I didn't want to offend her.

Two hours later Ashley and I were part of what had become a large meeting of law-enforcement officers from several agencies, including the National Park Service; the Lake Powell Police, which was a privately owned and managed department; sheriff's offices from border counties in Utah and Arizona; and some other agencies. A bomb squad was located and called in, and discussions went well into the evening.

It wasn't until after eleven that night that a plan had been formulated and assignments made to acquire the equipment needed to disarm the bomb and bring the bodies to the surface. No one believed the blanket-wrapped objects were anything other than bodies or that the small black box was anything other than a bomb, but we all hoped we were wrong on both counts. We all knew we could hope for the best but that we should plan for the worst.

Ashley and I were to be the divers since we knew the layout and no one else did and because no one else present was better qualified for the kind of dive we'd be doing. After talking it over, we agreed we had little choice but to do what we needed to do. Knowing we had a hard day ahead, we each got a hotel room and tried to get some sleep.

We were at breakfast early the next morning when I got a call from Corporal Jason Ott in Denver. "There were some useable fingerprints on the paper you found at the accident scene," he said.

"I expect you're going to tell me some of them are from JC Hass?" I said hopefully.

"Sure are," Ott said with triumph in his voice. "And, of course, Alvin Melville."

"That's good news," I replied. "I don't suppose we have any other lab results back on the samples we found in Stegner's truck."

"Not yet, but I'll give you a call when I know more. So what's going on with your investigation?" he asked.

I told him just enough to satisfy his curiosity while not releasing information we couldn't afford to have public yet and then ended the call. We were just finishing our meal when Denadene called Ashley. I could hear only Ashley's side of the conversation, but I could tell from the look on her face and the words she spoke that Denadene was not enjoying herself. Ashley assured her that law enforcement was working around the clock to try to find the three suspects who were left alive. And I heard her tell Denadene to stay where she was for the time being. After their call, Ashley said to me, "The poor girl. She says she's starting to go batty. She wondered if she should quit hiding."

"I'm glad you told her to stay put," I said. "Who knows where Bronson and the Hass brothers are now."

Keyes met us in the lobby of the hotel we'd stayed at. No one was with him. "Where's the bomb squad?" I asked. "There's no way we're going down there unless they can assure us it's safe."

"I have news. Some poor fish gave its life last night," he said.

"The bomb blew?" Ashley asked, astonished.

"I'm afraid so, but from what the ranger who was patrolling the area at the time said, it wasn't a huge explosion. Apparently it wasn't a very powerful bomb," he said.

"Was it strong enough to destroy the bodies?" I asked.

"I doubt it. It barely created a ripple at the surface. We'll go over the area with sonar before you guys go down, unless you've changed your minds," he said.

"I'll go down," I said. "I need to find out if Brea Burr is down there."

"And there's no way I'm letting this guy dive without me," Ashley said firmly.

"Are you sure, Ashley?" I asked. "You don't have to do this."

"I want to," she insisted. "I want to keep getting to know you, and frankly, I don't trust anyone else to watch your back like I will."

"And I'll feel better knowing you're close," I told her. Our eyes met, and, for a long time, we gazed at each other. I thought I may have found a soulmate in this beautiful woman with the almond-shaped green eyes and long dark-blonde hair. I hoped she was thinking similar thoughts about me.

"Okay, kids, let's get going," Keyes said. He was grinning widely at the two of us. "If and when," he said, "I'll expect an invitation."

Ashley blushed. I suppose I did too. As I watched Ashley walk ahead of me toward the door, I suddenly realized how important she was becoming in my life.

We were joined by two other men, one a local diver by the name of Tom Holz, the other Ranger Sam Connor, who had taken the first shift keeping the area secure. But the initial dive, it was determined, would be just me and Ashley. We would survey the scene inside the houseboat and then come back up and decide with Tom what to do.

The explosion, as far as we could see from the sonar, had not done any visible damage to the shell of the sunken houseboat. What it had done to the inside remained to be seen. I prayed the damage would be minimal. A few minutes later, while Keyes was in the cabin with the other men and Ashley and I were checking each other over to make sure everything was secure, Ashley leaned toward me and said, "Could we have a prayer together? I would feel better about this if we did."

I understood her apprehension. We no longer had to worry about the bomb going off, but the greatest danger now was that the structure of the boat may have been weakened. It could, with little warning, collapse around us. If that happened, we could be trapped and likely die.

"That's a great idea," I said as I felt myself drawn continually closer to this wonderful woman. "Would you like me to, or do you want to?"

"You, please," she said.

My prayer was short but from the depths of my heart. I had been praying silently all morning, but with Ashley listening, it was as if my prayer was more earnest and filled with greater faith. When I had finished, she said her amen and then added, "Thank you, Gage. We'll be okay now."

After an uneventful descent, we found ourselves once again facing the sunken houseboat. I couldn't see much change from the previous dive. It did seem like it was maybe tipped at a slightly different angle, but that was all. Ashley and I looked at each other, and I pointed toward the same opening we had used the day before. She nodded, and we swam toward it.

CHAPTER NINETEEN

ASHLEY AND I MOVED SLOWER and with even more caution than we had used the day before. I tried to think of the prayer we had shared and not of the danger we faced.

We found the door we were looking for, but it wasn't the only hole through the bottom of the room now. The explosion had ripped a new hole into the portside of the boat, far bigger than the one we had entered the day before. It looked to me like the main force of the explosion had been downward. I doubted that had been the intent of the killer who'd placed it there. At any rate, Ashley and I chose to go up through the opening we knew rather than one we didn't know and which had dangerous jagged edges that could rip our suits or pull our air hoses loose. Inside there was some debris we had to clear before we were able to get up to the bodies, which were still where they had been. The debris was mostly small chunks of material that had been torn from below us by the force of the blast. We moved it gently aside and let it float past us. The blankets had been badly torn, and a school of fish was feeding shamelessly on what we could now see were definitely human corpses.

I took pictures while Ashley watched the walls around us. Her job, as prearranged, was to warn me if there was any shifting in the boat, in which case we would leave immediately. I kept an eye out as well, but I concentrated mostly on taking pictures and doing so as quickly as I could. After I had put my camera away, I signaled that I thought we should take hold of the closest body and see if we could move it at all.

The blanket, though damaged, was still wound closely to the body, and we were able to tow the body down toward the opening with a lot of effort by both of us. We succeeded in getting it through, and then we let it rise to what was left of the starboard wall, where it settled fairly well. I checked my watch. We were out of time, so we left the boat and spent the next several minutes ascending. Keyes and the other men helped us into the boat.

"What did you find?" Keyes asked.

"A fish banquet," I said dryly. "But so far, they haven't done a lot of damage to the bodies, and they *are* bodies."

Ashley said, "The force of the blast did most of its damage below the bomb. It blew the portside wall apart. We had to clear some loose boards and junk to get to the bodies, but even though the blankets were badly ripped, we were able to tow one of them out of the closet. It's now resting against the roof or starboard wall or whatever," Ashley said. "It's so confusing when the roof and the floor are now the walls and the walls are now the floor and the roof. I hope we don't confuse you guys."

"We get it. Do you have pictures?" Keyes asked.

"We do," I said. "Should we use your computer again?"

After showing them the pictures, Ashley and I made a plan with Tom and helped him suit up. When we went down again, I went first, Ashley second, and Tom followed. Tom had a rope tied to him, which was secured in the boat and which we planned to tie to the corpses one at a time to get them to the surface. We took the first body and tied the rope to it, and with the three of us working together, we were soon able to get it out of the boat and near the anchor chain. Tom jerked on the rope, and then it and the body began to rise to the surface. We had to go up again before we could attempt to get the second body out of the houseboat.

The first body made its way to the surface much sooner than the three of us did. It didn't have to worry about decompressing like we live-bodies did. By the time we were all back to the surface and in the boat, Keyes and Sam had the dead person laid out on the deck of the boat. Together, the other men and I removed the torn blanket while Ashley photographed the process. The fish had not done a lot of damage to the corpse. The worst damage was done to its feet and legs. That was also where the blast had done the most damage. The face was chewed on a little, but not enough to keep me from identifying sweet little Selena's big brother, Randall, which came as no surprise at that point.

What did surprise me was that Randall's corpse still had on part of his diving equipment. "He had to have been murdered and wrapped in the blanket while down there," Ashley observed. "That must have been hard."

"Hard but possible, I guess," I said. "It had to have taken some time."

"I wonder if he was killed and then one of the others went up and got the blanket and heavy fishline or if that had been stored down there," Ashley said. "If so, Randall's murder was clearly planned ahead of time."

"Someone could have killed him by simply cutting his air supply. I don't see any evidence of knife wounds or bullet holes. I suppose a medical examiner can tell us that though."

"How are you going to tell Selena about her brother?" Ashley asked a few minutes later.

"I guess I have two choices: I would prefer to go up to Grand Junction and tell her in person because I don't think people should be given this kind of news on the phone. But I'm afraid I'm not going to have time to do that, and I'm pretty sure my boss won't authorize it at this point," I said.

"And your second choice?" Ashley pressed gently.

"Her bishop," I said. "He's a police lieutenant, so I know he's had lots of practice, and he's gotten quite close to Selena. I think that's what I'll do."

"When will you call him?" she asked.

"Not until we finish here," I said. "Because once she knows we found him dead, I'm sure she'll be calling me, and I want to have plenty of time to talk to her when she does."

"You're a good man," Ashley said as she reached out and touched me on the cheek, causing my skin to tingle rather pleasantly.

"I don't know about that, but I try," I said. "I guess it'll be your job to tell Denadene."

"And I'll have no choice but to do it on the phone when she calls me. Of course, it won't be as hard on her as on Selena, but I still wish I could talk to her in person," she said with sadness in her voice.

"Do you always keep in touch with your clients like you have with Denadene? I think that's going way beyond what's expected of you," I said.

"She's a special case," she responded. "Most of the time I'm glad when I don't have to deal with my clients anymore. I don't get to handle many cases in which my clients are innocent like she was. And, frankly, she's become a good friend."

"You're a good woman," I said with a grin. She touched my cheek again with such tenderness it sent sparks flying clear to my toes.

A few minutes later, the three of us went down again. This time we would have to get the body from clear back in that closet and then bring it up. Tom again towed the rope behind him as we descended. Then we had Ashley wait near the door as we went in, Tom still towing the rope. The fish that had been nibbling at the exposed parts of Randall's body had joined their friends, and they were doing some serious damage to the other victim. We were towing the corpse back out when Ashley suddenly appeared beside us. She was frantically waving at us to hurry.

I didn't take the time to figure out why; I just did what she indicated, and so did Tom. The body banged against the doorframe as we tugged it through. Ashley had joined us on the rope and helped us pull. Once the body was free of the doorway, Ashley pointed up. A wall was slowly collapsing toward us; only the water was keeping it from crashing down more rapidly.

We swam hard for our exit. The wall was coming at us slowly, but we weren't exactly moving quickly. I thought about leaving the body, but I couldn't bring myself to do that. I signaled for the others to leave me, but they wouldn't do it. The water was churning around, becoming murkier and making it that much more difficult for us. We swam hard and had barely cleared the boat when the top wall finally crashed to the lake floor. Debris shot like arrows in every direction.

Suddenly I was aware of Ashley slumping beside me, and my heart thudded in my chest. I grabbed Tom, and he saw instantly that she was injured. Without my having to instruct him, he took the body on alone. I grabbed hold of Ashley. She appeared to be unconscious, but a quick check showed she was still breathing through her regulator. Holding it in her mouth, I towed her through the water as more debris settled around us.

I was past the anchor chain before I dared to stop. At that point, I could see Tom's light near us, and I could tell he was letting the body rise above him.

Looking behind us, we couldn't see any sign now of the huge boat through the muddy water. We began our assent. I was still holding Ashley, and she was still breathing, but it seemed like her breaths were shallow. I continued to keep one hand around her mouth to keep her regulator from being expelled. I've prayed many times in my life, but never with the intensity and depth of feeling I did then.

I didn't know what the future held for Ashley and me. Perhaps there was no future for the two of us, but I knew now that I wanted there to be; I wanted it so badly it seemed to consume my soul. But even if we didn't end up together, I was determined to do anything I could to keep her alive. She had survived a shark. She just had to survive this recovery mission.

Tom had let the corpse go at its own speed, and it was rising faster than we could. The rope was tied to it and secured in the rescue boat above, so I didn't worry about that. But now Tom was free to help me with Ashley. I was grateful for his help; I couldn't have done it for much longer on my own. Suddenly her body shuddered, and her eyes behind her diving mask opened. She looked surprised, like she had no idea where she was, and she started to struggle. We had to hold her tightly to keep her from surging toward the surface.

When we had to stop to decompress the first time, the water suddenly began to move violently, and we had to fight to keep from being washed away. Mud and silt roared up and engulfed us and then kept going. For three or four minutes we couldn't even see each other or our lights. Ashley, apparently recovered enough to perceive what was happening, quit struggling.

I was so relieved when we were finally safe to start our ascent again, and it was hard not to hurry, although I was sure the worst of the danger from below was past. And even though Ashley was conscious now, I was anxious to get her into the rescue boat and check her out thoroughly.

Eternity is a long time; it has no end. I felt like our ascent to the safety of the rescue boat was an eternity. But finally, our ascent did end. Ashley and I broke the surface of the water together but slightly behind Tom. Sam pulled him aboard and Keyes reached for me. I signaled for him to take Ashley first. Then, a moment later, Sam helped me get aboard.

Ashley lay on the deck as we began to remove her gear. She took several long gulps of air, but she made no attempt to get up. I'd never been so exhausted following a dive before. I could tell Tom was equally exhausted. He lay on the deck too, letting his energy renew itself. Even though I wanted to lie down, all I could do was hover over Ashley.

"Is something wrong with Ashley?" Keyes asked with deep concern on his face.

"She got knocked out," I said.

"Gage saved my life," she said weakly. "He must have, because everything went black, and when I came to, he was helping me. So was Tom." Those few words exhausted her, and she lay still again.

"What happened down there?" Keyes asked.

"The boat collapsed," I said. "Ashley saved us. She noticed the top wall collapsing toward us. We barely got out before it hit the bottom, but we were close, and something must have struck Ashley."

"I'm glad you're all okay. You can give me a full report after you've all had time to recover," Keyes said. "Gage, the next time I call for help, I wouldn't blame you if you refused to answer your phone."

"You know I would never do that," I said. "There couldn't possibly be a more dangerous dive than this one." I grinned feebly at him, and then I asked, "Did you get the body Tom sent up?"

"We did. When you're up to it, I'll let you identify it if you can." He pointed across the deck from us. "Both bodies are covered with tarps over there now. Someone will meet us when we reach shore and take them to a medical examiner."

Ashley was stirring again, and she struggled for a moment, reaching for my hand. "Help me sit up," she said.

I tugged gently. Once she was sitting, Tom also pulled himself to a sitting position. Even though I felt like letting myself fall into a reclined position, I put an arm around Ashley to support her. After a moment, she said, "The last thing I remember was that huge towering wall collapsing toward us. Did it hit us?"

"We got clear before it hit the lake bottom, but pieces of it flew in every direction. You were the only one who got hit. I was more scared for you than I've ever been for anyone in my life," I said.

"You must have been praying for me," she said.

"Like I've never prayed before," I said. "I'm so grateful you're okay."

"I'm kind of glad about that myself," she said. "Thank you for whatever you did for me down there. The water must have gotten really muddy."

"Once that wall hit, there wasn't much visibility. If you hadn't been right there beside me, I wouldn't have known what happened to you, and I would never have been able to find you."

Tom spoke then. "I'm not a very religious man," he said. "But I would swear there were angels down there with us. I don't say that lightly."

Keyes said, "Look at the surface of the lake." There was a large debris field, and more items continually bobbed to the surface.

It was a good half hour before we had recovered our strength sufficiently to remove our diving gear and lay it on the deck to dry. Then I finally walked over to where the bodies lay covered on the deck. I pulled back the canvas Keyes and Sam had used to cover them. Randall's body was still Randall's body; there was no doubt about it.

I didn't have to look twice at the smaller one, the one I'd assumed was a female. I wasn't wrong on that count, and my heart sank. Brea Burr would never testify against Bronson Melville. I clenched my fists. Now, if I could just get my hands on those who were responsible for her death.

The blanket she had been wrapped in, Keyes told me, had made it to the surface, but not before it had come most of the way off her body. The turbulence down below had wreaked havoc on it. I was amazed Ashley, Tom, and I had each made it out of there and to the surface in one piece.

Ashley and I sat close together as we rode toward the marina. The other men were in the cabin, so we were alone on the deck—us and two dead bodies, who paid us no attention. Her hand was comfortably concealed in mine. She rested her head on my shoulder, and we talked softly from time to time. At one point she said, "I trust our diving date in a few days won't be as stressful as today and yesterday have been."

"I'm sure it won't, but now you and I have a diving experience few can match," I said.

She chuckled. "I have a previous one that was worse. I don't ever want to go through that close of a call again. Two is more than enough for me. First a shark bite and then a bomb scare and a huge boat collapsing around me. I don't want a third." She smiled at me. It was a tired but beautiful smile, one that gave me great hope of a bright future. I hoped I wasn't reading her wrong.

"I don't either," I told her.

Her smile faded, and she looked deeply into my eyes. Her distinctive, bright green eyes held me captive as she said, "I can only speak for me, Gage, but I think you and I have formed a friendship that could last forever."

"I sure hope so. I'm so glad to have met you," I said, feeling my way as I spoke and trying to keep from choking up.

"I think I want to move to St. George," she said. "I want to get to know you—really know you. Las Vegas is too far from you. And there'll soon be an opening for a defense attorney."

That made me laugh. "No one can ever replace JC Hass. He was nothing, so there's nothing to replace. You can make it on your own just fine. And I hope you do move. If not, I may have to see if I can work with the Las Vegas cops because I want to get to know you a lot better too."

She leaned snugly against me. I looked for a second at her lips and went for it. Wow! What a kiss. It was full of passion and hope. I was a lucky man.

"Gage," Ashley began after a few moments of blissful silence. "Do you think you should make some calls? I mean, Selena needs to know about her brother."

"And I guess I need to call my supervisors," I said.

"When you make those calls makes no difference to me, but I do think we need to let Selena know about her brother."

My first call was to Lieutenant Woodcock. I explained about Randall. "Selena needs to know," I said, "but I don't want to tell her over the phone. I was hoping you would break the news to her."

"I could do that," he said. "But you made quite an impression on her. If you could break free long enough to come up here and tell her yourself, I think it would soften the blow for her, even though it would delay things a little."

"I'll see if I can," I said. "I'll have to clear it with my supervisors."

"If it would help, I'll call your lieutenant and tell him I think you should come and see Selena personally. I think a conversation one lieutenant to another might smooth the way for you. Give me his or her name and number, and I'll call."

"His name is Lieutenant Bill Dollison. I'll give you his cell number since he probably won't be in his office today. I need to call either him or Sergeant Hanks and report what we found today," I said.

"Let me call first," Lieutenant Woodcock said. "I'll call you back after I talk to him."

I didn't have to call my lieutenant. He called me just a few minutes later. "It sounds like you've had an interesting couple of days, Detective. Why don't you take a break for the rest of the weekend and go talk to Randall Stegner's little sister. Then I'll see you in the office on Monday morning. I'll expect a full report then, but for now, give me a quick rundown on your activities."

Once again, I went over the events that had resulted in recovering the bodies of Randall Stegner and Brea Burr. When I had finished, he said, "It sounds like we have our work cut out for us. We need to find and arrest the Hass brothers and Bronson Melville. In the meantime, maybe you could get Kenny Keyes to fly you up to Grand Junction. Then you can take a commercial flight back home tomorrow sometime."

"We can't fly so soon after diving. I'll have to drive up," I explained. "And I'll want to get on it right away."

After that call was finished, Ashley pulled her head from where it had been leaning comfortably against my shoulder—comfortably for me, that is. I don't know how comfortable it was for her. "I take it you're going to Grand Junction," she said. "Would you like some company?"

I grinned at her. "Well, I guess I could see if Keyes would like to assist me. I could use another driver." Ashley playfully punched my shoulder. "Or if I'm really lucky, maybe I can persuade Miss Ashley Webler to go."

"You must be really lucky, then," she said. "Let's go talk to Kenny. It would be nice if we could get there before too late tonight, so we need to be on the road really soon. Selena deserves to know as soon as possible."

Ashley smiled and then tenderly kissed my cheek just as my phone rang.

It was a blocked number. I showed Ashley. "You'd better take it," she said.

"Hello?" I said.

"Hi, Gage. This is Denadene."

CHAPTER TWENTY

"Well, hi, Denadene," I said as I received an astonished look from Ashley. "I'm glad you called." I had quickly put my phone on speaker so Ashley could hear what Denadene had to say.

"I'm sorry," she said. "I know I've treated you badly, and you don't deserve that."

"Hey, you've been through more than anyone should have to go through. Please, don't worry about it."

"So are you going back to St. George now?" Denadene asked.

That wasn't going to happen, but I didn't tell Denadene that. "No, I have to drive back to Grand Junction first."

"Really?" What's going on there?" she asked.

"I need to speak with Selena," I said. "And I need to speak with you as well. I'd rather do this in person."

"Not unless it can wait," she said. "Please, whatever it is, tell me over the phone."

"I'm afraid it's about Randall," I said.

"What about him? Has he been arrested?" she asked.

"I wish that was all, Denadene. I'm sorry, but he's dead."

"Again?" she asked, surprising me.

"This time it's for real."

For a moment, she was silent. I was sure I heard her choke back a sob, but she finally said, "I lost my love for him a long time ago, Gage. He hurt me badly. I don't hate him. I guess mostly I pity him. What happened to him?"

"I have an idea," I said. "If you'll call Ashley, she can tell you everything." Ashley nodded at me but stayed silent.

"Okay, I'll do that. Or, after this, she can call me. I'll give you my number. I'm through hiding and running. I want JC and his buddies brought to justice for what they have done. I've thought about it, and I've decided the best way to do that is for me to let them find me. But, of course, I want you and some more cops there when they do."

"Denadene, I don't think that's wise," I said urgently.

"It probably isn't, but my mind is made up."

"It could be very dangerous," I warned her again.

"I feel like I have to do it, and I won't be talked out of it," she said firmly.

"If you insist, I'll do everything in my power to help you."

"I know you will. I'm sure you've been in dangerous situations before and survived them," she said.

"Not for over an hour," I said.

"What?" she asked, sounding alarmed.

My phone began to ring again. "I have another call coming in. What's your number?"

She gave it to me, and then I said, "Ashley will call you right now. Take care."

Ashley was already dialing as I accepted the other call, my phone still on speaker. This call too was from a blocked number. As quickly as I answered it, a familiar muffled voice said, "So far we can't find Denadene or Selena. But we will. You haven't done what I told you to do, and they will pay. I'm going to step the game up a notch."

"It's no game, JC," I said angrily. "I am going to find you, and when I do, you'll be facing murder charges and a lot more." I couldn't believe he had already forgotten I had figured out his was the muffled voice. I had always considered him dishonest, but until his slip-up, I hadn't thought he was stupid.

Ashley said something softly to Denadene and held her phone close to mine. I glanced at her, and Ashley turned her phone on speaker. She whispered, "Denadene is listening. Let her hear this." I nodded and held my phone closer to Ashley's.

"I told you to back off, but instead you interfered again. I don't know how you survived that bomb, but since you won't listen to me, I'll not only get you, Detective, but I'll get that pretty Vegas attorney you're hanging around with. Miss Webler, is it? Oh, she'll pay right along with you."

"Why don't you just turn yourself in—make it easier on yourself, JC. You know how it works." I was shaking with anger as I spoke.

"I don't know what makes you think this is JC. You've been warned again. I'm going to be gracious and let you have one more chance. Put those bodies back in the lake and give up on pursuing us." Then Hass hung up.

I quickly dialed the number I had called him on before, still keeping my phone on speaker so Denadene and Ashley could hear.

After five rings, he answered. "What do you need now, Detective?" Hass said. "I'm a busy man."

"Indeed you are," I said. "I'm going to find you."

"I already know where you and Miss Webler are," he said.

That made me nervous. I was afraid he did know. He knew about the bomb detonating and our recovery of the bodies. He must be flying over us somewhere or using a drone. I decided to try one more thing to be absolutely sure it was Hass who had called me just moments before. I said, "If I put the bodies back into the water and sink them, then what will you do?"

The idiot took the bait. "As you know by now, Miss Burr cannot testify," Hass said. "If you and Miss Webler both forget you found the bodies and put them back in the lake, I'll spare Miss Webler. But as for you, Detective, your death warrant has been signed."

I still shook with anger. "You'll be behind bars before long; I promise you that."

"You're too stupid to make that happen, Detective," he said.

"Says the man who calls me using that muffled-voice nonsense and believes I don't know it's been you threatening me. When I called you back on the number I found, you answered in your real voice."

For a moment, he didn't respond. Then he said, "I really don't want to hurt Miss Webler or Denadene or Selena. You turn yourself over to me, and I promise you, I'll leave them alone. But you will have to die. It's your life for theirs, Detective."

Suddenly a strong and angry voice came out of Ashley's phone. "JC, you are a pig. No, you're worse than a pig. There isn't any word that can describe how despicable you are. And let me tell you right now, I won't let Gage do that."

"Nor will I," Ashley chimed in.

"Give it up," Denadene said. "And just to make sure you know who this is, it's Denadene. I was stupid to have ever worked for you."

Hass suddenly shouted, "You're dead! You're all dead! I'll get you all for this. And Bronson, Alvin, Dwight, and I will all go free."

"You're delusional, JC," I said. "You know very well Alvin is already dead. Turn yourselves in. It's the only chance you have to try to make things better for you in court. If you make us find you, and we will, I'll resist anything but the death sentence for all of you."

Hass cursed and hung up. Denadene said, "He's gone over the edge. He's nuts, Gage, and he's dangerous. We need to get together and figure out how to find him."

"Leave that to me and my colleagues," I said. "You don't have to put yourself in danger."

"You and Ashley are, and there's no way I'm going to let you guys get hurt if I can do anything to stop it." I was about to protest again when Denadene suddenly gasped. "Gage, I just remembered something. Do you know Trey Overman?"

"Yeah, I know who he is," I said. "He has a plane at the airport in St. George."

"And he flies drones, and he's really tight with JC and with Bronson Melville. I know about him because JC got him off a federal firearms charge last year," she said. "And he flies Bronson around a lot."

I moaned. "So we *are* being watched by a drone or a plane. I was afraid of that."

"Yes," she said. "So keep watching the air."

"Thanks for the heads up," I said.

"You and Ashley stay safe. Which reminds me, Ashley—now I want to know what happened today that had Gage's life in danger," Denadene said, changing the subject.

"And nearly cost Ashley hers," I added. "You guys talk while I go into the cabin and speak with Keyes. We need to be very careful since we're being watched. I'll alert him about what you told me, Denadene, and then I'll call my office. We need to find out where Overman is." I glanced at Ashley. "When we get closer to shore, we'll all need to hunker down in the cabin, just in case."

I looked up and couldn't see anything in the sky but the early-afternoon sun, so I stepped into the cabin and told Keyes, Sam, and Tom what I had just learned. "Hass knows what we're doing?" Keyes asked in alarm.

"There's no question about it. I'm sure Overman has been flying up there, either in his plane or using one of his drones. There's no other way Hass could have known the bomb went off and that we have bodies aboard he didn't want found. Of course, I'm sure he thought whoever found them would not survive. That must have upset him. At any rate, we're probably being watched right now."

Keyes groaned. "This isn't good."

"It is worse than that," I said. "I would suggest we get an escort into the marina and have someone check for snipers around the area. I wouldn't put anything past Hass and his buddies at this point."

"Sam, you drive the boat while I make some calls," Keyes said to the other ranger.

I also had a call to make. I dialed and soon Sergeant Hanks answered. "Hey, I'm enjoying a rare day off," he said.

"Well, I'm not," I said. "It's been a horrendous day."

"That's what the lieutenant told me. He interrupted me as well. Now that you have me on the phone, what do you need?"

"I need someone to find out where Trey Overman is," I told him. I explained why.

"I'll get someone on it or do it myself. I'll get back with you when I learn something. But let me tell you this, Gage. If he's involved with JC Hass and company, that isn't good."

"Exactly," I told him. "Let me know as soon as you can."

A few minutes later we cruised slowly up to the boat ramp, accompanied by four other boats. "There are cops hurrying to cover us when we get off the boat, and others are looking for snipers. What else can we do?" Keyes asked.

"When these bodies are loaded, they'll need an armed escort to the medical examiner," I said.

"Okay, I'll see to it. What about you and Miss Webler?" he asked as we all huddled in the cabin of the rescue boat. I kept an arm around Ashley.

"We'll need to rent a car and drive, but we'll be going to Grand Junction tonight once we're debriefed about today's activities by whatever agencies need to hear from us. Ashley and I need to get to Grand Junction at a decent hour," I said. "I need to let Randall Stegner's little sister know he's dead. I asked her bishop to do it, but he thinks it would be best coming from me."

"I understand," Keyes said. "We owe a great debt to you folks. When you head out, we need to make sure Hass and his pals have no way of knowing what you're driving. We can't be too cautious at this point."

"I couldn't agree more," I said. "It looks like we're ready to dock."

"All right. You and Ashley stay here with me, Sam, and Tom until we have an armed escort to get you out of here. I'll make sure you know where the bodies are taken. And don't worry about your diving gear. I'll secure it, then fly it to St. George, and have the airport store it until you two get back there."

"That would be great," I said, and Ashley agreed.

I thought about calling Paige. I had made it clear enough to her earlier that I wouldn't be calling her about a celebration date, but I still figured I should call her. I needed to let her know Randall Stegner was dead. When she answered my call, I said, "I have some news, Paige."

"Have you changed your mind about celebrating with me?" she asked.

"No, and I won't even be back to St. George for a while," I said. "It's been a really bad day, and it's not going to get better. I have to drive to Grand Junction and give Selena Stegner some bad news."

"What kind of bad news?" Paige asked.

"That's actually why I called you. I wanted you to know some of the danger is gone. Randall Stegner is dead," I said.

"Are you sure?" Paige said.

"Very sure. A couple of other divers and I pulled his body from a sunken houseboat a short while ago, along with the body of the main witness in my murder case against Bronson Melville."

"Oh, Gage, how awful. I feel so bad for Selena. Denadene has told me what a sweet girl she is."

"She is that. And even though Randall wasn't a good guy, he was her brother and she loved him a lot. She'll be deeply hurt," I said.

"She doesn't know me, but tell her I'm sorry," Paige said.

"I'll do that. Now, you go celebrate your new job. You may still want to keep an eye out for Randall's friends, or I should say his enemies. We haven't found all of them yet. And good luck to you."

"Thanks, Gage. You're a great guy. I hope we can be friends."

"I'm sure we can," I said. "I need to get off the phone now. I'm waiting for a SWAT team to show up to escort Ashley and me off the boat we're on."

"Why do you need a SWAT team?" she asked.

"We're in a great deal of danger," I said. "We're lucky to even be alive after what we went through earlier today. Like I said, it's been a rough day."

"Can't you tell me about it? Wait, Ashley? Isn't that Denadene's attorney?

Why is she with you?" Paige asked.

"Aside from being Denadene's attorney, she's my rescue-diving partner," I said. "And she really put her life on the line to help me today. She helped me get the bodies from the sunken boat."

"She must be a good person," she said. "Tell her thanks from me for sticking with Denadene even though I know she didn't have to."

"Take care, Paige. I really need to get off the phone now."

Shortly after ending the call, a SWAT team, fully decked out and armed, arrived and escorted Tom, Ashley, and me to a waiting van. From there, with the SWAT team accompanying us, we were taken to the local National Park Service office. An hour later, after an intense debrief, Tom was escorted away, and Ashley and I were put into a rental car that had been arranged for us during the debriefing. Our overnight bags were already in it.

When we headed for Grand Junction, two officers in an unmarked car traveled with us. There was even a fighter jet circling high above us. Keyes had explained that since we had risked our lives assisting the federal government, the resources of the air force had been summoned to make sure no planes or drones could present a danger to us.

Ashley and I took turns driving. We were physically and emotionally drained. I was driving as we approached Grand Junction. We'd both had some power naps on the five-hour drive. I looked across the car and said to her, "Ashley, I'm sorry I got you into this. I had no idea I was subjecting you to so much danger."

She grinned at me, held my hand, and replied, "I think some good has come of it." I believed she meant us.

We were met a short distance from Grand Junction by not only Lieutenant Woodcock but another SWAT team, which he had arranged. An officer from Grand Junction drove our rental car so we could ride with Woodcock, and the officers who had followed us headed back to Lake Powell. He said as he drove, "I was fully briefed on the security in place. We'll be switching cars a couple of times, and eventually you'll end up at the safe house where Selena is being housed. Your rental car will be hidden somewhere out of sight, but your bags will be at the safe house when we get there."

It was almost nine p.m. when we finally walked into the safe house. Officers met us inside and assured us we would be protected there. Our bags were on the floor inside the door, where we could take them with us when we left. After we were both given a chance to freshen up, we went into the living room, where Woodcock and Selena were talking softly. Selena's face blossomed into a huge smile when she saw us, and she bounded to her feet, ran to me, and threw her arms around me. "Gage, I can't believe you're back already. What are you doing? It's so good to see you." She hugged me tightly, stepped back and looked at Ashley, and said, "Who's this?"

"This is Ashley Webler. She's the attorney who helped Denadene in Las Vegas," I said.

"Yes, of course. Denadene has told me all about you. She says she trusts you completely," Selena gushed.

"It's so good to meet you, Selena," Ashley said. "Denadene has nothing but praise for you."

Selena hugged her too and then said, "Come sit down. What do we need to talk about?"

Ashley and I sat across from Selena, who sat on the couch, and Woodcock sat in a chair next to her. "I'm sorry, Selena, but I have some bad news for you," I said a moment later.

Her eyes grew wide, and her face went pale. "Is it about Randall?"

I nodded and said, "I'm so sorry, but he's dead."

For a moment, shock came to her face. Then she covered her eyes with her hands and she cried.

Ashley moved next to her and put her arms around her. Then I moved to the other side and did the same. Selena sobbed for a long time. Finally, she stopped and wiped her eyes with the third tissue Bishop Woodcock had handed her. Then she asked quietly, "Can you tell me what happened to him?"

"It's not very pleasant," I said. "Are you sure you want to know?"

She looked me right in the eye and clutched my arm tightly. "Yes, I do. I know he wasn't a very good man, but he was my brother, and he treated me like I was special, even though he didn't treat his wife that way. Tell me, please."

She sat very still as the story unfolded from Ashley and me. Her pretty face was as gray as cold ash. Her eyes glistened with residual tears, and she worked her hands nervously on her lap.

"Those guys will find me, won't they?" she asked after we'd finished.

Her bishop spoke up then. "We will do everything we can to keep you safe while they're hunted down."

She glanced at him and forced a smile, but then she said with a trembling voice, "They'll find Denadene. Somebody has got to protect her."

Ashley and I exchanged glances, and she nodded almost imperceptibly, indicating to me that we should probably tell her Denadene's plan. "You're not going to like this any better than we do, but Denadene wants to be found," I said, "but only under controlled circumstances. And my fellow officers and I will be the ones controlling those circumstances. I wish she would wait, but she's insistent." I wasn't sure how that was going to work, but we had to keep Denadene safe and catch the killers at the same time. It was a very tall order, but with Denadene's determination to come out of hiding, it had to be done. And I could think of no other way.

"Doesn't she know how dangerous that will be?" Selena asked.

"Of course she does, but she won't be persuaded otherwise," Ashley said. "Believe me, I've tried."

"I want to try too," Selena said with determination in her voice. "She hasn't called me for a while, but when she does, I'll tell her I don't think she should do that. She needs to know that with Randall gone, she's the dearest person I have in my life. She's like a sister to me. I can't lose her too."

"We have her new cell number now," Ashley said. "Why don't you call her."

Selena's pain-filled face brightened a little. "You do? I'll call her now."

"Maybe you should wait until morning," I said. "It's kind of late."

But it wasn't too late for my phone to ring. It was Sergeant Hanks. "Sorry I've been so long getting back to you," he said. "No one has been able to reach Trey Overman. A couple of officers even went to his house several times during the evening, but no one was home."

"Okay, thanks. Could you have someone try again in the morning?" I asked. "I don't have a good feeling about the guy."

As soon as the call was over, Selena asked if we were going to stay in Grand Junction for the night. We assured her we were. Then she said, "Will you go to church with me in the morning? I really want to go. I'm going crazy here. And with my bishop being a cop, I'll be safe." She gave Bishop Woodcock a hopeful look. But he seemed worried.

"That'll be up to him," I said. "What do you think, Lieutenant?"

"Please," Selena begged.

"Selena, as bishop, I have to go early to church for my bishopric meeting," he said. "You understand that, don't you?"

"I do, but there's Gage," she said.

Woodcock looked at me. "Can you keep her safe, Detective?"

"I'll give it my best shot," I said, realizing my choice of words wasn't exactly appropriate.

"There's room right here in the safe house at the moment. Would the two of you consider staying here tonight?" Lieutenant Woodcock asked.

I glanced at Ashley, and she said, "I think that would be a good idea."

"Then we'll do it," I agreed.

"Great. Then, I'll make some further safety arrangements." He was thoughtful for a moment. Then he said, "I'll have a couple of officers pick the three of you up here in the morning at quarter to eleven. They'll have the address of the meetinghouse."

"I know where it's at," Selena said.

"You don't know how to get there from this safe house, though, do you?"

Sheepishly she admitted, "I guess I don't."

"Okay, so it's set. I'll have the officers come to the door to get you. There will also be a backup set of officers nearby. You might not see them, but they'll be there," Lieutenant Woodcock said. He turned to Selena. "You need to do exactly what Gage says. If at any point he thinks it's too dangerous, he'll have the officers bring all three of you back here. If all goes as planned, and I'm sure it will, Gage, I'll see to it you and Ashley have your car back and some security to follow you back to St. George or wherever you need to go."

Even though it was very late, Selena called Denadene. She had no more success than we'd had in persuading her to stay in hiding. I assured Selena again that I would do all that I could to keep them both safe.

We stayed up late talking to Selena, but finally, at midnight, after having a snack from the well-stocked kitchen, we all got some sleep.

CHAPTER TWENTY-ONE

ASHLEY AND I DRESSED THE best we could for church, though neither of us had planned for it. Ashley did have a dress. I had a pair of black slacks, a plain blue shirt, and a tan sports jacket.

I was dressed with fifteen minutes to spare before the officers were supposed to pick us up. Ashley and Selena were in their rooms getting ready. I was reading the Book of Mormon on my phone when I got a call from Sergeant Hanks.

"Gage, I just talked to Trey Overman's wife. Well, she's not actually his wife, but she refers to him as her husband. You know how it is these days. Anyway, she told me Trey had to fly to Lake Powell on Friday and she didn't have any idea when he would get home." The hair stood up on the back of my neck.

The rest of what Sergeant Hanks had to tell me wasn't what I wanted to hear either. Overman had not only flown his plane to Lake Powell but had also taken a small drone with him.

"What do you know about this guy's background?" I asked.

"I did some checking this morning. He's not a nice man," Jon said. "He has a criminal record, and from what I've been able to ascertain, he was very angry when you arrested Bronson Melville. Bronson flies all around the country with Trey. They're apparently good buddies. Trey's girlfriend made that very clear to me. She said she's glad Bronson got away because we had falsely accused him of murder and escaping was the only way he could avoid a terrible injustice. She even accused me of harassing her by coming to their house and said you and I should go jump off a cliff. Then she demanded I get out of her house. When I started to leave, she shouted at me that people had better quit messing with her husband or they'd pay," Jon said. "I turned back and asked what cops besides me were messing with him."

"Did she tell you?" I asked.

"Not specifically, but she told me enough that I understood. She said, and I quote, 'Those feds, that's who.' But when I asked her to elaborate, she wouldn't—just told me again to leave. I'll do some checking and find out if there are any federal investigations currently going on regarding him. I know there was one a year or so ago, but Hass managed to get him off on that one. I'll let you know what I find out."

"Thanks," I said, and we hung up.

Ashley and Selena came out of their respective rooms. Wow. They looked spectacular. "I'm going to be the envy of all the single men in your ward, Selena," I said. "You both look stunning."

Selena grinned. Ashley smiled, but she seemed self-conscious. I hugged Selena and then Ashley and received a modest kiss for my efforts. Selena gave a weak smile. "You two are into each other, aren't you?"

We didn't deny it. After a moment, Ashley said, "Does my leg look okay?"

I hadn't even noticed, but the artificial leg she wore now wasn't the one she'd worn diving. I remembered she'd told me her other one had a titanium core, but it actually looked like a real leg. Her dress came to well below her knees, but I could tell only by looking very closely that the color of the prosthetic covering was slightly different than the skin of her other leg. I doubted most people would even notice. "It looks wonderful. You look wonderful," I said.

Selena had grown silent. Suddenly she smiled brightly and said, "Are you the bionic woman? I didn't have a clue."

"I guess I am a little bit bionic," Ashley responded.

"You can dive with that?" Selena asked, pointing at Ashley's prosthesis.

"I use a different prosthetic leg for diving, but yes; it doesn't hinder me at all," Ashley said as the doorbell rang.

We had been instructed that no one but one of our officers, our protectors, was to respond to any knocking or ringing of the bell. One of the men stepped to the door while the other pulled his sidearm out and stepped to one side.

"Do you have a gun on you?" Selena asked me.

I pulled my jacket open to where she could see it, and she said, "A shoulder holster; that's neat."

The officer at the door unlocked several strong locks after viewing a small screen above the door that was connected to a camera outside. On it I could see two officers in suits with their shields displayed.

The ride to the meetinghouse was uneventful. The three of us mostly just talked. Selena, who was not at all shy, asked Ashley how she'd lost her leg, so we got the shark story, one that even having heard it already made me shudder. Selena said, "That must have been really frightening."

"It was that, but the Lord pulled me through—Him and some friends." She glanced at me as she made that remark and smiled.

The officers walked us to the door, both of them on the lookout for any danger. I kept an eye out too and noticed a second unmarked car a ways back on the side of the street. I was certain it was the one that had more officers in it. We entered the church, and our escorts returned to their car.

Inside the church, we were just in time to get seated before Bishop Woodcock stood and welcomed everyone to the meeting. It was a very large singles ward, not a lot different than the one I attended in St. George. I couldn't help but notice the looks we were getting. Well, the looks Selena and Ashley were getting. They were both turning guys' heads. After sacrament meeting, we were surrounded by a gaggle of young singles.

Selena introduced us as friends from out of town to a couple of her former roommates. She wisely made no reference to our respective professions, nor did she try to explain why we were attending her ward with her. We all three went with the others to a very large Gospel Doctrine class. I didn't respond to any of the questions the young woman who was teaching asked, but both Selena and Ashley did. I was impressed with the depth of gospel knowledge Ashley had. My fondness for her grew.

Selena was glad to be with her friends again. She was clearly a social creature, and people loved being around her. I could see where being alone the way she had been forced to be was very hard on her. I hoped and prayed we could soon end the danger she was facing.

When the two hours of church were over, I texted the officers, as per our previous arrangements. I was told to give them a couple of minutes to get the car in place as near to the door we were about to exit as possible. We stood inside, watching through the glass. Selena was standing quietly as a group of people chattered noisily. I touched her arm and said, "They're ready. I'll take the lead. You and Ashley stay close behind me."

The officers were leaning on their car. To the casual observer, they were totally relaxed—just two men in suits waiting for someone to come out of the church. But the truth was that they were very alert. A couple of rough-looking young men rode past on their skateboards. I suddenly had a very bad feeling and reached inside my coat. Our bodyguards did the same. Suddenly the two hoodlums stopped, and pistols appeared in their hands. "Get down," I ordered Selena and Ashley. As they dropped, gunfire erupted. My Glock was already in my hand, and I dropped one of the shooters. One of the officers stumbled and fell back against the car.

Then I heard gunfire from another direction and dropped down as the second skateboarder bit the concrete sidewalk. Two more similarly dressed young men were not far away on the other side of us. One of them was already down; the other one spun around, trying to see where the other officers were. Our backup officers were close to them, and in a moment, the second guy threw his gun down and raised his hands, screaming he gave up.

The gunfire was over as quickly as it had begun, but there were young people lying on the walkway to the church and on the grass. There was a lot of screaming. Bishop Woodcock burst through the door. "Officer down," I shouted to him, and then he slowly moved toward us, instructing his frightened young ward members to go back inside the church. The entire shootout had taken only seconds, so very few people had returned to the inside of the church. At the bishop's instructions, however, the lawn and walks cleared like magic. Ashley ushered Selena quickly back inside with them.

I approached the downed officer with my Glock in my hand, but his partner shouted that he was only hit in the vest, that he'd had the wind knocked out of him. He asked me to secure the two downed gunmen to our right. The one I had shot was as secure as he was ever going to be. The other man, however, was still alive. He had been hit twice—once in the stomach and once in his right thigh. I kicked his gun away from him and glanced toward where the other two gunmen were.

One was already cuffed, and the other was lying still on the ground. I watched as an officer felt his carotid artery and then stood up shaking his head. Just then I heard a buzzing sound and looked up as a black drone whistled past just a few yards above us. It disappeared beyond some trees. I was not surprised to also see a plane in the sky. Lieutenant Woodcock rushed beside me and said, "I saw them too. You get back inside and check the girls. My ward members are all okay, just shook up."

Sirens could be heard coming from all directions. I hurried back inside the meetinghouse, still alert to the possibility of other gunmen. I didn't holster my service weapon until I was all the way to the door. Selena and Ashley, both white-faced and wide-eyed, ran to me and grabbed me, holding me tightly.

"Are you two okay?" I asked as I became aware of others gathering close to us. I recognized the roommates Selena had introduced me to when we had first arrived. They were both crying, as were other young women. The young men were involved in comforting and otherwise acting protective of the girls.

Selena, in a shaky voice, said, "I can't believe we were attacked right here at the church. Who were those guys?"

"Hired guns, I would imagine," I said. "It's my fault. We never should have come here."

Ashley said, "I saw you hit one of them. How is he?"

"His criminal career is over," I said blandly—much more blandly than I was feeling inside. I had just killed a young man, and it was a terrible feeling. I felt sick to my stomach, but I tried to hide it from my two special friends. "Are you both okay?" I asked again.

"I'm sorry," Ashley said as she clung tightly to me.

"For what?"

"I'm sorry you had to shoot that guy," she said. "We're both okay. Well, mostly."

"What is it?" I asked. "Were you hit?" I felt a rising panic as I looked her over.

"Sort of," she said as she stepped back and lifted her dress almost to her knee. There was a hole in the material, and the outer shell of her prosthesis was cracked. I could see where a bullet had grazed it. She forced a feeble smile. "At least I'm not bleeding. But Selena is a little."

I turned quickly to her. She stepped back and held up her left elbow. "I got skinned when we went down; that's all," she assured me. I exhaled in relief as Selena continued. "You were amazing out there, and so were those other officers. But I don't understand. Did you just suggest that JC Hass and his friends hired those guys?"

"That would be my guess," I said. "I can't imagine any other reason they would've made such a brazen attack in broad daylight in front of dozens of witnesses."

"That seems stupid," Selena said, nodding.

"That's where I made my mistake. I didn't think he'd hire dumb kids. They must have had no idea we had protection. You'd think they would've assumed that," I said. "But I suppose whatever money they were offered was enough to stop their already-feeble brains from working. That's assuming, of course, they had any brains in the first place."

A good part of our Sunday afternoon was spent at the police department headquarters, giving statements. A search had been started for Trey Overman's plane. I was almost certain he had been in the area and that someone in the plane with him was operating the black drone that had zipped by us.

One of the surviving gunmen had been brought to the police station, and there he was questioned by officers, including Lieutenant Woodcock. Selena, Ashley, and I watched the interrogation through a one-way glass partition and could hear what was being said through a speaker in the wall near where I sat. He admitted he and his friends, all of whom were members of a local gang, had been hired to kill me, Ashley, and Selena. Pictures of all of us were found in the pockets of his baggy pants.

When asked who had hired them, he said he didn't have a name. He admitted we had been seen entering the church by someone in a plane and that their instructions were to come by on skateboards when the meeting ended and gun us down. I assumed that was supposed to make them look like they weren't dangerous. When shown photos of JC, Dwight Hass, and Bronson Melville, he picked out JC as the one who had hired them. When asked how much he'd been paid, the shooter said each of them had been given three thousand dollars.

"Just enough to make them stupid. To people like them, I suppose three thousand dollars is a lot of money," Ashley said. "I'm glad it's not going to be my job to defend that guy."

But my full attention was not on the interview. I was battling my own anguish as the face of the man I had shot kept running through my head. Ending a life was a terrible feeling, one I prayed I would never have to experience again. I supposed most officers were like me—they really don't expect to ever have to shoot someone. It was an awful thing to experience, and the fact that the gangbanger was trying to kill us didn't make it any more palatable.

A can of soda after the interview helped settle my upset stomach, but nothing could ease my mind, and I was afraid the feeling would linger for a very long time.

As I sat near Selena in a small conference room, holding Ashley's hand a few minutes later, Sergeant Hanks called. I had not yet reported to him or the lieutenant about the horrible day I was having. He didn't ask at first. He simply wanted to report that the FBI and other federal officers were investigating Trey Overman over allegations of selling firearms to a violent and very powerful cartel in Mexico.

"Has there been any evidence of his presence where you're at?" he asked me.

"I'm sure he's in the area," I said. I told him about the attack, but I couldn't yet bring myself to tell him I'd shot someone. "One of the surviving gang members identified a photo of JC Hass as the man who paid the four of them to eliminate Selena, Ashley, and me. He said we were being watched by someone in a plane." Before Hanks could say anything—I could tell by his spluttering he was trying to—I told him about the drone as well.

Finally, I gave him time to react. "You were attacked by a gang? Are you and the ladies okay? There's no way we can let you guys drive home now with Overman watching you from the air."

"Stop, Jon. I can only handle a few things at a time right now," I said. "We're all fine. Ashley got hit on her prosthetic leg, so it's going to need to be repaired, and Selena skinned her elbow when they dropped to the ground, but they're okay. I'm just glad we took precautions and had backup."

"You said a *surviving* gang member identified Hass as the one who hired them. I take it that means someone died," Hanks said.

"Two are dead, one is critically injured, and one surrendered," I said. "All four, it turns out, have extensive criminal records. The police here are relieved none of them got away."

"Did you have to engage or was it just the other officers with you?" he asked.

"I only fired one shot," I said. "I'm glad I have a second weapon with me because the police here need to keep my Glock until they're through with their investigation."

"If they kept your weapon, I take it you didn't miss with that one shot," he said.

"I was just trying to protect the girls."

"I know how well you shoot, Gage. I have to assume your guy is one of the two who didn't make it."

"I'm sorry, Sergeant, but I did what I had to do. I didn't have time to think about it. Now I'm going to see that guy's face in my nightmares for a very long time."

"You're a good man, Gage, and a good officer. Where are you and the ladies now?"

"We're at the police department," I said. "But I think we'll be able to leave pretty soon."

"Don't go anywhere until I get back to you," Jon said. "I need to make a call or two. I can't take a chance on someone shooting at you again."

As I finished my conversation with my sergeant, I could hear Ashley speaking on her phone. She said, "I'll have to have the outside part replaced, but it still works fine." She listened for a moment and then said, "Gage just got off the phone. Why don't I let you talk to him." She handed the phone to me as she said, "It's Denadene. She wants to come to Grand Junction."

I nodded and took the phone. "Hi, Denadene. I don't think you should come here. Please, just stay put where you are. We can come to you and make some kind of plan. Hass has gone crazy. He's a homicidal maniac, and he's having us watched with drones and aircraft. There's no way of knowing when and how he'll strike at us next," I said.

"I can't stay put much longer, Gage," she said, her voice earnest.

"Tell me where you are right now, and we'll head that way. We have a rental car, and we'll be fine."

"No, don't do that. Let me think about it for another day," Denadene said.

"Okay, but seriously, we can come meet you," I said.

"Let me think," she said. "And just so you know, I have a gun now, and I've been learning to shoot it. I can defend myself if I have to."

"You have a gun? How did you get it?" I asked.

"It's not important. I'll call you tomorrow," she said, and the line went dead.

CHAPTER
TWENTY-TWO

"WE'RE FLYING UP TO GET you," Sergeant Hanks told me a few minutes later. "Lieutenant Dollison and I are both coming. The chief wants you back here tonight, if possible. Then we'll all meet and plan what to do. Clearly JC has gone off the deep end. I think he'll do anything to get back at you."

"I can't argue with that," I told him. "Ashley needs to be in Las Vegas on Tuesday. It's been too recent since we dove, so neither one of us can fly today, but we can tomorrow. Otherwise we'll have to drive."

"I understand. So let's plan for you to fly home with us tomorrow," Jon said. "I'll explain to the chief why we need to wait a day, but we're coming to provide extra security. We'll rent a car at the airport and drive to the police department, so you'll need to wait there. If you need to eat, have food brought in. I don't want you guys leaving there for food or for any other reason until we arrive," he said. "We'll figure out what to do when we get there, but I think we'll all spend the night, as long as we can do so safely. With us there with you, I'm sure we'll be okay. I've got to go now. We'll see you as soon as possible."

Lieutenant Woodcock walked in just as I finished my call with Hanks. "Was that one of your supervisors?" he asked.

"Yes. My sergeant and lieutenant are flying up. We'll all stay another night and fly home tomorrow," I said. "They want us to stay here in your building until they get here."

"What's your sergeant's phone number?" he asked. "I want to talk to him for a minute."

He punched it into his phone and walked out of the room as he started to talk. I had no idea what he wanted to talk to Hanks about, but I was so emotionally and physically drained I didn't much care. What I cared about right then was that Ashley and Selena were both okay. Ashley was beside me right now, but I was also worried about Denadene. I wished I could convince her to stay put, but I wasn't at all sure she would, no matter what I or anyone else said.

If she decided to try to drive to St. George on her own without giving me time to help her, she would be putting herself in terrible danger. She seemed convinced Hass couldn't figure out where she was or, if she rented a car, what she would be driving, but after all that had happened that day, I wasn't so sure. He seemed to have all the help he needed when and from wherever he wanted it. I thought about all the evil people he had managed to get off serious charges over the years. It wasn't too much of a stretch to think he was, at this very moment, calling in favors from some of the worst of them. The questions were how many, who were they, and where were they?

"You look worried, Gage," Ashley said, taking hold of my hand and squeezing.

"Denadene is in danger," I said. "So are you and Selena."

Selena had left with her bishop and a couple of other officers a couple of hours earlier and returned to the safe house. She had called Ashley and me a couple of times, worried about us. We worried about her too.

"I suppose so, but we're being watched over."

"We can't have a bunch of cops around us all the time," I said.

She smiled at me. "That's not what I meant. The Lord is looking out for us."

"I'm sure He is," I agreed, but after the close call at the church, I had to admit I wasn't at all sure He wouldn't let things happen that might be detrimental to us. After all, God didn't stop bad people from doing bad things to good people. He allowed them their agency. But despite that, I had a prayer in my heart that He would help us avoid our enemies.

I was glad when Lieutenant Dollison, Sergeant Hanks, and the sheriff's pilot who had flown them up in their department plane finally walked into the police station a few hours later. They had been met by a couple of officers at the airport and had been handed the keys to our rental car. I guessed that was what Lieutenant Woodcock had talked to Hanks about earlier.

After chatting briefly about the events of the day, Lieutenant Dollison said, "We already booked hotel rooms for all of us. The chief wasn't excited about the expense, but we convinced him it was necessary. We'll fly late tomorrow morning to St. George. Does that give you time enough between your dives and flying?"

"Yes, that'll be fine," I said after glancing at Ashley and getting her nod of agreement.

"Have you two had something to eat?" Lieutenant Dollison asked.

"I haven't been all that hungry until now," I admitted.

"Neither have I," Ashley added. "But I think I could eat now."

"Then, that's what we'll do. After that, it's off to the hotel. You guys look like you could use a lot of rest," Dollison said.

I had a decent night's rest, disturbed only by recurring thoughts about the young man I had killed and worry about Denadene and Selena. We slept in the next morning and joined the others for an unhurried breakfast at about ten. After we'd eaten, we got into the rental car and went to the airport. We hadn't heard from Denadene, and when we tried calling her, we got no answer. My worries escalated. Surely she wouldn't try to drive to St. George without telling us.

We hadn't been in the plane long when my cell phone rang. I answered it, and my blood pressure spiked when I heard the now-familiar sound of JC Hass's voice. He must have finally figured out I was onto his attempts to keep me from knowing it was him calling, because he didn't even attempt to hide his identity this time.

The words he spoke drove terror to my heart. "We're following a tan Jeep," he said, laughing. "You lose again." Before I could respond, he ended the call.

A tan Jeep? Had Denadene rented a vehicle? I tried her number again. This time she answered. "Denadene, tell me you're not driving a tan Jeep," I pleaded.

"How did you know?" she asked.

"Hass just called me. You're being followed."

"Oh no," she said softly.

"Where are you?" I asked.

"I'm on I-70 headed west. I'm coming to Grand Junction from Denver," she said.

"We'll come to you," I said. "Keep driving. I need to make another call, but I'll have Ashley call you. Whatever you do, stay on the phone with her. We need to be able to find you."

"Okay," Denadene said, her voice shaking. "I will."

I hung up and shouted to the others, "Head for I-70! Denadene's in trouble. She's headed our way in a tan Jeep. Hass has figured out what she's driving and said he's following her."

No one doubted my word. Dollison had the pilot head north in the general direction of Grand Junction until we knew exactly where on I-70 Denadene was driving. Ashley was already on her phone talking to Denadene before the plane had completed its turn. I called Lieutenant Woodcock, who answered on the second ring. I told him about Hass's call, and he promised to alert cops along I-70 to attempt to locate Denadene.

When I ended the call, I looked at Ashley. She was still on the phone. She asked Denadene, "Are you sure you don't see a vehicle behind you that's been there for a while?"

Ashley switched her phone to speaker mode in time for me to hear Denadene say, "I'm sure. Believe me, I'm being careful. But I don't know how he could possibly know I'm in a tan Jeep if he's not following me. I paid for the rental with cash. Does he have people watching all over the area?"

"I suspect he knows a lot of criminals who would help him if he offered to pay," I said. "You worked for him for a while. You know who some of those people are. There are a lot of people he might think owe him favors. Think about where you've been and see if you can come up with any former clients who live in or near that area."

"He has defended people from all over the western U.S. After all, St. George is an area lots of people pass through, and occasionally some of them get into trouble there, as I'm sure you know. But how would he know I've been in Denver and have someone looking for me there? That's a huge city."

"Maybe he's called people in lots of areas. The point is, Hass found you and clearly wants to do you harm. How he did it isn't something we need to worry about right now. We need to get help to you. Where are you, exactly?"

Before she could respond, I heard what I was sure was a gunshot. Denadene screamed. "He's found me!" she said between screams. "He shot my tire out! I have to stop."

"Don't do that. Keep driving, flat tire and all. Where are you?"

"I don't know exactly. I left Denver, heading west, over an hour ago," she said as another shot rang out. I expected another scream, but after a pause, her tone took on an eerie calm. "He got another tire. He's not alone. I can't keep going. But I can take care of myself." She wasn't screaming now. She seemed to have made a determination to do something, and I remembered her gun. "I'll leave my phone on."

We all listened, spellbound, helpless, and sick at heart as we heard the sound of tires on gravel as she left the pavement. More shots rang out, very close to Denadene's phone. The sound of traffic could also be heard, along with heavy breathing. I held my breath. Ashley gripped my arm. My superior officers were both on their phones.

Suddenly Denadene was back on the phone. "I think I just killed a guy! He's lying on the ground behind my car." She was speaking rationally but not calmly. She was almost shouting.

"Where is Hass?" I asked.

"He drove off when I shot his friend," she said.

"What was he driving?" I asked.

"I don't know. It was white. I think I blew a hole in his windshield," she said. "The guy on the ground isn't moving."

"Are you out of the Jeep?" I asked.

"Yes. There are cars stopping. People are running toward me," she shouted.

At that point I could hear a man ask if she was okay. She said she thought so, and he said he'd called for the police to come, and an ambulance. She said she didn't think the guy needed one. Then I heard him say it was for her, that she certainly was not okay. "Gage, I'm hurt, but I'm safe for now. Can you guys find me?" she asked.

Lieutenant Dollison spoke up. He identified himself to Denadene, and then he said, "Sergeant Hanks and I are coordinating with officers on the ground. Thanks to several 911 calls, there will be officers there shortly."

"Thanks," she said, her voice becoming weak. "You've got to find JC."

"I'm working on it," I said as I entered Hass's number and listened to the ringing on my phone. I told everyone else in the plane to get off their phones or at least cease to speak. Hass wasn't answering his phone, but I supposed he could have wised up and gotten a different one since he knew I had his number.

But he hadn't wised up. A moment later he answered. "That you, Overman?" he asked. At my signal, everyone else quit talking. "It sounds like you're still in your plane. I need you to do something right now."

It was a little hard to hear Hass, as I could hear what sounded like the rushing of air. I guessed it was from the windshield Denadene had shot out. "Yeah, I'm flying," I said, trying to make my voice sound like anyone's but mine and hoping he wouldn't recognize me. Like his, the number of the phone I was using was blocked.

"I almost got her," Hass said. "But she shot Jimmie. Can you believe that? The little witch had a gun. I put a bullet in her car as I drove away. I'm pretty sure I hit her. I was hoping to catch her and make her suffer before doing away with her, but that didn't work out."

"Where are you, JC?" I asked. I wasn't sure how I was doing masking my voice, but it must've been convincing enough.

"I'll worry about me," he said. "I'm on I-70." He gave an approximate location and then said, "See if you can fly over and figure out if I got her or not. And see if you can tell if Jimmie's dead."

"You left him?" I asked, trying to sound angry like I thought Overman would be.

"I had no choice. He jumped out of the car, and she was shooting at both of us. He went down, and I had to get away. There was other traffic. Call me back as soon as you know something."

The others were all looking at me. Even the pilot glanced back for a moment. I quickly explained the conversation I'd just had with Hass.

"He thought I was Overman and that I was flying. Trouble is, we don't know where Overman is. Hass thinks he told Overman to fly over the area where the shooting took place."

We gave quick instructions to the pilot, and he flew in Denadene's direction, but we were a long ways away. I told Ashley to try to get Denadene on the phone again. She had her in a moment and put her phone on speaker. Denadene sounded like she was in pain. We could hear lots of other voices. Ashley asked Denadene if she'd been shot. Denadene said she guessed so, but she hadn't realized it until just a moment ago.

While Ashley continued talking to Denadene, Dollison broke in and said, "I have good news, folks. Overman's aircraft has been located. I just talked with Lieutenant Woodcock. It's on the ground in an airport in Pueblo. It's being watched. When he shows up there, he'll be arrested."

"That's great," I said. "But as soon as Hass tries to call him, he'll know he was fooled. I think I'll call him again to keep him from calling Overman. We all need to be silent again. But first, Ashley, how is Denadene?" I asked as soon as her call was ended.

"They have an ambulance there now. She's getting very weak. I think she's losing a lot of blood," Ashley said.

I made my call and almost instantly Hass answered. "You there already, Trey?"

"Yeah. It looks like you shot Denadene, all right."

"Good. Now I need to find that idiot Tipton. I'll need another car before I go after him. Where can I meet you? We'll fly somewhere and rent one. I'll just leave this one when I see you." The rushing air I'd noticed the last time I'd talked to him had gotten louder. No wonder he didn't know who he was talking to.

"Meet me at the little airport in Glenwood Springs," I said. I knew that was probably near where Hass was currently located.

Our pilot heard what I said and changed course. In the meantime, Hass asked, "Are you sure the Stegner woman is dead? Or is she just injured?"

"There are two bodies covered by blankets on the side of the road," I lied. "I'll see you in a little while."

"Speak up, Trey. I'm having a hard time hearing you with this broken windshield," Hass said.

"She's dead," I said louder. "I'll see you in Glenwood Springs."

"Great. She finally got what she had coming," Hass responded and ended the call.

"He still doesn't realize he's not talking to Trey Overman?" Sergeant Hanks asked with a strained chuckle.

"Thanks to Denadene," I said.

"I don't suppose you can call Denadene again?" I asked Ashley.

"No, but I have the number of an officer who's there. He said to call him later and he'd let me know where the ambulance takes her," she responded.

Lieutenant Dollison had been following our conversation, but he looked deep in thought. His brow was wrinkled, and his eyes were narrowed. He spoke up now. "If an officer spots a white car with the windshield broken, maybe we should have them follow it to the airport. And perhaps some others could go there directly and watch for his car to arrive. I think it would pay to have some other officers meet us there. Hass isn't going to want to get caught if he can help it, so we need to expect the worst."

We all agreed with him, so he again got on his phone. Ashley spoke up. "I don't know where Denadene was hit by the bullet, but she seems more concerned that she had to shoot someone than she is about how badly she's hurt."

"I can relate to that," I said as my stomach twisted at the thought of the gangster I had shot just the day before.

Ashley reached over and touched my arm. "I'm sorry," she said.

We flew as fast as the aircraft would go. Lieutenant Dollison's phone rang. He answered it and listened for a moment. We all watched him anxiously. Finally he said, "So Overman is no longer a threat?" He listened again. "Good," he said a moment later. "Keep a close eye on him. We're hoping to catch JC Hass at the airport in Glenwood Springs. He thinks Overman is flying there to pick him up."

As soon as his call ended, he said, "Overman tried to shoot it out with the cops in Pueblo. He's on his way to the hospital. He got hit twice, but the cops are all okay. Let's hope that Hass doesn't try the same thing."

I called Hass's number a few minutes later. Fortunately he was still driving when he answered; I could still hear the wind coming through his windshield. I asked him how far from Glenwood Springs he was, and he told me he thought maybe fifteen minutes at the most. "Okay, you'll beat me there," I said in my Overman voice.

"Be ready to pick me up the moment you land," he said and ended the call with a chuckle. At least, it sounded like a chuckle.

Something didn't feel right. The chuckle didn't fit. I had a feeling Hass suspected it wasn't Overman he'd been talking to. I could only hope I was wrong. But to be on the safe side, we alerted other officers that he might not show up at the airport but to keep watching for him. Shortly after that, Ashley learned Denadene was being taken to a hospital in Glenwood Springs. She asked the officer she was talking with to make sure Denadene was protected and that JC Hass was not the only one who presented a danger to her. She described him, Dwight Hass, and Bronson Melville. Ashley was also informed that Jimmie, who had been shot by Denadene, was dead, as she had suspected.

When we arrived at the airport, as I feared, JC Hass was not there to meet us. An officer who was there told us a white car with a broken windshield had been abandoned in a grocery store parking lot nearby.

"He probably stole another car," Sergeant Hanks said. "He could be anywhere now."

Lieutenant Dollison walked a short distance from our plane as he made a call. When he rejoined us, he said, "I just talked to my contact in Pueblo. He said he has Overman's phone, and it's been ringing."

I nodded. "I guess Hass must have tried to call him, and when Overman didn't answer, decided he'd better not come here."

Ashley said, "If that's the case, he might have guessed Denadene is alive. We'd better get to the hospital, just in case."

Local officers gave us all rides to the hospital. Denadene was in surgery when we arrived there. There was no sign of Hass. But that didn't mean he wasn't lurking nearby, perhaps watching us and perhaps not alone. At least with Trey Overman out of commission we didn't have to worry about drones spying on us. But there was no way we could leave Denadene without protection.

After some discussion, it was determined that I would remain at the hospital in company with a couple of local officers and that Ashley would fly back with my lieutenant and sergeant. "We'll take her home," Lieutenant Dollison promised.

"And I'll check with you regularly," Ashley said. "Don't you dare get hurt."

CHAPTER TWENTY-THREE

DENADENE CAME OUT OF SURGERY, and I was able to see her late that Monday night. She was still groggy when I stepped into her hospital room. I left an officer outside the door to watch for any of her enemies. "How are you feeling?" I asked.

"I'm in a lot of pain, but I'll be okay," she said. "The doctor said the bullet didn't hit anything too important."

"It hit you, and you're important," I said.

"Thanks, Gage. I'm sorry I've been such a jerk to you, but I just think we aren't right for each other. But I'm glad you're here. Maybe together we can figure out how to lure JC to come see me," she said. "Then maybe you guys can catch him."

"You need to let us find and deal with Hass," I said sternly. "You had a close call this time. Next time it might not turn out so well. You just need to rest and get better, and then we need to hide you again."

"I wish it would have been him I shot instead of that other guy," she said with a sudden touch of bitterness. She looked up at me. "Do you think he knows I'm here?"

"We have to assume he does. We need to quietly move you to a different hospital."

"No, I won't do that. Let him come and find me. Then you and your colleagues can end this once and for all."

"Denadene, please, we can't take any chances. Let me make the arrangements."

It was to no avail. She had her mind made up, so there was nothing more to say except to promise we would do our best to catch Hass if he came to the hospital. No one saw him that night or the next day. But then

I got a very disturbing phone call from Detective Butler in Las Vegas. He said, "I thought Ashley Webler was going to be back before today."

I felt the bottom drop out of my stomach. "She returned the night before last," I managed to say past the bile rising in my throat. "She called me shortly after she got back to her apartment late Monday night."

"She didn't appear in court today. The judge wasn't happy."

"She went back when she did for that purpose," I said as my anxiety mounted. "Have you tried to call her?"

"Only about a hundred times," Butler said. "Now I'm really worried."

"Have you been by her apartment?" I asked. I was feeling panic set in.

"I have and she wasn't there, but I'm heading there again," he said.

"Thank you, Marcel," I said. "Please call me right back after you get there."

"Will do," he promised.

Fear shot through me like a speeding freight train through a tunnel. I didn't have to stretch much to imagine that the worst had happened to her. I prayed like I had seldom prayed before. I begged the Lord to take care of her. I had never been one to beg, but I did so now out of sheer desperation.

I was called over the hospital's speaker system and asked to report to Denadene's room immediately. I had spoken with her about an hour prior to let her know we hadn't seen anything of Hass at that point and to again offer to move her. Not surprisingly, she had stubbornly refused.

The panic from the news about Ashley hadn't abated and now I wondered what was wrong in Denadene's room. I hurried from the waiting area where I had been lounging and to her room. She was whiter than she'd been when I saw her just a short while before. "Denadene," I said in alarm. "What's the matter? Why didn't you just call me?"

"I needed to see you face-to-face. I need your help again. Please, don't be angry with me," she said.

"I'm not angry—just worried. What's the matter?" I repeated.

"It may be nothing, but I've been trying to call my parents for several hours now—I need to tell them what's happening to me and try to help them not worry—but they aren't answering my calls," she said.

First Ashley and now the Garfords were not answering their phones. I felt myself getting angry, the anger overriding my worry. "Have you tried all of their phones?" I asked.

"Yes, over and over again," she said. "Gage, JC wouldn't do something to them to get to me, would he?"

Of course he would, I thought. Instead I said, "I would hope not. I'll have a cop drive by the house right away."

"Please do," Denadene said. "I'm so scared for them."

"I'll be right back," I said as I started to work my phone and walk to the door. I didn't want to be with her when Detective Butler called me back. She had enough to worry about without me adding to it with letting her know about Ashley.

I called the police department in Cedar City and asked them to send an officer to the Garfords' house. I explained the urgency of the matter and asked for a call back the minute anyone knew anything.

I paced the hospital hallways while waiting for my calls. Detective Butler was the first to call me. "Ashley still isn't home, but I checked and found her car in her parking area. Her door is locked, and her curtains are closed."

"Considering all that's happening, maybe you'd better find a way to have a look inside," I said urgently.

"Tell me what's happening," he said. "I need to know to justify going in."

I gave him a quick summary of the latest developments. "See if you can get the apartment manager to let you in," I said after stunning him with the somber facts.

"I'll see what I can do and call you back," he promised.

I next got a call from an officer with the Cedar City Police, who informed me there was no answer at the Garford home and that their vehicles were there. They said the doors were locked and they couldn't see any movement inside through any of the windows.

I thanked him and returned to report to Denadene. As I walked her way, I called Sergeant Hanks and quickly brought him up to date before hanging up again. There was a doctor in Denadene's room, and I went to back out, but Denadene said, "Don't go, Gage. I was just talking to the doctor about whether or not I can be moved. He says I can be flown to a hospital in either Cedar City or St. George, but only if it's really important."

"It is important," I said to both of them as I wondered about her change of mind. "I sent an officer by your parents' house, and there's no one there. But their cars are."

I didn't think she could get any whiter, but she did. "He's got them, hasn't he?" she said. "JC is going to use them to get to me."

"I hope that's not true," I told her as my phone began to ring. Before I answered it, I asked the doctor to make arrangements to move Denadene as soon as possible and to let me know where she would be going so I could have security set up for her there upon her arrival.

I didn't recognize the number on my phone screen. "Hello?" I said.

I nearly passed out with relief when I heard Ashley's voice. She said, "I need help, Gage. I think I just killed a man."

"What?" I exclaimed. "Where are you?"

"I have no idea," she said. "But I don't think I'm too far from Las Vegas."

"Are you safe?" I asked with almost overwhelming relief.

"I don't know. I only ever saw this one guy, and I have his gun now. But I don't know what to do," she said. She sounded shaken, on the verge of panic.

"Did you shoot him?" I asked as my mind raced.

"No, he was the one with the gun," she said.

"So how did you kill him?" I asked. "And who is he?"

"I don't know who he is. I haven't touched him, except to check his pulse. I can't find one. I really think he's dead," she said, sounding rattled. "I took his cell phone from his shirt pocket to call you. The gun was lying on the floor where he dropped it when he fell."

"Ashley," I said, trying to gain her focus, "if he had the gun, how in the world did you—" I began.

"I hit him with my leg," she interrupted.

"You mean you kicked him?" I asked, baffled.

"No, he made me take off my prosthetic leg. After I got it off, he started to laugh at me and lowered his gun, so I just swung it at him with all the strength I had. It wasn't easy standing on one leg. But I guess I hit him too hard. Like I told you before, the leg is made of a titanium alloy."

"Good work, Ashley," I said stupidly. I didn't know what else to say, but I quickly found my words. "Okay, we need to get someone there right away."

"I don't know where I am," she protested.

"Are you in a building? Look outside. Maybe that'll give you a clue, but be cautious just in case he has helpers nearby."

"Okay," she said.

"Before you do that, check his pulse again."

"He's dead," she said a moment later. "He has no pulse and no breath."

"You're sure?" I asked. I didn't want her to be surprised if he wasn't really dead.

"I'm sure, and I have his pistol," She reminded me. A minute later she spoke again. "This is some kind of old cabin in the desert. I can't see any other houses or anything. The only thing I see is a car—the one he brought me here in, I suppose."

"Was it dark when he brought you?" I asked.

"It was for me. He blindfolded me before he forced me out of my apartment and into the car. He bound my hands and put me in the backseat. It was a miserable ride."

"That sounds awful. So you saw him but didn't recognize him?" I asked.

"That's right. I just know it's not JC Hass," she said.

I wasn't surprised. I had a feeling Hass was the one who had kidnapped Denadene's parents. But I didn't mention that to Ashley. "Okay, here's what we'll do," I said. "Hang up and call Detective Butler. Maybe he can figure out where you are from the phone's GPS, if it has it. If that doesn't work, maybe you can get the car keys from the dead guy and start the car. Maybe it has GPS," I suggested. "If nothing else works, you can drive away from there."

"Okay, but I already searched him, and I don't know where his keys are," she said.

"Maybe he left them in the car," I suggested.

"Yeah, maybe. We are alone out here in the desert, so it wouldn't be in danger of being stolen," she said.

"Okay, you check and see," I said. "But let's stay on the phone together."

"I wish you were here, Gage," she said soberly. "I miss you."

"I wish I was too, but this is the best we can do. At least we can hear each other's voices."

"I'm glad there's that. I feel better being able to talk to you," she said. "Okay, I'm outside now." I waited for a minute, and then she said, "You were right. He left the keys in the car."

"Okay, let's call Butler now," I said. "Instead of you calling, let me put you on hold and I'll call. If I lose you, I'll call you back."

"Okay," she said.

I put her on hold and dialed. "Detective Butler," he answered.

"It's Gage," I said. "I heard from your missing attorney."

"Where is she?" he asked quickly.

"Somewhere out in the desert at an old cabin. Her captor is dead. She has no idea who he is," I said.

"How did he die?" Butler asked.

"She hit him in the head with her titanium leg," I said.

"What titanium leg?" he asked.

"The one she uses to walk with," I said.

It was silent for a moment, and then Butler said, "Okay, you guys can explain that later. How are we going to locate her?"

"Okay, let me get back to her. I think I'll have her call you from the dead guy's phone. That way you can trace it. If not, she has the keys to his car," I said.

"Good. Then she can drive out of there if she has to."

"Let me take her off hold and have her call you," I said.

"Okay," he said.

"Are you there, Ashley?" I asked a few seconds later.

"Yes, but I'm standing outside in the heat. I don't want to be inside with that guy."

"Okay, I spoke with Detective Butler. Go ahead and give him a call. Let me give you his number." I read it off to her.

"Got it," she said.

"I need to make some more calls, but I'll be waiting for you to call me back. Are you sure you are safe?"

"I'm safe—just missing you terribly," she said with a catch in her voice. "But I'll call you soon." The call ended and left me with a feeling of loss. I was relieved Ashley was okay, but I was still worried about her.

I went back to Denadene's room. The medical staff was already preparing to move her to St. George. I was glad she'd chosen that location; it would be easier for me to provide security for her there. "This is going to be expensive," she said, "but the doctor spoke with my insurance company and convinced them this was best for my health and well-being, and they agreed to cover it."

"That's good. How soon will they be moving you?" I asked.

"About an hour," she said. "I asked, and they said you could ride with us as security."

"That's great. That way I can get protection for you set up right away in St. George. You're an intelligent woman, Denadene."

"Not very," she said, "or I would've quit working for JC Hass a long time ago."

"You couldn't have known what he would do," I said. "I'll stay close until they're ready to take you to the plane, and I'll ask the officers providing security for you here to take us."

She agreed to that. My phone rang, so I again stepped out to the hallway. I was relieved to again hear Ashley's voice. "Hi, Gage," she said. "I guess I'll have to drive out of here. This phone doesn't have GPS, and neither does the car. Detective Butler is notifying several cops who are within an hour of Vegas in one direction or another. I know it wasn't longer than that from the time he abducted me until we reached this place during the night."

"Okay, then get moving," I said as my phone again began to ring. "I have another call coming in. Give me a few minutes, and then I'll call you back."

"Okay, I will. I miss you, Gage," she said again.

"I miss you too. I'd better take this call. Talk to you soon."

I answered the other call. "Detective Tipton. Have I got a deal for you," Hass said in a mocking tone. He laughed. "I have your lovely attorney and Ms. Stegner's parents. I want to propose a trade."

CHAPTER TWENTY-FOUR

So HE DIDN'T YET KNOW Ashley had overpowered whichever of his cohorts had abducted her—that was to my advantage—but he apparently did have the Garfords, and that was a serious problem. "What kind of trade do you propose?" I asked.

"I'll trade Miss Webler for you and Denadene for her parents. That sounds pretty generous, don't you think?" It sounded anything but that to me, but I didn't want to prod him right then. Ashley was almost safe, but the Garfords were not, so I said nothing. I just waited for him to go on. "Yeah," he finally said. "I have you over a barrel now, you jerk." All the humor was gone from his evil voice. "You'll do exactly as I say, or I will summarily execute the three of them and then come after you and Denadene. Either way, you lose. But this way, at least you can save the lives of Miss Webler and the Garfords."

He stopped talking. I supposed he wanted a response from me, so he got one. "I have a counterproposal," I said. "I'll turn myself over to you, but you have to release all three of them and leave Denadene out of it from this point on. You already injured her, and there's no way she can leave the hospital for days, if not weeks. So let's do it. It'll be just me for the three of them."

"That's no good, Tipton," Hass snarled. "She'll come with me. I don't care how badly she's hurt. She hurt me too, you know."

"How did she hurt you?" I asked, trying to remain calm.

"She refused my affection," he said. "I would have made her happy."

I wanted to say something about how he apparently had not made his previous wives happy, but I refrained.

He went on. "Here's what you are to do. Have them put Denadene in an ambulance. You drive it. I'll let you know where to meet me."

"Hang on a minute, Hass," I said. "I haven't agreed to the trade, and anyway, unless you have the other three where my colleagues can collect them at the same time you take me and Denadene, I definitely won't agree."

"Tipton, I am holding all the cards. You'll do it my way, or the three of them die."

Fortunately, he wasn't holding all the cards, but he was holding enough of them to make him dangerous. "Let me talk to Denadene first," I said.

"No, I need to talk to her. Give me her number."

"No. She can call you if she wants to, but you're wasting your time. She'll never agree to your deal," I said. That, I was afraid, was not true. I feared she would want to try to trade herself for her parents. I couldn't let that happen.

For a moment Hass didn't respond. Then he finally said, "Okay, have her call me, but she has only ten minutes. If she doesn't call me by then, I'll call you back, and people will start to die."

"People have already died, thanks to you and your friends," I reminded him angrily. "Just call this deal off. You release your captives, and I'll give you twenty-four hours to get lost before I start looking for you. That'll give you time to get away. There's a deal you can't pass up."

He didn't even respond to that. "Have her call. Ten minutes. I mean it, Tipton. I'm calling the shots here, not you," he snarled and hung up.

I slowly walked back to Denadene's room. "What's happened now?" she asked from her bed. "It's something bad; I can tell by your face."

"Hass wants you to call him. I have the number. He says he wants to make a deal. If you don't call him within ten minutes, he says people will start to die," I said glumly. I gave her a quick rundown of what Hass was proposing. "We'll think of something."

Then she said, "They have Ashley too? I'm so sorry. I have a feeling the two of you have a future."

"Maybe," I said. "Now, make the call. The ten minutes he gave us are almost up."

Denadene put her phone on speaker and had me dial the number. It rang only once. "That had better be you, Denadene," Hass said.

"It's me. Gage said you want to make a deal. What is it?" she asked. "I just want my parents and my friend back."

"They'll live—if you and Gage turn yourselves over to me," he said.

"So you can kill us?" she asked bitterly.

"That remains to be seen," he said. "You know I love you, Denadene. You spurned me, but if you were to change your mind, you and I could leave the country together and make a wonderful life for ourselves somewhere else."

"I'd rather be dead," she said, and there was no doubt in my mind she meant it. "And what about Gage?"

"We'll see. Maybe I can find a use for him, if he cooperates."

"Sure you will, Hass," I broke in. "Tell Denadene your proposal, and we'll go with whatever she decides. But like I said earlier: the exchange has to be simultaneous."

"We'll see about that," he said. "So, my dear, here's what I propose."

I could see that Denadene was nearly gagging, but she forged gamely ahead. "What?" she said.

He then proceeded to tell her what he'd told me earlier and what I had already quickly discussed with Denadene. After he had finished, she said, "I'm really sick, thanks to you."

"One of my friends, an old client, is dead because of you," he retorted.

"I'm badly injured. I can't leave the hospital unless it's in an ambulance."

"And that's what I expect. You'll be on a stretcher in the back, and Tipton will be driving. We'll meet tonight at midnight. I'll call Tipton back with the details in an hour or two. I have to have time to get your parents in place."

"And Ashley Webler," Denadene reminded him.

"Once I have Tipton, she'll be released. That's the best I can do. I'll have your parents where you can see them, and as soon as Tipton steps out of the ambulance, unarmed and with his hands in the air, I'll check to make sure it's you on the stretcher, and then your parents will walk away, and my guys will take Tipton and disappear. I'll drive you to a safe place where I can take care of you. That's the deal. Midnight. I'll call with the location. And Tipton, since you're listening, let me make it clear that if you try anything, if you have any other cops around or if you try to pull a gun, you die and so do the Garfords and Miss Webler." With that, the call was terminated. That was fine by me. I didn't have anything else to say to him.

I sat down beside Denadene's bed and put my head in my hands for a moment. Finally, I looked up and said, "I need to find someone to ride in the ambulance."

"You already have someone. It'll be me," she said.

"You know I can't risk that," I told her.

"You have no choice, Gage, but I'll have a little surprise for him."

"What's that?" I asked.

She told me, and I said, "I don't know about that."

"That's how it's going down," she said stubbornly. "Now, I need the doctor in here. Our trip to St. George is off, and we have to convince him to let us take an ambulance. Maybe we can tell him I need to go to a hospital close to here before I make the trip to St. George."

"He won't believe us," I said.

"Then we'll tell them why we really need it. They need to know that lives depend on us doing this," Denadene said bravely.

"Okay, we can give it a try," I agreed reluctantly. Putting Denadene in danger, on the front lines as it were, did not appeal to me, but she was headstrong and determined. I grudgingly admired her for that.

My phone rang. "Ashley, are you safe?" I asked.

"I am," she said. "I'm with Detective Butler. And we know the identity of the man I killed."

Denadene's eyes were like saucers. "That's Ashley?" she asked with disbelief on her pain-filled face.

"She escaped," I said. Then, to Ashley, I asked, "Who was it?"

"You won't have to prosecute Bronson Melville," she said with a touch of emotion in her voice.

"Melville! You killed Bronson Melville with your prosthetic leg?" I said as calmly as I could.

"I guess I did," she said. "I had no choice. Now I know how you felt after what happened yesterday morning in front of the church. It's a horrible feeling, but at least I'm alive."

We talked for another couple of minutes, and then I said, "Listen, Hass called me. He says he'll trade you and Denadene's parents for me and Denadene."

"But he doesn't have me," she protested.

"He doesn't know that yet," I said.

"Gage, that's nuts. You can't agree to that," she wailed. "There's got to be another way to get the Garfords back."

"I can't think of one. I don't think we have a choice, but we do have a plan. Hass is going to lose again. Trust me."

"I guess I have no choice either," she said. "Take care of yourself though."

Ashley and I said goodbye, and Denadene smiled—the first one I'd seen on her face in a long time. "I saw your face when you were talking to Ashley. I think you and she are going to end up together."

"Time will tell," I said. "We hardly know each other. Now, let's get that doctor in here."

Before we did, Denadene's phone rang. She looked at the screen and frowned. "I don't want to talk to him right now," she said and let her phone keep ringing.

"Who is it?" I asked.

"One of the other guys I was dating when you and I started going out," she said with a sheepish grin.

"Why aren't you answering?" I asked.

She went red. "I don't want to talk about it anymore."

"I get the feeling you like this guy."

"I do, but I also like you."

"Come on; you know what I mean," I said, smiling at her.

"Okay, fine. The past few days he's been on my mind a lot. He and I have a lot in common, but I don't want to worry him right now. He doesn't know what's going on. He doesn't even know I've been shot."

"Denadene," I said sternly. "Listen to me, please. I didn't know what was going on when you'd been abducted. I wish I'd known sooner. And I have a feeling this guy, whatever his name is, would feel the same."

Her eyes became moist. "His name is Isaac Sparks," she said. "I guess you're right. I'll call him back while you go find my doctor, but I won't tell him what we plan to do. That would really freak him out."

"I understand," I said. "Tell him I said hi."

"You know Isaac?" she asked with a look of surprise on her face.

"I've met him," I said. "When you first went missing, I talked to a lot of people. Someone steered me to him. I didn't get the feeling he liked me very much, but I know he would have liked to help if he'd had any idea what might have happened to you."

"He's jealous of you, Gage. But he doesn't need to be. He's a good guy. Go. Find the doctor," she said. "I'll call Isaac if you think I should."

Thirty minutes later the doctor and a couple of other medical personnel were in the room with Denadene and me. We were waiting for the Glenwood Springs chief of police to join us. I had talked to him on the phone to briefly explain what was going on, and he'd immediately offered help and support. He suggested we use one of his female officers to take Denadene's place. I wished Denadene would allow that, but I didn't think that would happen. I figured we'd see what happened when they met.

Denadene was adamant. No one was happy about the plan, but no one could come up with a better way to secure the release of Denadene's parents. The police chief assured us he would have people nearby but well-hidden and offered to put a tracking device on the ambulance. After further discussion, we decided to attach one to Denadene as well. The doctor insisted they also have medical personnel with the police. Once the treacherous plan was as firm as we could make it, we had but to await for the appointed hour.

Time dragged interminably. I was sitting with some local officers in a waiting area of the hospital. To say I was not a nervous wreck would be untrue. I wasn't nervous for me; I was nervous for Denadene and her parents. Denadene's role was key to the success of the operation. She was putting herself in a dangerous position, but she wouldn't back down, despite the pain she was in and the arguments that were strenuously made by me and the police chief. Denadene blamed herself for much of the trouble that had occurred and said she could never live with herself if she let something happen to her parents that she could possibly help prevent. She also argued that Hass was a shrewd man and might find out a way to be sure she was in the ambulance; if he wasn't convinced, her parents would die.

I was also nervous because I hadn't heard back from Hass yet, and it was well beyond the hour or two in which he'd promised to contact me with a location for the trade. Of course, a lie from Hass shouldn't surprise me. But it was getting late, and I began to wonder if he'd changed his mind. At eleven thirty, he finally called. I had barely answered the phone when, to my amazement, Ashley walked into the waiting area, limping but with a smile that lit up the room.

I returned her smile and pointed with my free hand to my phone. She nodded and stepped close to me, giving me a kiss on the cheek. I said, "Hello, Hass," and Ashley's eyes grew wide. She sat beside me and leaned close to my head so she could hear what he was saying. He was short, terse, and to the point. He gave me a location and then said, "Be there in thirty minutes. You'll leave the ambulance and walk away. I'll drive it away from the meeting point. Denadene's parents will be sitting in an old Ford Bronco. They'll be secured, so getting them free will be your problem. The keys will be in the ignition, but don't even think about driving away until I call you and tell you to go. You will be watched. And if you don't do exactly as I say, the couple will die." What he didn't say but I was sure he was thinking was that I would die regardless of what happened with the exchange.

Before I could say a word, he ended the call. We sprang into action. After trying once more and failing to persuade Denadene to allow the female officer to take her place, we began gently slipping her into the ambulance. Ashley wanted to come with us, but I explained there was no way she could. Within five minutes of Hass's call, we were rolling out of the hospital parking area. I drove the ambulance to the location Hass had mentioned. It was out of town a ways, on a mountainous road. I wasn't surprised, as I hadn't expected him to name a location that would be populated with cars. The twisty road was in a heavily wooded area.

Our backup had to stay much farther back than I had hoped, but I knew that if Hass or anyone assisting him spotted any of them, disaster would strike. They all knew that too, and I had made sure they understood the danger of not following Hass's orders. My phone rang again, and Hass said, "Pull off the road just a few feet past where you are. You'll be able to see the old brown Bronco about twenty-five yards to your left."

I did as instructed, and then he said, "Stop right there."

It was dark, but I could see the interior light of the Bronco. There were two people sitting close together in the back seat. I could only pray they were the Garfords.

"Leave the ambulance running," Hass said. "Put your hands on the steering wheel, and there'd better not be anything in them but your cell phone."

I did as instructed. My phone was on speaker. The window from the driving area of the ambulance to the patient area in the back was open so that Denadene could hear my phone.

"Good. Now, remember, no weapons. If I see you go for a gun, my men will shoot you. Got that?"

"Got it," I said.

"Is Denadene in the back?"

"Of course she is."

"If it's not her when I open the door, whoever it is will die instantly."

"It's her," I said, wishing it wasn't.

"It better be. But just to be sure, since I'm sure she's listening, tell her to say her name. I know her voice."

"Denadene Stegner," she said, but it was very weak.

"I can barely hear her," he growled.

"If you remember, she's been shot," I said angrily. "She's dying, Hass. She can barely respond."

"I need to know it's her. Denadene, what color folders do I file cases for my theft clients in?"

Denadene said, "Purple."

"In case you couldn't hear her, she said they're purple," I said as I realized Denadene had been right. Hass was shrewd—that was a question an impersonating officer could never have answered.

"Very good. Now, Tipton, you keep your hands above your head and step out of the ambulance and walk away from it," he ordered. "One wrong move, and you're a dead man."

CHAPTER TWENTY-FIVE

My heart was in my throat as I stepped out, leaving Denadene alone on the stretcher in the back of the ambulance. I could only pray everything would go as we had planned, but in order for that to happen, Hass had to do what I had anticipated he might.

He continued to speak to me on the phone. "Keep walking, but don't go near the old Bronco," he said.

I did as he instructed. I neared the trees at the side of the turnout, and someone stepped into view. It was dark, and there was no way I could tell who it was. I assumed it was JC. I assumed wrong.

"Keep your hands up," the familiar voice of Dwight Hass said.

I could see in the dim light that he was holding a pistol and it was pointed at me. "Where's Ashley?" I asked.

"Probably dead by now," Dwight said with a laugh.

"She'd better not be," I growled. My performance had to be believable.

"Or what?" Dwight sneered. Then, in a louder voice, he called out, "I got the cop covered, JC. Go ahead and get in the ambulance."

"I just want to look in the back first," JC said, making my stomach twist.

"Are you going to ride in the ambulance too?" I asked Dwight.

He laughed again. "I'll be driving the Bronco," he said. "And you'll be staying here. Oh, and I'll be taking your phone with me. You won't be needing it. Drop it on the ground at your feet." I did as instructed, hoping I didn't damage it.

"But the Garfords," I said as I realized what I had already suspected was true—that the Hass brothers had no intention of letting me leave here alive. I could only pray the body armor I was wearing would protect me.

"Yeah, too bad about them, huh? They'll be going with me."

"JC and I had a deal," I said.

"Yeah, but the deal just changed, you fool," he said, and a shot rang out.

Dwight instinctively turned toward the ambulance, where the shot had come from. When he did, I dropped to my knees and pulled a pistol from my boot. Dwight turned back toward me, and when he did, I fired. It was too dark to be terribly accurate, but I knew I'd hit him because he fell like a rock. I wanted to run to the back of the ambulance, but I didn't dare turn my back on Dwight, even though I knew I'd hit him. So I ran toward him, my pistol aimed at his dark bulk on the ground. I heard a groan from him, and then his hand came up.

I leaped to the side as he fired, and then I returned fire. Even as dark as it was, my aim was good at such a short range. I knelt beside him but kept an eye out toward the ambulance where the first shot had occurred. Dwight was still breathing, but he didn't seem to be a threat to me at that point. I picked up his gun and stuffed it into my waistband, and then I headed quickly for the ambulance, my pistol held out in front of me.

I hadn't yet reached the ambulance when I heard sirens and could see red and blue lights flashing through the trees. I stepped to the back of the ambulance and said, "Denadene? Are you okay?"

She groaned. "I think so, but what about my parents?" she said in a weak voice as I spotted someone on the ground just a few feet from the back of the ambulance.

The door was hanging open. There was movement on the ground, but light from the inside of the ambulance gave me enough visibility to see a gun slowly being raised by JC, who was flat on his back. I was close enough I didn't have to fire again. I simply kicked the gun from his hand. Then I knelt beside him and said, "That was a stupid move, JC."

"I'll kill you for this," he said.

"You'll have to survive first," I told him coldly as an officer stepped up beside me.

"You can have him for now," I said. "I need to check on the patient and find the hostages."

A nurse who had accompanied the officer beat me to Denadene, so I stood back, and as the second police car arrived, I waved at the officer in the car and directed him to follow me. A woman got out with him, and they followed me toward where I had left Dwight. "Is he alive?" a voice I was beginning to adore asked.

I turned toward her. "What are you doing here, Ashley?" I asked.

She stepped close to me, and I could see her face faintly from the light of the officer's flashlight. "I hitched a ride," she said.

I breathed deeply. "I'm glad you're here," I said. I pointed to where more officers were running toward us. "Let's let these officers take care of Dwight. We need to see if Denadene's parents are in the vehicle over there and find out if they're okay."

Ashley activated the light on her phone, and together we approached the old Bronco.

The Garfords were in the back seat, tightly bound and gagged. We quickly freed them, and a couple of officers soon joined us. Denadene's father asked with a raspy voice, "Where is Denadene? Is she okay?"

"She's in the ambulance. She says she's all right," I told him. "Why don't we go over there and make sure."

I spoke briefly with the nurse, who asked me to drive the ambulance back to the hospital, as Denadene needed to get back there quickly. I explained it to one of the officers, who okayed me to leave but asked me to return as soon as I could.

Denadene's parents had crowded into the ambulance with their daughter. The nurse gave them just a moment with her before she asked them to step out. "I'll see that you get to the hospital in a little while," I said.

Just then I heard Hass say weakly, "Your girlfriend is a dead woman."

Ashley stepped back to where he was—he was surrounded by officers—and said, "If you're talking about me, I'm just fine. But I'm afraid your client Bronson Melville is not."

She turned and hurried back to where I was still standing at the back of the ambulance. JC muttered something, but I couldn't tell what he said. As I turned to go to the front of the ambulance, an officer asked me who had shot JC. "I did," the weak voice of Denadene came from inside the ambulance. "That's JC Hass. He pointed a gun at me. I was ready for him, so I fired. He stumbled back and fell."

The officer asked for her gun, which she gave to him. Then I said, "I shot the other guy," before the question was asked. "He tried to shoot me but missed. I'll be back shortly to give a full report."

"I'm going with you," Ashley said as the nurse shut the back door to the ambulance and sat down next to Denadene.

"Then let's go," I said, and I helped Ashley into the passenger side before hurrying back to the other side. Before I climbed in, I said to the officer, "I'll have Miss Webler call my cell phone. It's somewhere over there." I pointed. "When you hear it ringing, will you get it so I can get it from you when I get back?" He nodded. To Denadene's parents, I said, "These officers will take care of you. I need to get your daughter back to get the treatment she needs."

When we arrived at the hospital, there were a number of people waiting near the emergency room entrance. Hospital personnel quickly but gently removed Denadene from the ambulance and headed for the door. I saw Isaac Sparks walking beside the stretcher and speaking to Denadene. The crew moving the stretcher suddenly stopped, and I heard Denadene call out, "Gage, can you come here for a moment?"

Ashley and I looked at each other. "You come too," I said softly to her.

We hurried because I knew this had been an extraordinarily tough experience for Denadene and she needed medical attention. As I stepped beside the stretcher, she looked up at me and said, "Thanks, Gage. I guess you already know Isaac. He flew all the way from St. George to be with me." She smiled at Isaac and then spoke again. "Isaac, you know Gage, and this is our mutual friend Ashley Webler. She flew up from Las Vegas." And with that, the medical attendants moved the gurney forward, and Ashley and I stepped back.

***

I was seated behind my desk two days later working on my backlog of reports when I was summoned to the police chief's office. I had reported everything that had occurred to my sergeant, lieutenant, and captain, but I had not spoken to the chief since my return, as he had been in Salt Lake at police chief meetings. I spent an hour with him before returning to my desk. He had been very complimentary of the work I had done but reminded me that even though Bronson Melville was dead and that case closed, I still needed to wrap up the matters of the deaths of Randall Stegner and Brea Burr.

He realized those cases would fall under other jurisdictions but reminded me that I was central to the successful prosecution of the guilty parties. I returned to my desk, thinking about what I had learned from Dwight Hass. JC had attempted to put the blame on him for most of the crimes that had occurred, and Dwight had reacted. He was angry at his critically injured brother over that, and he, in turn, opened the floodgates to Sergeant Hanks and me. I recalled his words during the interview as he'd said, "I did all this for my brother. It was his idea. It's always been his way or no way."

When I had asked him what he meant by *all this*, he had replied, "JC ordered Alvin and me to break Bronson out of jail. He was being paid by Bronson's family since they realized he'd probably be convicted."

I had then asked, "What about the deaths of Randall and Miss Burr? I already know you and Alvin have considerable diving experience, but tell me exactly who did what in relation to their deaths." I had been bluffing. I'd assumed they had both dived and that they were the ones responsible for the two murdered bodies in the sunken boat.

"Of course we are divers," he admitted. "Alvin killed Brea because he said Bronson and JC told him to. It was Alvin's idea to put her body in that old sunken houseboat. I didn't help with that," he'd said. "I mean, you know, I didn't dive with Randall and Alvin that day. They were the ones who took her body down and hid it."

"But Randall didn't come up," I'd reminded him as I thought about the statement of the witness who had watched them through a spotting scope. The witness had said two people had gone down and one had come back up.

"That's because JC and Bronson wanted him dead. He had been blackmailed into doing what they asked. They threatened to destroy his little sister if he didn't do what they told him to do. The dummy finally said he couldn't do it anymore. He agreed to bury the woman's body in the water but that after that he was through and wouldn't do anything else for them," Dwight had explained.

"How was Randall killed, and who did it?" I had asked.

"It wasn't me," he'd said quickly. "It was Alvin. He did something to stop his airflow. He probably cut his line. Anyway, that was how he killed him. That's all I know."

I hadn't for one minute believed that. I'd said, "Dwight, someone placed a bomb with the bodies and attached the line to the triggering device."

"That was Alvin. He and Randall took it down with them when they took the girl's body down," he'd said. "It wasn't me."

We had asked Dwight more questions, but he'd never once admitted he was involved in any murders. According to him, it was all the other men's faults.

I looked over at my computer screen. I had already typed all of that up. When our investigation was through, prosecutors in St. George, at Lake Powell, and in Colorado would have to decide what charges to bring against the Hass brothers and their pilot friend, Trey Overman. One thing I was quite certain of was that all three of them were looking at many long years behind bars—very possibly the rest of their miserable lives. They had earned it.

I hoped and prayed Denadene would heal from the terrible things she had gone through because of those selfish and evil men.

As for me, I was planning to get to know Ashley Webler a whole lot better.

EPILOGUE

Six months later

IT WAS NICE TO HAVE a day off. My new wife, Ashley, was busy in her St. George law office but had agreed to go to lunch with me. The upcoming Friday and Saturday, we planned to do some relaxing diving at Lake Powell, far from the sunken houseboat.

I walked into her office. Her legal secretary, Denadene Sparks, smiled at me and said, "Why, hello, Detective Tipton. What brings you in today?"

"I have a lunch date with my wife," I said. "She's working too much. You need to see what you can do about easing her caseload a little."

Denadene chuckled. "As if I have anything to say about that. She is a hard worker. Anyway, it's your and your colleagues' faults. If you wouldn't arrest so many people, she wouldn't be so busy."

"I guess you got me there," I agreed.

Just then Ashley came out. As always when I saw her, she almost took my breath away. I couldn't believe she had agreed to marry me. She was way too good for me. She walked up to me and kissed me lightly before turning to Denadene. "I think I'll take the rest of the day off. You can do the same, if you'd like."

"That would be great," Denadene said. "Isaac and I want to look for some furniture. This would be a good chance to do that. But remember, Mr. Kilpatrick may want to talk to you about the Anders case that's set for a hearing on Monday."

"If he needs me, he has my cell number," Ashley said as I steered her to the door.

"What if you need me?" Denadene asked.

"If I do, I'll call you." A shiver ran up my spine as she said those haunting words. I just hoped eventually the phrase would cease to bother me. It didn't seem to bother Denadene or Ashley at all.

I opened the door for Ashley, waved back at Denadene, and stepped out into the reasonably comfortable early-December air.

ABOUT THE AUTHOR

CLAIR M. POULSON WAS BORN and raised in Duchesne, Utah. His father was a rancher and farmer, his mother, a librarian. Clair has always been an avid reader, having found his love for books as a very young boy.

He has served for more than forty-five years in the criminal justice system. He spent twenty years in law enforcement, ending his police career with eight years as the Duchesne County Sheriff. For the past twenty-plus years, Clair has worked as a justice court judge for Duchesne County. He is also a veteran of the U.S. Army, where he was a military policeman. In law enforcement, he has been personally involved in the investigation of murders and other violent crimes. Clair has also served on various boards and councils during his professional career, including the Justice Court Board of Judges, the Utah Commission on Criminal and Juvenile Justice, the Utah Judicial Council, the Utah Peace Officer Standards and Training Council, an FBI advisory board, and others.

In addition to his criminal justice work, Clair has farmed and ranched all his life. He has raised many kinds of animals, but his greatest interests are horses and cattle. He's also involved in the grocery store business with his oldest son and other family members.

Clair has served in many capacities in The Church of Jesus Christ of Latter-day Saints, including full-time missionary (California Mission), bishop, counselor to two bishops, Young Men president, high councilor, stake mission president, Scoutmaster, high priest group leader, and Gospel Doctrine teacher. He currently serves as a ward missionary.

Clair is married to Ruth, and they have five children, all of whom are married: Alan (Vicena) Poulson, Kelly Ann (Wade) Hatch, Amanda (Ben) Semadeni, Wade (Brooke) Poulson, and Mary (Tyler) Hicken.

They also have twenty-five wonderful grandchildren and a great-granddaughter.

Clair and Ruth met while both were students at Snow College and were married in the Manti Utah Temple.

Clair has always loved telling his children, and later his grandchildren, made-up stories. His vast experience in life and his love of literature have contributed to both his telling stories to his children and his writing of adventure and suspense novels.

Clair has published more than thirty novels. He would love to hear from his fans, who can contact him by going to his website, clairmpoulson.com.

Enjoy this sneak peek of Gregg Luke's April 2019 release,

PLAGUE

Portland, Oregon

MITCH PINE DREADED THE AMOUNT of death that was coming. He hated death. He'd seen too much of it.

Standing in front of a rain-spattered glass wall at Portland International Airport, Mitch stared out at the large jet preparing for its morning flight to Denver, where he had a brief layover on his way to his final destination: Atlanta. In his briefcase was a thick report he'd been working on for the past ten years, along with his laptop and two cross-sections of ancient wood supporting his theory. The chiefs of epidemiology at the Centers for Disease Control needed to see his report. The world needed to know what was coming.

"Dr. Pine?"

Mitch turned quickly to see a United Airlines attendant smiling prettily at him. "Yes?"

"May I see your boarding pass, please?"

"Is there a problem?" he asked, handing the woman his ticket. He noticed her eyes flick to the short chain securing his briefcase to his left wrist. Reaching into the side pocket of his cargo pants, he pulled out the security clearance that allowed him to carry such an item. "Do you need to see this too?"

"No, sir. I'm merely exchanging your ticket. You've been upgraded to first class."

Mitch frowned, not upset, just confused. "Why?"

"You don't have to accept, but doing so will open a seat to someone on standby. This is a full flight, and we have at least a dozen passengers needing to get to Denver."

"Do I have to pay for the upgrade?"

"No, sir."

Mitch glanced around, half expecting to see a dozen men in black suits and dark glasses striving to look inconspicuous. But he saw no one fitting that description, nor anyone he deemed unjustifiably questionable.

"Um, okay, I guess. What do I need to do?"

"Nothing, sir. It's all taken care of," she said, handing him a new boarding pass. "Did you check any baggage?"

"No. I just have my briefcase and this overnight bag," he said, nodding at the carry-on at his feet.

"Fine. If you'll come with me, please, we're boarding first-class passengers now."

Walking through the jet bridge to the plane, Mitch scrutinized the people in front and behind him. He saw nothing dubious about any of them. No one exchanged more than a cursory glance with him. Few smiled.

He shook his head shortly, chastising himself for being so paranoid. Yes, something terrifying was coming. Yes, it was probably something many people would pay big money to know about in advance. But that didn't matter to Mitch. He wasn't doing this for the money. Besides, once this information was made public, everyone would have a chance to prepare.

Stowing his carry-on overhead, Mitch dropped into the wide seat next to the window and settled his briefcase on his lap. He'd never flown first class before. The seat was amazingly comfortable and provided plenty of legroom. Watching the other passengers file by, he smiled at the backward logic airlines used when loading a plane. First-class travelers were always allowed to board first and were always seated at the front of the plane. The remaining travelers were then forced to shuffle single-file past those who'd been treated preferentially, like peasants obliged to parade past the condescending appraisal of their nobility. But Mitch didn't consider himself particularly noble. What he was doing now was what anyone with a moral compass would do. Ignoring the slow-moving stream of passengers, he pulled out his phone and switched it to airplane mode.

"Good afternoon," a very attractive woman said as she loaded a bag into the overhead compartment and eased into the seat next to Mitch.

"Hi," he answered with a grin.

The woman looked to be roughly his own age, in her late twenties, and moved with the confidence of a seasoned traveler. She had a wide mouth that framed a brilliant smile. Her eyes were deeply brown, almost black, as was her hair; her skin was bronzed and flawless. She wore a trim blazer over a light silk blouse tucked into a short pencil skirt that showed off an acceptable amount of toned leg without being risky. Mitch guessed her profession to be a business exec or a high-end sales rep. She radiated that kind of assuredness.

"Got business in Denver or family?" Mitch asked, trying to sound laid back. In truth, attractive women unsettled him.

"Business," she said, buckling herself in. "You?"

"Just a layover. Heading to Atlanta."

She smiled kindly. "Well, it's two-and-a-half hours from Portland to Denver. We might as well exchange names. I'm Kiana."

"Mitch. Mitch Pine—*Doctor* Mitch Pine," he stumbled.

"Doctor? You must be pretty smart, then," she said with seemingly honest appraisal.

"I know many who would argue with that," he said, feeling his face redden. "Kiana—Is that Polynesian?"

"Hawaiian, yes. On my mom's side."

"You have the look."

"So I've been told."

As Mitch struggled to come up with a topic of conversation, Kiana pulled from her purse an iPhone and earbuds. She tucked her purse under the seat in front of her before fitting the buds into place and selecting something on her phone. Leaning her head against the back of her seat, she folded her hands in her lap and closed her eyes.

Mitch sighed in defeat and gazed out his window at the light drizzle. Struck out again.

"Sir? Can I offer you a headset?"

From the aisle, a flight attendant held out a clear plastic parcel. Inside was a set of Bose headphones. "There's a selection of music choices listed on the information pamphlet in the pouch in front of you. Just plug these into the armrest."

"Thanks," he said, accepting the gratuity. He chose some classical music, wishing he'd brought his own MP3 player or, like Kiana, had some music on his phone. Classical was the closest thing to his collection of Zen music he always listened to on flights to help him relax. The takeoffs and landings set his nerves on edge.

A long taxi, an even longer wait in line, and a shuddering takeoff preceded a mercifully smooth flight. After accepting a soft drink, Mitch settled back into the comfortable seat. He had not planned on falling asleep, but sometime later the static *pop* of his headphones being unplugged jarred him awake. With a gentle smile, Kiana held up the end of the plug and her iPhone, as if explaining to Mitch what she was doing. She plugged the headset into her phone and pressed the screen.

"Hello, Dr. Pine," a man with an English accent said through the headphones. The strained, wheezing tone in his voice intimated an advanced age. "My name is Edgar Montrose. I will dispense with formalities and get straight to the point. Simply put, I am greatly intrigued by your research conclusions, but I cannot allow them to go public."

Mitch frowned at Kiana. Her kind smile never faltered. Her liquid-brown eyes penetrated his with a look of simultaneous challenge and finality. *Resolute* was the word that came to mind. She turned the volume up a notch.

"To that end, and to show you the magnitude of my convictions, your assistant has something to say." Mitch heard the brief rattle of a microphone being adjusted. "Ms. Nakamura, please tell Dr. Pine what is happening here."

Mitch's frown deepened. He heard a sharp intake of breath.

"Mitch. It's Suko."

His mouth dropped open. It *was* her. He'd recognize her voice anywhere.

"I don't know who these *baka* are, but don't do anything they ask—" Her words cut short as something covered her mouth. He heard sounds of a struggle, some garbled expletives, and a squeaking door.

The old man cleared his throat and continued. "As you can tell, your research assistant is being less than cooperative. What you need to understand is that I have her in a secure location and will not hesitate to do her harm if you do not do precisely as I say."

Kiana tipped her head slightly to one side and continued to smile. She couldn't hear what was being said, but she clearly knew.

"I am sending you on a quest. If you refuse, Ms. Nakamura will suffer. Why I am doing this will be revealed at a later time. For now, here are your instructions: You will accompany Ms. Rosemont on a connecting flight in Denver. Your passage has been prearranged. It is imperative that you not make mention of this recording or my demands to anyone. The moment you suggest to anyone that you're under duress, Ms. Rosemont will transmit a signal, and Ms. Nakamura will die. It's that simple. Do not test me on this, Dr. Pine, as I am deadly serious. As deadly as the information you now carry. Goodbye."

The recording ended and Mitch shakily removed the headphones. "What the heck was that about? What's going on here?" His voice trembled, but he didn't care. It was as if his worst nightmares had come true.

"The recording was quite explicit," Kiana said, unplugging her phone and flipping through the menu. "Just remain calm and do as I say, and everything will be fine."

"Remain calm? You throw down death threats on my assistant, tell me to not publish my research, and then order me to remain calm?" He gasped loudly, struggling to control his breathing.

She tipped her head back and laughed as if Mitch had just said something delightfully funny. In a softer voice she said, "Yes. That is exactly what we ask. And please, keep your voice down. I will not hesitate to send the signal if I feel we are compromised."

"Look. You've got the wrong guy," he balked. "I don't even know what research you're talking about."

Her false benevolent smile inched wider. Her eyes narrowed in mockery. "I believe it's the information chained to your wrist, Dr. Pine."

Mitch reflexively pulled his briefcase tighter against his lap. "So what— you expect me to just hand over ten years of research? I take it you're Ms. Rosemont."

"I am. But Edgar doesn't want you to hand over your research; he wants to prevent it from going public."

"So he said. And what the heck is this quest he mentioned?"

"I don't know those details. I'm simply your handler. I'm here to escort you and make sure you're as comfortable as possible."

"Gee, thanks."

She leaned on the armrest between them. "Rest assured, Mitch, my employer will carry out everything he says he will if you do not comply. If you try to run or cry for help, my employer will know immediately. He has links to any form of communication you might try to access, including the computer in your briefcase and the Galaxy Note 8 in your pocket."

Mitch flinched. He was in shock, his thoughts a jumble of anxiety and frustration. This was crazy. His fear quickly morphed into anger. He glared at his seatmate as she sat back and waved a flight attendant over. "Two flutes of champagne, please."

"I don't drink," he grumbled, not wanting to do anything that hinted at compliance.

"You will this time. After all, we just agreed on a marvelous business transaction. We need to celebrate."

"*We* didn't agree on anything."

"For the sake of your assistant, I maintain we have."

After the attendant delivered the drinks, Mitch placed his left hand on his briefcase. "This research isn't complete, you know."

Kiana sipped her champagne. "That's not my concern. I'm just a handler and, for the next several hours, your host. Remember, Mitch, I make the rules until your assignment is fulfilled." Her smile held no anger, no hint of animosity or evil intent.

A few minutes later the fasten seatbelt light flashed above them with an accompanying soft chime. The captain announced their beginning descent to Denver International Airport. The temperature there was a balmy forty-two degrees. Partly cloudy skies. Seventy percent chance of light flurries. The flight attendant cleared the champagne glasses and asked Kiana to secure her tray table.

As the airliner gently slipped from cruising altitude, Mitch muttered, "This is insane."

Kiana again leaned her head back. "Edgar thinks otherwise."

"What do I care what he thinks?" he growled.

"Because he has Ms. Nakamura."

None of this made sense. How did the old Brit on the recording even know about his research? None of it had been published yet. Mitch *had* found evidence of someone hacking into his computer files at the university but had assumed it was merely a crafty student hoping to change his grade. And what was this stupid "quest" about? Even more concerning, what was Montrose going to do to Suko?

CHAPTER 2

Denver, Colorado

MITCH FOLLOWED KIANA DIRECTLY TO the loading zone, where a bulky man with a shaved head opened the trunk of a luxury town car. As they handed the man their luggage, Kiana's cell phone pinged with receipt of a text.

While she read her phone, Mitch glanced down the loading zone at the throng of travelers. There was plenty of airport security. Would they help him if he yelled? Would they protect him if he ran? He was a bit out of shape, but he was sure he could outrun the big bald guy.

"Don't even think about it, Mitch," Kiana said without looking up, as if reading his thoughts. "Just get in the car."

He turned back to her. *Focus, Mitch!* "Wait a sec. Can I listen to that recording again? I'm not sure it was Suko I heard," he lied.

"It was."

"Says you. I need verification."

She turned her phone toward him, and his breath caught. On it was a picture of Suko sitting on a metal folding chair, her hands and feet bound, duct tape covering her mouth, her eyes filled with anger and fright.

Mitch let fly an expletive. "When was that taken?"

"Probably last night," Kiana said, pocketing her phone. "Call it verification."

The big man cleared his throat and cocked his head toward the open car door. Kiana nodded and crawled inside. After a slight hesitation, Mitch followed.

As they pulled away from the terminal, Kiana asked, "Are you comfortable?"

"Swell," Mitch grumbled. He then asked the driver, "Hey, buddy, where are we going?"

The man glanced back via the rearview mirror but didn't respond.

"You don't need to know," Kiana answered.

"But I'd *like* to know," he countered. He was scrambling for something, anything that would take his mind off the image of Suko bound and gagged.

Kiana pulled out her phone and began scrolling through her emails.

From the corner of his eye, Mitch scrutinized the woman next to him. She was fit, pretty, clearly high-class. She certainly didn't look like a stereotypical kidnapper or a mob crony. How could someone like her be involved in something like this? Who were these people?

"You do realize I have an appointment with the Centers for Disease Control in Atlanta this evening?"

"You did," she said with a lift of her eyebrows. "Your personal secretary called and cancelled for you."

Mitch snorted. "I don't have a personal secretary."

"They don't know that."

"When did that happen? The call, I mean."

She gave a light shrug. "Doesn't matter. Your time is free now."

"What about my classes? I have to get back to the university soon."

"Mitch. It's November twentieth, the beginning of Portland State's holiday break. Classes won't resume until the twenty-sixth. And don't use the excuse of Thanksgiving dinner with your family. You have no siblings, you were with your dad when he died in Africa, and your mom passed away a year after that from breast cancer."

Mitch fought the sensation that he was trapped in a narrow hole rapidly filling with sand. His clothes felt coarse and heavy. A dry, acrid bitterness coated his mouth. He didn't know where to turn, what to do next. He felt a need to stall for time but wondered if doing so would further endanger his research assistant.

"This isn't happening," Mitch groaned softly.

"Rest assured, Mitch, it is. My employer will follow through on everything he says. I've worked with him for a long time. His resolve is absolute."

Her tone was so poised and confident; he had to believe her.

"Why are you doing this?"

"It's my job."

"How long have you worked for Montrose?"

Her bearing took on a harsh edge. "You sure ask a lot of questions."

"I'm an epidemiologist. I ask questions to save lives."

"Asking too many questions can get people killed," she amended, returning her gaze out her window.

Mitch pursed his lips in an effort not to scream in frustration.

Fifty minutes later the car circled into Boulder Municipal Airport. The driver opened the door on Mitch's side, and he and Kiana scooted out. She headed directly into the terminal without a word. Mitch followed, equally wordless. The bald man followed with their carry-ons.

Stopping at a kiosk displaying flight times, Kiana taped the screen of her phone and waited. When it pinged with a response, her eyebrows arched sharply, as if surprised. "I guess we're headed to Iceland."

Mitch frowned. "You mean you didn't know that?"

"As I said, I was asked to accompany you to a destination. I'm not involved in the planning. I simply go where they tell me and make sure you come along."

"So that's what escorts do, huh?"

"I prefer the term *handler*, but yeah, mostly."

"Why Iceland?"

She shrugged. "I thought maybe you'd know."

"Why would I know?" Mitch snapped. "Do you even know what this research is?" he asked, holding up his briefcase.

"No."

"Then . . . then, why are you involved?"

"A hundred thousand to accompany a nonviolent person to an undisclosed location, all expenses paid? Not a bad day's pay."

His eyes narrowed. "How do you know I'm not violent?"

She favored him with a look that cried, *Really?* Then, with a jerk of her head, she said, "Come on, Killer. My phone says we catch Southwest to Las Vegas, a connection at JFK, and then on to Reykjavik."

Three more takeoffs and landings, he thought, raking his fingers through his hair. *This just keeps getting better.*

CHAPTER 3

Portland, Oregon

SUKO NAKAMURA'S EVENING DEFINITELY DID not end how she'd expected. She'd agreed to a date with Jared, a guy she'd met in a PetSmart. They were both buying feeder crickets for tropical amphibians. He raised painted turtles; she had a pair of red-eyed tree frogs that matched a colorful tattoo on the nape of her neck. He'd asked if paying for her crickets could count as their first dinner date. That had made her laugh. His sense of humor—and the fact that he was six foot nine—boded a fun evening. She was barely five foot one. They'd look ridiculous walking side by side, talking about unique and endangered species. She couldn't wait.

Stepping from her car in front of her apartment, she was suddenly grabbed from behind and forced into a waiting panel van. She struggled initially, viciously kicking one in the ribs, but then realized she had little recourse other than to wait and see what happened. Two large thugs in dark sweaters made quick work of stuffing a gag into her mouth, duct-taping her mouth closed, and binding her hands behind her and her ankles together.

They weaved through the city for what felt like an hour before coming to a stop. The panel door opened to reveal the interior of a dark, empty warehouse.

The larger man tossed her over his shoulder and strode up a flight of metal stairs to a small office, which contained a desk and two metal folding chairs. An old man sat behind the desk. He had sparse silvery hair and opaque sharklike eyes—eyes that revealed no emotion, no insight as to what he was thinking. The thug unceremoniously dropped Suko onto one of the folding chairs while the other thug snapped her photo with a phone.

Leaving her wrists and feet bound, the first thug ripped the tape from her mouth and pulled out her gag.

"Where am I?" Suko immediately demanded, blinking away tears of pain, feeling too angry to be intimidated.

The old man sat perfectly still, staring at her, saying nothing.

"What do you creeps want from me?" she continued with increased venom.

After a full minute of complete silence, the man finally spoke. "Good evening, Ms. Nakamura. I trust my associates have not been too rough with you?" A clear English accent rounded his vowels, but his thin voice remained even, very businesslike, with little fluctuation in tone.

"Who are you?" she spat.

"My name is Edgar Montrose."

"What do you want with me?"

"Merely your cooperation."

"You have a lousy way of asking for it. And if I refuse?"

"Then you will compel me to be more persuasive."

Suko forced herself to remain calm. She couldn't let these men get an emotional upper hand on her. True, she was their hostage, but she'd be dipped in frog scat before they got anything from her. She was as frightened as she was angry, and she was determined to draw energy from both emotions.

"Bring it on, old man."

The man's left eyelid twitched briefly before he gave a soft, closed-lip harrumph. "Yes, I have heard your temperament can be quite caustic."

"You have no idea, Ed. Get me out of these restraints and I'll show you how *persuasive* I can be."

One of the thugs slapped the back of her head with enough force to nudge the chair forward an inch. She gritted her teeth against the pain.

Edgar withdrew a small digital-recording device from his pocket and placed it on the edge of the table.

"I want you to speak to your employer on my behalf."

"The university?"

"Dr. Pine."

"To Mitch? Why?"

"Because he has something I very much want in my possession. More to the point, I want it out of his possession."

Suko glared at Edgar for a moment before responding. "No."

The old man leaned forward and fixed her with his milky eyes. His lifeless stare made her skin crawl. "Ms. Nakamura, I assure you this will go much easier if you cooperate."

"Oh, since you put it like that . . . no *way*."

After a long pause and another eyelid twitch, Edgar looked beyond Suko and gave a single nod. With her arms pinned behind her, she didn't see the needle jab into the crook of her elbow, but she recognized its sting. She drew a sharp hiss through her teeth. "What the—?"

"My associate just pierced your median cubital vein with a hypodermic syringe filled with a powerful neurotoxin. I will instruct him to depress the plunger if you do not cooperate."

Suko's determination instantly evaporated. "Fine, fine," she said quickly. "What do you want me to say?"

"Simply follow my lead." He cleared his throat and pressed a button on the recorder. "Hello, Dr. Pine," he said in a businesslike tone. "My name is Edgar Montrose. I will dispense with formalities and get straight to the point. Simply put, I am greatly intrigued by your research conclusions, but I cannot allow them to go public. To that end, and to show you the magnitude of my convictions, your assistant has something to say."

Edgar pushed the recorder closer to the lip of the desk. "Ms. Nakamura, please tell Dr. Pine what is happening here."

Suko drew a quick breath, her anger returning at Edgar's insistence. "Mitch. It's Suko. I don't know who these *baka* are, but don't do anything they ask—"

A beefy hand clapped her mouth from behind, making it hard to breathe. Edgar's jaw clenched a few times before he gave a slow nod. Suko felt intense burning as the contents of the syringe emptied into her vein. She screamed a number of expletives, but the thug's hand muffled all sounds. Almost immediately the room began to sway. Edgar waved her away with a flick of his wrist.

The larger thug picked her up and flung her over his shoulder as the other one opened the door. She desperately wanted to scream, but the pressure of the thug's shoulder in her gut prevented her lungs from cooperating. She heard the old man continue to speak, but his words were unintelligible. It all sounded like garbled mush in an echo chamber.

Darkness began to creep in from her peripheral vision. She tried to fight it but couldn't. She was out cold before they reached the bottom of the stairs.

CHAPTER 4

Las Vegas, Nevada

McCARREN AIRPORT, NEAR VEGAS, WAS a hopeless maze of three chaotic terminals. Luckily, Kiana's employer had arranged for skycap to shuttle her and Mitch to their connecting flight. They spoke only a few words to each other. Mitch battled mental numbness fraught with anxiety and confusion, but he tagged along without complaint. What else could he do?

It was fully dark by the time their 737 lifted into the dense overcast. When the captain switched off the fasten seatbelt sign, Kiana turned to Mitch and fixed him with another of her resolute gazes. "May I ask you a question?"

It surprised him that she would make the request instead of simply demanding an answer. "Okay."

"What do you teach at Portland State?"

He blinked. "You don't know? You seem to know everything else."

"As I said—"

"You're just an escort," Mitch cut across.

"A handler."

"Right, right," he groused. "Fine. I teach various courses in epidemiology, but teaching isn't my focus. I mostly do research. Some consulting too."

"So your education is a PhD, not an MD?"

"Yeah. Why?"

Her brows pulled together. "Earlier you said you ask questions to save lives. If you're not a medical doctor, then what did you mean?"

It surprised him that she knew so little about his educational background, considering the familial details she had mentioned earlier. He considered her silently for a moment, wondering where this line of questioning was headed. "Why do you want to know?"

"Just curious."

"Why should I tell you anything? You're the enemy, remember?"

She let out a huff of air. "On the contrary, Mitch, I'm your best friend. Your actions will determine everything. I don't know exactly what my employer has in mind for Ms. Nakamura, but I can guess it won't be pleasant if you don't comply. As a handler, I prefer not to know such details. Suffice it to say, my word can spare her a world of hurt."

"Like I said: you're the enemy."

She folded her arms. "Look. This is a long flight. We can be rude to each other, or we can be civil. I'd much rather pass the time understanding why you're so important to my employer. Why?" she said before he could respond. "Let's just say I'm inquisitive by nature. And . . . well, you're different from other men I've handled."

"Am I?"

"Yes. In a good way. When you do this as long as I have you learn to read people pretty well. You're not overly belligerent or rude, even though you have a right to be. You've seen the situation for what it is and are being quite cooperative." She shrugged. "You've got me curious."

Mitch deliberated for a moment. What would it hurt to explain what he studied? It *was* a long flight. But how much should he tell her? How could he explain more than a decade's worth of research to a layperson in a way that would make sense—that would not sound totally crazy?

"Fine. I got into epidemiology because of my dad. As you obviously know, he died in Africa, but do you know how he died?"

Her eyes filled with pity. "No."

"He was a civil engineer who specialized in water management. The summer after I graduated high school, he took me to Africa with him to help several remote towns and villages assemble water-filtration systems. It was there I first saw unbridled disease and death." Mitch rubbed his tired eyes. "Anyway, the last job was in Mutala, Mozambique. Their water supply was infected with shigella bacteria. Dysentery was epidemic. By the time we arrived the town had already lost half its population, seventy percent of those being children. The conditions were appalling. People would bring out their dead and just lay them in the street because they were too weak to bury them. The stench was unbearable." He paused and looked out the window. "Dad accidently cut himself on some machinery, and it got infected. Necrotizing fasciitis—flesh eating bacteria. The most horrible thing I've ever seen. No one there knew what it was until it . . ." He paused again and swallowed. "He lasted only five days. Dad was my hero."

"I'm so sorry," she said with sincere emotion.

"Thanks. I wanted to prevent that kind of death, that kind of sorrow. In epidemiology, we study every aspect of the disease—how it's spread, if it can be controlled, and most importantly, its etiology—its origin."

"And that saves lives?"

"Only if the recommendations from the findings are followed. It's usually suggestions like proper sanitation, washing food before eating it, sourcing clean drinking water, stuff like that. Later my focus turned to paleoepidemiology. I study what happened hundreds of years ago—sometimes millennia ago—to determine what happened in various cultures, particularly those that had unexplained, massive death tolls."

"And that's what's in your briefcase?"

Mitch again stared out the window at the moonlit cloud cover below for a time. If Edgar already knew about his research, why go to all these coercive tactics? Why insist Mitch undertake a quest? And why involve Suko? She was merely an assistant, an innocent bystander. She had nothing to do with his conclusions. Unable to stop his anger from building, Mitch chose to remain silent, to not even look at Kiana.

"Look, if you'd rather not talk about it, fine," she said. "But rest assured, this *is* between you and me. I'm not carrying a wire or any hidden recording device. You saw me go through TSA scot-free, just like you. I have a phone, but it's off right now. See?" She handed him her iPhone, but he didn't take it. She sighed and nestled it back in her blazer pocket. "Suit yourself."

Mitch didn't want to reveal anything more to this criminal, but it suddenly occurred to him that if they kept talking, *she* might reveal something to *him*—perhaps even Suko's location. He turned to face her. "So you're not tasked with finding all my dirty dark secrets?"

"Do you have any?" she asked with an eyebrow raised playfully.

He merely stared at her.

"Look," she said as if fed up. "I told you: I'm just your handler. But that doesn't mean I can't carry on an intelligent conversation. I do have a brain, you know."

Was she trying to be funny? Perhaps she was simply being affable. Another minute passed before Mitch said, "Fine. Have you heard of the Black Death of 1347?"

"Sure. The bubonic plague," Kiana said.

"Exactly. It was one of the most devastating pandemics in all of history. Some mortality estimates are as high sixty percent of Europe's total population. No one knows for sure."

"Yeah, it was spread by rats—well, the rats spread it, but the fleas on the rats carried the disease."

"Flea bites *are* the predominate theory. We know fleas can transmit a bacterium called *Yersinia pestis*, which causes bubonic plague. But there are several inconsistencies with the bubonic theory. For instance, we now know that there are other forms of *Yersinia*, airborne through saliva droplets and blood-borne via mosquitos. My epidemiologic question is, was there only one factor that caused the death of nearly two-thirds of medieval Europe? Or was there more than one?"

"More than one plague?"

"More causes of death than just the plague."

Kiana thought for a moment. "Perhaps. But don't medical records back then prove it was bubonic plague?"

"Surprisingly no. There are no definitive medical records from back then. Germ theory wasn't even confirmed until five hundred years *after* the Black Death."

"Are you saying they didn't know about germs back then?"

"Not really. Microorganisms were thought to be mostly ethereal and were not considered disease-causing. It wasn't until around 1850 that Louis Pasteur first proved germ theory. He also developed the first practice of vaccination. But that was long after the Black Death. What most physicians and researchers go off of are the *symptoms* mentioned in journals and such: fever, malaise, headache, blindness, respiratory failure, black splotches on the skin, and the infamous pustules—weeping sores known as buboes in the armpits and groin."

"Isn't that sufficient evidence?"

"Not really. See, a lot of diseases can cause those same symptoms. Bacteria and viruses can both cause a runny nose and diarrhea. Blood poisoning can cause swollen lymph nodes, just like the plague. Frostbite and gangrene can both blacken the skin. In this case, *bubonic* plague caused buboes and fever but not respiratory failure. That came from *pneumonic* plague. Other journals tell of delirium, seizures, and people bleeding out, which had to be *septicemic* plague."

"Bubonic, pneumonic, septicemic—is it really that important?"

"In the world of epidemiology, yes. *Every* factor matters, even the nonmedical stuff. For instance, the rate of transmission is the second clue bubonic plague may only be a minor part of a bigger picture. *Yersinia* simply doesn't spread that fast, especially in a cold, temperate climate like Europe. At least not as fast as was reported in 1346 and '47."

"I thought once people caught it they were dead the next day," Kiana argued. "That seems pretty fast to me."

"Untreated it can kill within seventy-two hours, yes. But the theory is, as you stated, that it was *spread* by rats. The infrastructure of medieval Europe simply wouldn't accommodate that. In urban areas, maybe, because it was prime breeding ground for the black rat. But back then Europe was mostly rural. Roads, bridges, and such weren't well-developed, and travel was limited. Rivers and mountains were actual barriers—many impassable. Add to that the fact that only five percent of rats themselves ever survive the disease, and you find that, clearly, there had to be other factors behind the devastation."

"Okay . . . so why do textbooks maintain the Black Death was the bubonic plague?"

"It's their best guess. There are only three DNA analyses of the fourteenth century I know of that are verifiable: one in 2000, one in 2010, and one in 2016. But there are counter arguments for those findings as well, many with good scientific backing. In fact, most skeletons from that period don't show *any* sign of *Yersinia* at all. So all anyone can definitely say is that *Yersinia* was *present* during the Black Plague but not necessarily the *cause* of it."

"Huh. I'm surprised I haven't heard any of this before . . ." Kiana mused, tapping her index finger against her lips, thoughtfully taking it all in.

Mitch wasn't sure what to make of her reaction. She seemed truly interested, which surprised him, but perhaps it was just an act. Maybe she was playing the part of the good cop instead of the coercive kidnapper, trying to get him to spill his secrets. *Well, let her try.* He was determined to get a few secrets from her as well.

"So is that what this is all about?" she finally asked, nodding at his briefcase. "You have a different theory on the Black Death?"

"Oh, it's more than that, I'm afraid."

"How so?"

"Classic epidemiology says that if you can find out how a pandemic started, there's a good chance you can prevent it from happening again. That's why I was meeting with the CDC—to get their epidemiologists' take on my conclusions and hopefully get their confirmation."

Kiana looked at him from under arched brows. "And if they don't agree with you?"

Mitch absently slid his hand across his briefcase. "What I've found is irrefutable. I wish it weren't, but . . ."

"But what? You have proof, right?"

He nodded. "That's why I can't understand why Edgar doesn't want it to go public."

She tilted her head to one side. "Is it bad?"

He nodded. "It's the end of the world."